CW00376993

Simon —

A great British drama!

THE LONDON CONNECTION

AN OLIVIA STREETE MYSTERY

best wishes

M. F. Kelleher

THE LONDON CONNECTION

M.F. KELLEHER

Copyright © M.F. Kelleher 2022

The right of M.F.Kelleher to be identified as the author of this work has been asserted in accordance with the Copyright, Designs and Patents Act 1988.

All rights reserved. No part of this publication may be reproduced, stored in or transmitted into any retrieval system, in any form, or by means without the prior written permission of the publisher. Any person who does any authorised act in relation to this publication may be liable to criminal prosecution and civil claims for damages.

This is a work of fiction. Names, characters, businesses, places, events and incidents are either the products of the author's imagination or used in a fictitious manner. Any resemblance to actual persons, living or dead, or actual events is purely coincidental.

ISBN 9798356401251

Cover artwork by Claire Meczes

CHAPTER ONE

The South Bank of the River Thames is bursting with shoppers as Olivia Steele walks back to her flat near Tower Bridge. Her mind is slightly panicked with the thought that it is a month to go before Christmas and she has yet to buy anything for anybody. Her mother will be messaging later today, just as she has done every other day for the last week, trying to find out what plans her daughter has over the holidays. Olivia has, as she does each year, avoided the question.

As she reaches the front door to her block of flats, she can feel her phone vibrating in her pocket. She pulls it out of her pocket and sits on one of the chairs in the reception area that are hardly ever used. She looks up at the doorman to the block. They exchange weak we-are-strangers-but-feel-we-should smiles.

There are two messages on her phone, neither from her mother. The first is from Poppy, her daughter who has left a voice message. Olivia puts her phone to her ear.

"Hi Mum, you know that guy I was seeing, well it didn't work out and he was all weird in the end so I dumped him the other night, I had to get an Uber at two in the morning. Dad got in touch and invited me to his for Christmas but his girlfriend is proper weird to be honest, so I was thinking of coming to you. What are you doing, you going to Grandmas? Gotta go, Mum, message me. Love you."

Olivia considers replying but isn't sure what the answers are.

The second message is from an agency that she uses for work telling her that there is an urgent need for a corporate lawyer in a government office in Whitehall, starting immediately. Olivia hasn't worked for a month, so replies saying she's interested then goes to the lifts and up to her flat.

By the time she wakes up the next morning, there is a message back from the agency with details of who to meet about the job. She dresses in a black suit and pulls her hair back into a low ponytail.

The address is on the other side of Whitehall to Downing Street. She gets there ten minutes early and is shown into a dark-wood panelled room to one side of a cavernous entrance hall.

A short, dark woman walks around the corner. Her hair in a chignon and her blouse buttoned up to the neck.

"Miss Streete?" she says. "Follow me, will you?"

The woman leads Olivia through the glazed double doors next to the security guard and they disappear into the bowels of the building.

They turn sharp left and ascend a staircase to the first floor, then turn sharp left again into a corridor that is fifty yards long. The woman doesn't talk to Olivia as they walk. When they reach the far end, the woman opens door and lets Olivia go in first. The meeting room is equally as Victorian as the reception waiting area had been.

The woman leaves her without further words and shuts the door behind her. The sound of the traffic is muted behind the glass and Olivia walks to the window and looks out at the cars, taxis and buses crawling passed along Whitehall.

After ten minutes a man in his forties enters and walks over to her. He has brown eyes and dark hair cut short.

"You must be Olivia Streete?" he says.

She extends her hand and they shake. He puts his laptop on the table next to him but doesn't open it.

"I'm Stephen Boyd, I'm a Deputy Director here in BEIS."

"What's that?"

"Business, Energy and Industrial Strategy."

She raises an eyebrow but he doesn't notice.

"You were recommended to us," he says.

"Good to know I have friends in the right places." She smiles, and he echoes it after a second wondering if he should. "What's the work, Mr Boyd?"

"We have some particularly sensitive challenges concerning negotiations that the Minister is doing with large electronics companies."

"Which companies?"

"Has anyone got you to sign the Official Secrets Act declaration yet?" he says. She shakes her head. "Then, I'll wait to tell you any names. Safe to say, we need someone who is going to operate quickly and discretely in support of the Minister."

"This is Heather Wells?" says Olivia.

He briefly closes his eyes in acknowledgement.

"Can you tell me in outline what the legal work is?" she says.

"Sorry, I can't yet," he says. "I'll ask Jeanette to get the paperwork. It may be an hour or so. Do you want to wait or come back?"

"I'll go for a walk in that case," she smiles politely and he shows her back down to corridor to the entrance.

"Could you give me your number?" he says as they reach the main doors. "I'll message you when she's sorted it." They exchange numbers and Olivia walks out to Whitehall. She turns left towards Parliament Square and finds a coffee shop while she waits.

The message from Boyd comes an hour later and he suggests that they have lunch so that he can brief her. He has booked Kerridge's on Northumberland Avenue.

Olivia arrives two minutes before he does and is shown to a table in the corner. The waitress says that this is 'Mr Boyd's usual table'. When he arrives, he is more confident than before, but hurried. He puts his briefcase on the floor and rummages around in it then produces a stapled four page document and hands it to her. Olivia reads the document as he orders water and bread for the table and a bottle of Château Grand-Puy-Lacoste Bordeaux without asking her.

"Do you have a pen?" she says after a couple of minutes and he produces a pen from his jacket pocket. Olivia signs the document and hands it to him. "I'll need a copy."

"I'm having the lamb, hence the Bordeaux," he says. "I hope you don't mind." Olivia picks up her menu and the waiter brings the wine. She orders sea bass and flicks her eyes to him as she does so. She can't tell whether he has the slightest hint of a smile in the corner of one eye.

"Tell me about you," he says.

"I'm a corporate lawyer, I've done a lot of buy-outs and mergers work, and some criminal defence. I'm licenced in the US and the UK."

"You went to Cambridge didn't you?" he says, indicating he probably knows the answers to whatever he is going to ask her.

"Girton."

"Didn't want to go into chambers?"

"I don't like the stuffiness of all that barrister work," she says.

"I'll make sure I'm not too stuffy then."

She ignores the flirtiness. "Tell me about the job."

"The Minister has been talking to three suppliers for a year. She wants to move all government communications to be managed externally to improve the environmental footprint."

"What do they get in return?" says Olivia.

"Aside from the contract, we would work with them on their foreign investments."

"Where?" she says.

"All over, Canada, South Africa mostly."

"What does 'work with them on their investments' actually mean? Government subsidy?

He stops and scans her face, realising that she is as good as he has been told.

"There may be a financial element."

"I signed your piece of paper, Mr Boyd," says Olivia. "You can be open with me."

"Let me tell you about what we need from you," he says. "You will attend the talks with the suppliers and you will be the Minister's eyes and ears in the room, then oversee all of the contractual paperwork."

"Don't you have staff lawyers who do this normally?"

"She would rather have someone from outside," he says.

"She doesn't trust the staff?"

"I didn't say that, of course she trusts all of her staff."

"Fine," says Olivia. "I can do that. Is it you who decides if I get the job?"

"Oh, you've got the job, Miss Streete," he says. "You had the job before you arrived this morning."

CHAPTER TWO

The Jubilee Line carriage is full the next morning and Olivia has to push between a Japanese businessman and a woman with a bright yellow hat trying to message someone on her phone. The five minute journey seems to take longer than that, before she emerges into daylight at Westminster tube station.

She has never liked commuting, there is something about the repetition that gets to her. Part of the reason she had chosen corporate law was because of the variety. The same woman who met her yesterday is waiting in the reception area trying not to look flustered but failing. Once she sees Olivia the woman is highly focused but insincere as she goes through what seems like a dozen forms that need to be completed to allow Olivia to get a door pass and a laptop. After forty minutes, with her pass around her neck, Olivia is shown to a desk in a large office on the long corridor from yesterday. There are two other desks in the office, both unoccupied. The windows look out over Whitehall Court, a street lined with white stuccoed buildings down both sides.

On Olivia's desk is one thin, blue folder. Inside are two pieces of paper. The first giving her instructions to get into the laptop, and the second is a list of appointments for today that someone has typed up. The first on the list is for 10am and according to the silent clock above the door, that is in five minutes.

The door opens with a rush and a man enters. He is in his early thirties with a mop of blond hair, and his green eyes betray an intelligent mind beneath a reticent demeanour. She checks her list.

"Are you Tom Adams?" she says, standing up behind her desk.

"And you must be Olivia?" They shake hands. "I'm here to brief you on this GreenLink work."

She goes to her bag and fishes out a notebook and pen, then he leads them to a table under the window with four chairs around it and they sit.

"What do you know?" he says.

"Nothing."

"OK then," he begins and gives her a tiny smile. "The Minister has been talking to three suppliers for six months. The current communications contract we have covers four ministries and they want to provide services for the whole of the civil service. That is one of the biggest contracts we have aside from the military spending."

He pauses for any reaction, so she raises her eyebrows and nods but says no words.

"You will appreciate that the scale of the contract means that there has been much scrutiny over this work, and sadly accusations of preferential treatment from other companies."

"Are those justified?" she says.

He stops again, assessing her question, then finally says, "No, of course not." Another little smile.

"Can I ask, Tom? He is not used to pcople using his first name so soon after meeting. "Why did you call it the GreenLink work?"

"GreenLink are bidding."

"But others are too?"

"Of course."

"So…?"

"They're seen as the front-runner," he says. "The Chief Executive of GreenLink is Jeremy Alpin, are you familiar?"

"Only from the news."

"You'll know that he has been subject to some criticism for his outlandish personal life in the past, but we have been speaking to his team to ask that he keeps that out of the papers, as it doesn't look good if we're contracting with a…, with a…"

"Playboy?" she says. Tom doesn't react, but his lack of denial she takes as acceptance. "Who is doing the negotiation from our side? Surely not Heather Wells herself?"

"No, I have been covering the contractuals, and Ellen Hill is leading on the requirements. You'll like her, she's…, she's…"

"A woman?"

A little smile. "We have a meeting with GreenLink this afternoon," he says.

"I saw," she says. "Who organised all of these meetings?"

"That's Gia," he says. "Very good, forgetful but thorough." Olivia wonders whether someone can be forgetful and thorough at the same time.

They talk on about the details of the contract and another man turns up an hour later to see Olivia. He is short and fine with a shaved head and large glasses. He introduces himself as William from Finance as though it is his name. He takes her through the cost and payment schedules.

Olivia's afternoon is equally packed with people telling her things. The GreenLink people at the meeting are both enthusiastic but forgettable men. By the end of the working day, she slams out of the building into the already dark streets of London and turns away from the river towards the centre of the city. Her brain is tired and she needs to unwind. She had promised to meet Poppy for a pizza but her daughter had messaged her an hour ago saying, 'some cute guy at school' had invited her to the cinema and 'life is too short not too, eh Mum?'

Olivia keeps walking and ends up going through the St James's district and up onto Piccadilly. She passes the Royal Academy that has closed for the night when she hears her name called from behind her. She turns.

"It is you, Miss Streete?"

"Hello, Mr Boyd."

"Are we going the same way? I am headed for Browns Hotel and the bar there."

"I wasn't."

"Would you like to join me, in that case? We can catch up on how your first day has been. I'm meeting Ellen Hill, did you meet?"

"No, she's probably the only person I haven't met today." She smiles and he does too.

Ten minutes later they arrive at the Donovan Bar within the hotel. A tall, dark-haired woman in her early thirties is sitting on one of the tall chairs at the bar. She has blue eyes and has slow and deliberate movements of a woman used to her own attractiveness. She is wearing a dark suit with a skirt and court shoes. When Stephen arrives with company, Olivia senses no disappointment in Ellen's manner so dismisses the idea they may have any personal relationship outside work, either that or Ellen is an excellent actress.

They order cocktails and talk about work for a while, then move on to their personal lives. Olivia talks about Poppy and getting pregnant at university. It's part of her life that strangers and friends alike always seem to be fascinated by.

Stephen was married two years ago but they have no children. Olivia notices that Ellen's face is unemotional during this part of the conversation. The topic reminds him to go and call his wife from a payphone as he left his mobile at home this morning.

Ellen talks about herself after Stephen has gone. She's single and has been for four years, she had a boyfriend but he became controlling and she left before the whole thing deteriorated further, which she had sensed he might.

"There's been no one since?" says Olivia.

"No one serious," says Ellen. "I dated a couple of guys, but they didn't want to commit to anything. What about you?"

"I split from my boyfriend a few months ago. We weren't spending any time together. I don't keep men for long, for some reason," says Olivia. "And I travel a lot with work. I always seem to be somewhere in Europe or the States, that doesn't help."

The women talk on until Stephen returns. They all have a couple more drinks and the group splits up at about nine o'clock. Olivia goes home, orders a food delivery on the way then eats her Udon noodles with beef and red onions while watching a movie online which she has seen before.

*

It is completely dark as Olivia is pushed out of sleep by her phone ringing. Before waking, her subconscious tries to switch off the noise as her brain thinks it's her morning alarm, but through the blur her mind finally engages and she sits up suddenly and grapples with the mobile.

"Yes? Hello?"

"Is this Olivia Streete?"

"Yes, that's me."

"This is Sergeant Collins from the British Transport Police. We're outside your flat and we rang to doorbell but didn't get an answer."

"It's the middle of the night, sergeant." she keeps her frustration out of her voice tone. "I was asleep. What's this about?"

"Could you let us in, miss?" he says. "And we'll go through it with you."

She walks to the door. There are two police officers on the video screen by the door and she buzzes them in to her block of flats.

Two minutes later, after throwing on leggings and a t-shirt, she answers a knock on her door. She ushers in Collins and a female officer and the all sit on her sofas.

"We believe you were with a Stephen Boyd earlier this evening, miss?" says Collins. He has kind, pale eyes.

"Yes, that's correct."

"Can you take us through your movements this evening, miss?" says Collins. The woman pulls a notebook from her top pocket and licks her pencil, which Olivia has only ever seen happen in films before.

Olivia explains what she did and where she was from the time she left the offices off Whitehall to when she arrived home.

"What's this about, sergeant?"

"A couple of other questions," says Collins. "Did My Boyd seem himself? Did he seem happy?"

"He appeared to be happy enough. I've only known him for twenty-four hours so I can't tell if he was himself. Ellen Hill would be able to answer that as she has known him for longer."

"Yes, we've asked her."

"So, what's he done?" says Olivia. "Has he been arrested?"

"Mr Boyd was found dead earlier this evening," says the woman. Her blonde hair is short but her fringe is long and hides her eyebrows. "What's your relationship with the dead man, miss?" says the woman, who doesn't have as sophisticated an ability with subtlety as Collins.

"Not much," says Olivia. "He is a senior civil servant in the department where I have just started working. I know nothing about him, but he said tonight that he has been married for two years, that's all I know."

"You're single aren't you?" says the policewoman.

Olivia frowns. "How is that anything to do with anything?"

"He was a successful man, and handsome," says the woman.

"I don't know what you're getting at."

The woman doesn't continue but smiles to herself.

"So, you didn't see him after he left Browns Hotel?" says Collins.

"That's right, sergeant."

"Are there any witnesses we can confirm that with?"

"As your colleague said, I'm single so there's no one in this flat but us. The food delivery guy can confirm I was here if that helps."

She gives them the receipt for the food and they say they'll follow it up. Collins is appreciative but the policewoman doesn't show any humanity and gruffly tells Olivia to come in to the station and make her formal statement within the next 48 hours.

They leave and Olivia shuts her front door, then makes tea and sits watching the dawn come up over the water as she wonders if anything Stephen Boyd said to her was true.

CHAPTER THREE

Olivia's phone lights up with a text message as she walks towards the office the next day. She looks at the screen, it's from the personal assistant to Heather Wells, the Minister, telling Olivia to attend a meeting in fifteen minutes.

The office suite for the Minister is at the far end of the long corridor and Olivia only just gets there before the appointed time. Heather's assistant, Millie, is the smallest woman that Olivia has ever seen, with sharp green eyes and a brunette bob. Millie shows her into the inner office. Olivia recognises Heather Wells' from the television. She's younger in real life, with a face that is continually enquiring. Opposite her is standing a tall man with a wave of black hair and an expensive suit.

"This is the new lawyer, minister," says Millie.

Heather stops her conversation and turns to Olivia, her eyes flitting up and down before landing her gaze on Olivia's face. She smiles, genuinely, and holds out her hand.

"Heather Wells," she says. "It's Olivia, isn't it?"

"Hello, yes, Olivia Streete."

"You come highly recommended," says Heather.

"Who by?"

"A good friend of mine," she says. "Let me introduce you to Jeremy."

The man's face breaks out into a huge smile, but this time it's not genuine.

"Pleased to meet you," he says. His voice is smooth and his eyes sparkle. The voice of a rich man, she thinks. They shake hands and his skin is cold to the touch.

"We need your advice on the news overnight, Olivia," says Heather.

"We could have done without something like this," says Jeremy.

Olivia looks at Jeremy without an emotion on her face, trying to assess the psyche of someone she has only just met. Why would someone who is patently not stupid really be so crass as to position someone's death as merely a problem that needs to go away? She makes a mental note to research more about Jeremy Alpin.

"We do need to say something to the press," says Heather. "I've had calls to this office already this morning, the police must have leaked it."

"Can't we put a stop to that?" says Alpin, turning to Olivia. "I have friends at the top of the Met Police."

"It was the British Transport Police who dealt with it," says Olivia.

They both look at her. "How do you know?" says Heather.

"They called at my flat in the middle of the night."

"Why?"

"I had drinks with Stephen last night."

There is a pause, as the Minister and the CEO both try and work out what this means for their own interests.

"You knew him, then?" says Heather.

"Barely, I only started working here yesterday."

"How did you end up having a cozy chat with a man who is now dead?" says Jeremy. "I bet he took you to the bar in Browns Hotel? He took all his women there."

"I'm not one of his women," says Olivia, her voice rising slightly with frustration.

"You would have been," says Jeremy. "That's the way he worked."

"We just need to decide how we respond to the press," says Heather.

Whenever she works as a freelance lawyer, she Olivia has become used to her clients involving her in many things that aren't anything to do with legal matters. They see a lawyer as objective, a safe pair of hands and trustworthy, which gives her a carte blanche to stick her nose into anything in her view.

"Don't you have a press officer, minister?"

"I don't trust them." A second awkward pause sits between the three of them.

"I can draft something," says Olivia. "Factual, brilliant career, personal tragedy, our thoughts are with his family – that sort of thing?"

"Perfect," says Heather with relief in her voice. "If you do that and get it to Millie by twelve?" A question disguised as a command. "If both of you would excuse me, I have a meeting at Number 10 in half-an-hour."

Jeremy and Olivia walk into the outer office and Millie goes into Heather with her coat and papers.

"I'm having a small gathering at my London house tonight," he says to Olivia once Millie has gone in. "A few friends, do come if you're free."

Olivia smiles at him. "Thank you, I'm not sure what I'm doing tonight yet."

"Take my card." He hands her a business card, gold lettering on a black background. "There's my personal number on there. Let me know later."

He gives a small head bow then walks out before she can respond.

*

As the taxi drops off Olivia in front of 22 Hereford Square in South Kensington, the half of her brain that controls her pride is resisting going into the Alpin's house and the half that controls her inquisitiveness drives her on across the pavement and up to the front door.

A woman wearing a black dress and white apron opens the door and smiles professionally, raising her arm up to direct Olivia inside. The house is festooned with expensive glass and original features with deep fabrics, placed creatively. A hallway leads into a long lounge that ends in a covered-in verandah overlooking a garden that is big for London. Olivia can see a dozen people grouped around chatting with glasses in their hands.

The maid takes her coat and hangs it on a wheeled hanger to one side. As Olivia emerges into the light, a tall woman strides over to her and gives her a hearty hand-shake.

"I'm Greer Alpin, Jeremy's much better half," she says. "You must the new girl. Olivia isn't it?"

"That's right." The woman is impressive socially. "How did you know?"

"Jeremy tells me all about the Department and your little contract."

"It's quite a big contract actually," says Olivia.

"Where did you work before?" says Greer, and Olivia rattles off the summary of her CV. "Useful. I hear you're good."

Olivia can see Jeremy approaching across the room and he calls out to her. "I wondered if you'd forgotten me when you didn't message." A waiter offers her a tray of drinks, from which she takes one. Olivia notices that Greer had already made a beeline for someone else in the room before Jeremy arrives.

"I always like to keep people guessing," says Olivia, and smiles briefly. "Aren't you going to introduce me?" She waves her glass at a group near them and Jeremy doesn't lose his polite veneer to cover any disappointment.

By the time Olivia has met enough people to start forgetting the names of the first ones, she goes to the bathroom which is back through the house near the front door. As she comes out, a woman is waiting.

"I haven't met you before," says the woman. Her voice is deep and velvety and her eyes rise up towards the outside to give her a permanent smile.

"I'm Olivia Streete," she says. "I've just started working with Jeremy on the government contract." The words intentionally constructed to get a reaction.

"He didn't say."

Bingo.

"I'm Violet." The woman puts out a long arm and they shake weakly.

"Do you work at GreenLink?" says Olivia.

Violet smiles beautifully. "I'm more of a personal support to Mr Alpin."

"What does that involve?" says Olivia.

Violet grabs hold of the door to the bathroom and starts to go in, just before the door closes she looks up. "Mostly, that involves screwing him while his wife is away," she whispers. "Lovely to meet you."

Olivia has grown used to not reacting to outrage from her days in court in America. She returns to the party and notices Tom from the office has arrived and is standing in a corner of the room looking uncomfortable.

"Were you invited too?" says Olivia as she approaches.

"Jeremy expects us to be here."

"Who?"

"The people in the Department who are dealing with his contract."

"But he *is* just one supplier," she says.

"He's powerful, Olivia. He can get anybody to do what he wants in Whitehall."

She decides to test something.

"Even kill?"

Tom doesn't react the way she thought he would. She had expected him to be shocked, but the calm surface of his demeanour barely registers a faint breeze blowing across it.

Tom turns his eyes to her. She can tell he wants to say many things but also she can tell that he won't, not here anyway. This is a steady man, behind the scenes, in the shadows, always there, like a reliable butler.

"Nothing's impossible," he says.

"Tom, you and I need to become best friends," she says.

"We all just need to be careful."

She continues her innocent bravado act. "About what?"

"Just do your job, keep your head down," says Tom.

"Is that how you've survived in your time in the civil service?"

"I don't want to see other people get hurt," he says.

Olivia rolls on with her strategy of shock and awe. "You mean Stephen?"

Tom looks at her and stops for a second, his eyes looking at hers, trying to find something without saying any words. This is a man who is not used to this type of risky conversation.

"We all liked Stephen." Olivia's eyes are locked on his face to reap any truths that slip out non-verbally. "Go and talk to Claire," he says. "Stephen's wife. She knows more than anyone."

Before Olivia can ask anything more, a woman and man come up to them and introduce themselves. The conversation diverts to the new people. Olivia looks around five minutes later and Tom has quietly slipped away.

By the time the couple say they, 'need to circulate', Olivia wants to go. She calls a cab on her phone app and makes her way through to the front door. As she enters the hallway, she can hear raised voices coming from a room to one side that she guesses might be a dining room.

"Just get your bloody tart out of my house, Jeremy."

"She is my personal assistant, and that is no way to talk about my staff."

"So funny, the way you say 'my staff'. You know the saddest thing about you, is not that you need to pay that woman to fuck you, but you think no one else notices. You're such a prick. Christ, my father was right!"

"Your father?" he says, his anger rising. "That's the man who has a reputation for destroying people when he disagrees with them, is it, my darling?" he says.

"You snide bastard." Greer's voice is a mixture of fight and genuine sadness.

At that moment a voice comes from behind Olivia. "Madam?" It's the maid, holding her coat up for Olivia to put on. She accepts the coat and the maid quickly opens the front door and looks expectantly at her.

Olivia steps out into the cold air and across the pavement to the waiting taxi.

CHAPTER FOUR

As she approaches the conference room the next morning, Olivia can't help thinking about Stephen Boyd. She tries to recall the details of the three conversations they had: the interview; the lunch at Kerridge's; and the drinks with Ellen in the bar at Brown's Hotel. Did he give any clues that might connect to his death? What does she already know about him? By all accounts a ladies man, however that is defined these days; married but with some questions over their happiness. His death could have been an accident of course, but her legal mind already suspects it isn't. Had he slept with someone's wife or girlfriend and they had sought revenge? Or was there something that connects his death to the contract he was managing and the bidders? Both Jeremy and Greer seem confident, driven, and conniving. Did Stephen cross them and end up risking his life?

She can't answer any of these questions before she reaches the meeting room. Heather and Millie are at the front on a raised stage. Forty chairs are laid out before them. Millie is pointing out parts of the documents that Heather is holding and is nodding as she listens.

After a few seconds, Heather sees Olivia. "Good," she says brusquely. "Can you read this and give me your comments please?"

She hands the papers to her. Olivia sits on the front row and reads the document, which is a statement on Stephen's death.

After a minute, Heather says. "Thoughts?"

"It's a bit impersonal," says Olivia. "You need more on Claire and his personal qualities before you get to this long list of his career highlights."

Heather frowns. "Mmm." Olivia writes some words on her copy of the papers and some arrows to restructure the speech, then hands it back to Heather. The Minister scans the changes and says "Right," after a few seconds.

"Shall I get them in, minister?" says Millie. "It's ten."

"Thank you."

Millie goes out and a minute later, the door opens and she leads in journalists who sit near the front of the room. Olivia takes a seat to one side.

After Heather has read the prepared statement and, 'said a few words personally' about Stephen that were not on the papers, she asks if there are questions and the journalists don't disappoint. What will happen now? Is she back-filling the job immediately? Does this affect her agenda for the coming parliament? Heather answers them all with aplomb, having been a marketing director before her parliamentary career.

"Any more?"

A man who is half-way down the room and has clear blue eyes puts his hand up.

"Yes?"

"Ethan Poole, The International Courier; does the Minister think that Stephen Boyd's death is connected to the other deaths of people close to companies run by Boyd's wife's family over the last ten years?"

Heather stops. For two seconds that seem like more, she looks at the journalist without speaking, but she isn't nervous, she's a master class of calm composure.

"Mr. Poole, Stephen Boyd was a remarkable civil servant who served this country for over a decade. He leaves a young wife and colleagues who are mourning him. I find it distasteful that you might try and use this personal tragedy to further a campaign that, if I am not mistaken, you alone have been waging over these past few years. I am not going to give your question the credibility of a response. Thank you, everyone."

Heather picks up her papers and walks directly to a side door, and Millie follows her out.

Olivia stays seated and watches the journalists. Most of them start to chat about the press conference, but the man who asked the question at the end stands up and hurries out on his own.

There is a note on Olivia's desk from Gia when she gets back saying that the police have called to remind her to go in and give her formal statement, so she decides to go to lunch then on to the address written on the note.

*

The British Transport Police HQ is a grey, square block on a cross-roads in Camden. Olivia calls in at the reception and is escorted to a grey, square room on the fourth floor and told to wait. After ten minutes a fair-haired man in a new light-grey suit carrying a tablet computer comes in and introduces himself as Inspector Savage, but he's the opposite of his name.

Savage listens while she recounts the events of the evening with Stephen and then he types some words that summarise her story and turns the tablet to her.

"Read that and sign electronically at the bottom, if you would." She reads and signs. "That's it then," he says with a slight smile.

"How the investigation going?" says Olivia.

"Well, officially all I can say is that we're following up a number of leads." He smiles again.

"And off the record?"

He looks around to check the door is closed. "There isn't a great deal of evidence to be honest."

"Where did they find him?" she says. "On a station presumably, hence you being involved?"

"On the tracks outside Clapham."

"Any forensics?"

"Got your lawyer nose on?" he says.

"There must have been some." She widens her eyes, knowing that this man wants to talk more, despite it being against the rules.

"I've seen a few bodies on the tracks over the years," says Savage. "Not like this one."

"How was he different?"

"Well, I don't want to be too graphic…"

"I'm a big girl, Inspector."

He pauses then says, "Normally, they get mangled a bit, you know? This one had no signs of any fall, but his face had been completely disfigured, we only ID'd him by his driver's licence in his wallet."

"What did he die of?"

"I can't tell you, sorry."

"What time did he die?" says Olivia.

"About one, they reckon."

"Who found him?"

"Night workers, repairing the track by platform 4. Just lying there, they said, like he was asleep."

The door opens and a young female officer with short, red hair comes in.

"Guv, the wife of that Clapham body is here," she says, then when she sees Olivia. "Oh, sorry."

"Thanks, Lois," he says then turns to Olivia. "I'd better be going."

"Do you have a card, Inspector?" she says.

"Sure." He pulls out his wallet and produces a card for her. "It's straight along to the lifts," he adds as he opens the door. She shakes his hand and walks down the corridor.

In the reception, a woman sits on one of the plastic chairs. Olivia takes a punt. "Are you Claire Boyd?" she says to her.

The woman is dark and her eyes show sadness. "Yes, are you the Inspector?"

"No, no," says Olivia. "I worked with Stephen, I've just been giving my statement."

The woman visibly relaxes. "Did you know him well?"

"Not at all really, I'm new," says Olivia. "He seemed like a lovely man, Mrs. Boyd."

The woman smiles. "He could be." She pauses. "What's your name?"

"Olivia, I'm a lawyer."

"Did you see him on that last day?"

"Yes, we had drinks after work."

"Was he happy?"

"I think so. He called you, didn't he, on that evening?"

"No, he didn't," says Claire.

"Sorry, my mistake," says Olivia.

The lift doors open and Lois appears. "Would you like to come with me, madam?" she says to Claire.

Claire stands up. "Mrs. Boyd," says Olivia. "If you'd like to talk, then, here are my contact details." Olivia holds out a business card to her. For a second, the woman hesitates, then takes the card.

"Thank you. I'd like that."

Olivia is taken aback an hour later when a message arrives on her phone from Claire Boyd inviting her to the family home this evening.

*

The walk from Hampstead tube station takes Olivia down roads of large Victorian terraces and mature trees, now bare from the coldness. The road leads in the direction of the Heath and she checks the numbers off on the houses to find the one on the message that Claire had sent her. Most of the houses are apartments now and the Boyds' flat had once been the basement kitchen of an eight bedroom house. Inside, it's a large and spacious modern space with ownership of the garden. Lights are scattered across the outside shrubbery highlighting features and fountains through the darkness. Claire shows her into a long living area of muted tones. She pulls two wine glasses and a bottle of red from a cupboard and they sit opposite each other on two squashy sofas. Olivia waits while the woman pours the drinks, hands her one, then sits back down and takes a large gulp of wine.

"What did you think of him?" says Claire.

"Your husband?" Claire nods. "Like I said this afternoon, he seemed kind."

"He wasn't," Claire nearly whispers.

Olivia continues. "He seemed good at his job."

"He was."

"He seemed to care about you."

"He didn't."

"Tell me about him," says Olivia.

"He was ten years older than me," she begins. "We met at some business event. I do design work. He was charming." She pauses. "And he got on with my family."

"Why did you say he wasn't kind, just now?"

"It wasn't part of his make-up. Charming yes, kind no."

"What else?" says Olivia.

"He liked women," says Claire. "I don't think he was faithful to me."

"Did you tell him?"

"No."

"What did you think when you heard he'd died?" says Olivia.

"I thought something had finally caught up with him."

"What?"

"A husband maybe," says Claire. "Or someone he'd got on the wrong side of."

"What do you mean?" says Olivia.

Claire stands up and picks up a letter from the sideboard.

"I received this yesterday," says Claire handing the paper to Olivia.

Olivia reads the lines on the sheet. "Your bloke was in deep shit, it all may come out unless you cooperate."

"Special courier," says Claire.

"Do you know what they're referring to?"

"No."

"You need to go to the police," says Olivia.

"I can't," says Claire. "You don't know my family. We're well-connected. My mother's a judge and my father's in the House of Lords. It would be a scandal if anything like this got out."

"You have to do something," says Olivia. "People can't go around just threatening you, and you do nothing."

"I'm not going to the police," says Claire.

"Who might do something like this?"

"No idea. Stephen was a private person, particularly when it came to his business dealings either in the Department or outside."

"What sort of business dealings did he have outside?" says Olivia.

"I don't know really. He was often on his phone, late at night," she says. "Or hiding his emails if I came into his study."

"Excuse me for saying this, but could those have been other women he was talking to." Claire's eyes are heavier in that second.

"I should look through his laptop," says Claire. "His solicitor gave me the password to his computer this afternoon, but what am I looking for?"

"Anything you didn't know about, that would be a good place to start."

Claire knocks back another mouthful of wine. "I've never done anything like this, but you have."

"What do you mean?"

"Lawyers, they do that don't that don't they?" says Claire. "You must know about researching what happened in cases like this, when someone gets killed."

Olivia doesn't answer, but stops to think. She knows how own her mind works and no matter how much she pushes this away as someone else's problem, the fact is that she could help. Her resistance is poor when there's something she can do, and one of the reasons Olivia got into the legal profession in the first place was to see people brought to justice. She takes a deep breath.

"When you search the computer, if anything looks untoward, why don't you send it to me?"

"Thank you," says Claire. "I want to be able to tell the truth to our child."

"I thought Stephen said you don't have kids."

Claire pats her stomach. "We will in seven months' time."

"Did he know?"

"No," says Claire.

Olivia leaves the Boyds' house later in the evening and walks back through the streets towards the tube station. The night is deathly quiet, no sound breaks through despite traffic running down the hill at the road junction up ahead. The only sound is her heels on the paving.

Then she hears something else. Is that steps behind her? She turns to look but there's no one there. She tells herself off for being paranoid.

After another minute, she hears them again.

This time, she is not mistaken. She looks around and sees man in a dark overcoat in half shadow on the opposite side of the street. As she sees him, he stops and steps back under the trees that overhang the path on that side.

She walks on, more briskly this time. In another minute, she can see the tube station and its red and blue sign glowing in the December evening. Her mind is latched on to the sound of the footsteps behind her, and now she can tell the man is quickening his pace.

Olivia gets to the main road and walks out from the kerb. A car is suddenly right in front of her, the headlights in her face. The driver lets off a long horn blast in anger. Olivia puts her hand up in apology, continues to the far side and walks into the station. Just inside the doorway, she grabs a free paper from the stand and turns to the wall as though she is reading. The man enters within thirty seconds. She waits until he's gone through the gates and he is waiting for the lift. Olivia plants herself at the far side of a crowd of six people. The lift arrives and the man goes in first, Olivia waits and goes in last, keeping hidden from his view. They all descend to the track level and the man seems to be nervous, willing the car to go faster. He pushes the doors open and rushes off to the platforms. Olivia follows at a safe distance. She can see him scouring the faces of the people on the platform as the train arrives. He waits, not getting on but watching all those who do. As the door closing alarm sounds, Olivia moves rapidly across the platform into a carriage. The man sees her, starts to move towards the train himself, but the doors close and he bangs on the door to get it to open. There's a second when Olivia feels safer, then the door open again, the man gets on the train further down from where she's standing. The door alarm starts again, the doors move to lock her inside. At the last possible second, she puts her foot forward, blocking the door, then pushes through as the doors force themselves shut. She lands on the platform and the train moves out of the station. She scans the windows for the man. Then she sees him, staring at her through the rushing glass. As he passes her, he keeps his eyes locked on her all the way until the tunnel mouth swallows him and he disappears into the inky blackness.

CHAPTER FIVE

When Olivia arrives at the office the next morning, Tom is already at his desk. She puts her belongings down and logs in to her machine.

"Tom?" she calls across the space to his desk, twenty feet away. "You sounded knowledgeable about the Alpins the other night at the party. What else do you know about them?" She walks over to him. He lays down a pen he has been using and takes a sip of coffee from a cup next to him.

After a moment, he begins. "Do you remember when Jeremy was in the papers a few years back?"

She shakes her head. "I was in the States then," she says.

"It was the first time I'd ever heard of him. His father was a member of parliament and Jeremy did a big deal to provide some government services, can't remember what. A journalist dug into his past thinking his father had fiddled it."

"And had he?"

"It seems not, it all went quiet. His dad lost his seat at the next election anyway and set up GreenLink with his son. The father, Sir Bruce Alpin is a bit shadowy and uses his old status as a lawmaker to wheedle cozy advisor jobs."

"Doesn't Jeremy have a reputation as a party animal?" she says.

"A few years ago he did. But he settled down, got married to Greer.

"And what do you know about her?" says Olivia.

"She's led a much more interesting life. Her father made money out of sugar and her mother spent it," says Tom. He does his little smile that Olivia has grown to like. "Greer aspires to be a member of parliament, I think."

"I met her," says Olivia. "I don't think the two of them get on."

"Wouldn't surprise me."

"What else do you know about them?"

"Jeremy has no siblings but his wife has a brother, can't remember his name. Public school idiot by all accounts," says Tom. "He got a job as a researcher in Westminster straight out of uni, helping a junior minister. Being the second generation of a rich family he generally behaved appallingly. He didn't have his father's business expertise, but what he did have was an inflated view of his own skills, he was in the papers a lot."

Olivia laughs. "I'm getting the vague impression you don't like him."

"Merely reporting facts." He smiles at her. "Anyway the house of cards came falling down when he was caught after hours with a lady of the night inside the chamber of the House of Commons." Tom raises his eyebrows as a finale to the story.

She pushes on with her plan. "Did Stephen know the Alpins?"

"Our Stephen?" Tom's brow furrows. "A bit, but not socially I think. Stephen was from a very different mold

- Grammar School boy from Manchester. His wife's family is well-connected though. Everyone was surprised when he ended up with Claire. She's a member of the Harwell family. He did well for himself, until..."

Words are not needed to finish the sentence and they pause as it sits in the room between them.

*

By the end of the working day, Olivia just wants to have an evening in. She arrives home at six, dumps her coat and shoes and changes into jeans. She starts to make food. Almost immediately her doorbell sounds and she walks over to the entry-phone screen. A black-helmeted motor cyclist in captured on the video. She presses the door open button and waits, but doesn't open the door to her flat.

After less than a minute, a fist bangs on her front door.

"Parcel!" the man shouts from outside.

Something about what Claire had told her, and the man following her last night has made this caller feel more risky.

She approaches the door. "Leave it outside will you, I'm just out of the shower."

"It needs to be signed for."

She stops and thinks, then remembers something she has done a couple of times in the past when she was involved with certain where she had started to feel her own safety threatened. She goes to the kitchen and pulls a knife from the kitchen drawer and stuffs it into the back of her jeans. Then she turns the lock on the front door and depresses the handle.

The man is tall anyway, and even taller with his crash helmet on. The visor is up but he has a balaclava on underneath that obscures his nose, leaving just two blue-grey eyes staring out of the helmet at her.

"Here," he mumbles, and hands her a small electronic device with a screen.

She signs with her finger on the screen but it's nothing like her real signature. She hands it back to him and he looks at the screen. For a second, he pauses, not moving. She can feel the hairs on the back of her neck flick up and a shiver run through her skeleton. The cold blade of the knife is pressed into her lower back. The man moves his arm behind him.

He produces an A4 envelope. "Here you go. Cheers." He turns away and through the door to the stairs. Olivia can feel a single bead of sweat drop down from her forehead to her eyebrow.

She returns to the kitchen, pours herself a large glass of red wine, goes into the lounge, sits on the sofa and tears open the envelope. Inside, there are six sheets of paper and a note from Claire saying, 'This is all I could find'. Olivia gets her notebook and opens a clean page. She reads the documents and makes notes to decipher what they tell her.

The papers show that Stephen Boyd had been in contact with a man called Evan Rice at various times over the last six months. At first, exactly what they were discussing isn't clear to her, but in the string of emails that Claire printed off, it seemed as though Rice was selling something. Neither Stephen nor Rice ever described what it was they were buying and selling, once Rice used the phrase, 'the goods will be ready for you to collect after Friday,' and on another document, Stephen had written, 'there's a need to retain the merchandise a little longer'. From her experience, this does indicate something that could be construed to be underhand, or even illegal, but it's not evidence.

There's a further two pages of messages from a phone, this time between Stephen and someone called Jas. Again, they tend to talk in vague language but towards the end of the last page, Jas had typed, 'you realize the consequences of your actions here, do you, S?' Stephen's reply comes five minutes later, 'Of course'. Then Jas comes back, 'Security is such an important matter these days'. There are no further response from Stephen to this message.

Olivia checks the date and timings of the messages against her calendar. It doesn't seem to make sense, and she re-checks the dates. But it's suddenly clear to her - the messages between Jas and Stephen were sent when Stephen went off to apparently call his wife, while Ellen and Olivia chatted in the bar on the night of his death. Jas had given Stephen a warning only a few hours before his dead body was found on the railway.

There's no more in the documents, so Olivia gets her laptop and searches for Evan Rice. There are many men with that name and she laboriously goes through websites and social media pages to find some link to Stephen Boyd. Most of the men she finds have little information about them online, or what she can find doesn't link. Her eyes start to hurt from the screen after a long day in Whitehall, but she ploughs on.

She says to herself that she'll look at one more 'Evan Rice' then call it a night. This last one is British, he went to a private school, and he had a privileged childhood by the looks of it. She finds a link to a charity dinner where he spoke, it doesn't look like there are any links to the Boyds. Olivia reads the start of the speech, 'It is a great pleasure to be here tonight, and there is only one woman that I can really thank for my receiving this invitation at all, that is my darling sister Greer.'

Her heart skips a beat. To double check what he brain has already concluded, Olivia does another search, this time for 'Greer Rice'.

There, in the first search result, she sees the words she has been looking for, dated seven years ago. 'Mr. and Mrs. Lionel Rice are pleased to announce the marriage of their daughter Greer to Mr. Jeremy Alpin at The Sacred Heart Church, Angel Street, Petworth, West Sussex'.

Stephen was messaging the younger brother of Greer Alpin, right up until the day he died.

Olivia's mind races on. The next questions that she needs to answer are what sort of business were the two of them part of? And did the messages that Claire found on the laptop lead to the untimely death of Stephen Boyd, implicating the Alpin family?

CHAPTER SIX

The note from Gia on Olivia's desk is short and sweet. 'Heather wants to see you'.

Millie's eyes give away nothing as Olivia reaches Heather's office. The Minister of Business, Energy and Industrial Strategy is standing looking out of her office window.

"Minister?" says Olivia.

The woman turns to her. "Olivia, I had a call from Lord Chatwood."

"I don't know who that is."

"Claire Boyd's father." The woman's eyes explore Olivia's demeanour. "He was raising a complaint to me."

"OK."

"You have been bothering his daughter, apparently."

"Bothering?" says Olivia, her brows dropping. "We met, certainly."

"How did you meet?"

"At the police station, I was there to give my witness statement and…"

The woman interrupts. "I take it you aren't planning to see her again?"

"Possibly, why does it matter?"

"Lord Chatwood doesn't want his family brought under any pressure at this delicate time."

"Mrs Boyd asked me to visit her, minister, not the other way around. I didn't pressure her into anything, and I got the impression she wasn't being bothered by my being there, quite to opposite in fact. She is feeling in need of support after Stephen."

"And that support is being fully provided by her family," says Heather.

"What did you say to her father?"

"I assured him that my staff will do as he wishes."

"Can I ask a question?" says Olivia. Heather's slight frustration starts to show, brought on by Olivia's refusal to be a doormat.

"Of course."

"Do we know anything about the circumstances of Stephen's death?"

"The police are dealing with all that," says Heather. "We don't need to concern ourselves with it."

"Aren't you curious?" says Olivia. "It would look bad if it turns out that it was suicide rather than an accident, wouldn't it? Reflect badly on the Department?"

"What makes you say that?" Heather is suddenly more engaged with the conversation.

"What Claire told me is that Stephen had a tendency to be secretive, he kept things from her. Maybe he got in over his head and chose to end it all?"

Olivia's expertise from dealing with witnesses and clients gives her a heightened ability to see how behaviour gives away thought, and Heather's whole attitude has shifted in the last minute from reprimanding boss to self-protective politician.

"Let me make a suggestion, minister," she says. "Whilst treading very carefully, obviously, if I happen to find out any more about the circumstances surrounding his death, I could keep you updated."

Heather's eyes move into a smile, acknowledging Olivia's perception of the issues. "Yes," she says slowly "I think that would be a good idea."

*

Shaftesbury Avenue is busy with traffic as Olivia makes her way along the pavement and turns up Great Windmill Street then left into Ham Yard. Ellen is sitting in on one of the soft seating areas in the Ham Yard Hotel with half a margarita in front of her when Olivia arrives.

As she sits down, Olivia can see that this is quite a different woman from how she was on the night of Stephen's death. Then she was calm, confident and happy; now she is broken. A waitress comes up to them and Olivia orders a glass of Malbec.

"How are things?" says Olivia.

"Difficult," says Ellen.

"Is it Stephen?"

Ellen takes a gulp of her drink. "He wouldn't have killed himself," says Ellen. "I've known him for over six years."

"It's officially an accident."

"I know."

"You don't believe it?"

"No I don't. I miss him."

"What do you know about his background?" says Olivia, sensing this woman will know more about Stephen's private life.

"Ordinary - he grew up in the north, middle class. Went to uni, came out, got a job in the civil service straight away; worked there all his life."

"And what was he like?" says Olivia.

Ellen can't help face revealing tender memories as she thinks about Stephen. "He was a kind man," she says. "Thoughtful."

"Perfect then?"

Ellen looks at her, directly in the eyes. "He had his weaknesses." Ellen has slowed down her delivery as she remembers. Olivia waits for more. "He could be overly protective, and he went into panics sometimes when he couldn't control everything at work."

"Control freak?" She's being intentionally spiky.

"Could be," says Ellen quietly. "He did get passionate about some things and then, yes, he wanted everyone to do it according to his plan."

"Did that extend to his private life?" says Olivia.

"You writing a blog post on him or something?" says Ellen, smiling.

"Just nosey," says Olivia. They both laugh but she doesn't let go of her line of questioning. "What about his wife, what do you make of her?"

"I knew Claire before she met Stephen, sort of introduced them. She's a cold fish though," says Ellen. "When she was in her early twenties she slept around, a string of blokes, all sorts too. She just dumped each one when the new one came along."

"She's rich, isn't she?"

"From a rich family, sure. Her mum and dad used to be plain old Gerald and Patricia Harwell. She's a judge and he was an MP years ago in Devon, they made him a Baron when he retired, so now they're Lord and Lady Chatwood.

"You know them?"

"I used to go around to her parents place in Mayfair, a big fuck-off house. They had a place in Sussex too. They were alright, but I was, maybe, twenty-one when I used to go there. They always seemed a bit distant really, like they had fingers in loads of pies and they weren't going to tell you about them."

"Think they had something to hide?" Ellen shakes her head and shrugs her shoulders.

"You trust Claire?" says Olivia.

Ellen considers the question and finishes her drink as she does so. "Probably not." She looks up at Olivia. "Another drink?"

*

It has started to rain on the windscreen of the black cab as it turns into Drury Lane. Greer pays the driver and runs across into the glazed doors of The Delaunay restaurant and disappears inside. The place is nearly full but the maitre d'hotel is the essence of calm generosity as he shows her to a table tucked away to one side that he keeps for his special guests.

Greer orders a bottle of Sauvignon and looks around at the clientele. After five minutes, the man walks in who she is waiting for. Tall, he is wearing a bespoke Ozwald

Boateng suit in dark blue under his mackintosh. As the man is shown to her table, Greer's mind can't help thinking that this man, Adrian Gilbraith, editor of the news app 'newsource', is going to be very useful to her.

"Greer, my darling, you look fabulous."

"You always do, Adrian." He widens her eyes in recognition of the words.

They order starters. "I saw Jeremy in the news the other day - saying something about that civil servant chap who died. We didn't run the story."

"He was just buttering them up, as usual," says Greer. "He's good at that."

"You don't often compliment him, Greer."

She smiles politely. "He has his moments."

"Still fucking that tart, is he?" Adrian takes a mouthful of wine.

"I didn't come here to talk about my husband," she says. "I want your help."

"Above board or underhand?"

"Both."

"Intrigue. Lovely."

Their starters arrive, they both have Dorset Crab Salad.

"How can I help?"

"I want to be an MP, Adrian."

"How can *I* help with that, darling?"

"Pull strings, run some stories about me," says Greer.

"You *do* know you need to be voted in, don't you?"

"No need to be rude, darling. Sir Bruce is sorting that."

"Jeremy's father?" says Adrian. "The old member of parliament helping the next generation?"

"He's finding a safe seat and convincing some old boy to retire."

"And you want PR cover from me to position you as the next best thing since sliced bread?"

Greer drinks her wine and looks over the glass at Adrian as he eats his crab.

"I think we can do something," he says.

"I'd be indebted to you."

"An interesting choice of words you use," says Adrian. "There is a quid pro quo."

"What?"

"In exchange for supporting you unequivocally as a candidate, you'll owe me one."

They smile at each other, then Greer picks up her Sauvignon again and Adrian does the same. They chink glasses and make slight nods at the other.

*

Ellen has to go and leaves Olivia to finish her drink. She moves around to where Ellen had been on the bench seat, gets out her laptop and starts to see if she can build a file on Evan Rice to help her think about the questions she has in her mind.

Evan Christopher Rice is the son of Lionel and Delia Rice. He is the younger brother to Greer. After attending Winchester College he went to Durham University where he studied Art History. As Tom had told her, Evan got a job as a researcher in the Houses of Parliament but was sacked after being caught having sex in the Commons Chamber one August evening.

He disappeared for a couple of years then emerged as a lobbyist working for Anstone Lobby Partners. There is little on the clients of Anstone which doesn't surprise Olivia as lobbyists don't like the glare of publicity. There's a very short profile piece on the Anstone website that says hardly anything about Evan's expertise. Olivia suspects his social skills and ability to drink, learnt at school and university, may be his major contribution to Anstone profits.

She searches again about the scandal but there's nothing, which makes her think it was hushed up. Olivia searches, 'Evan Rice girlfriend', and finds one Facebook entry with pictures of a party on a beach four years ago. Evan is there with his arm around a woman. The caption reads, 'Evan Rice and Cat Beecham, can she really be his girlfriend?'

Olivia writes it all down in her notebook.

"All alone, Ms Streete?" The voice comes to her across the table. She looks up.

"Violet. How are you?"

"Can I join you?" says the woman.

"Please." Violet seems to pour herself into the chair opposite without spilling a drop of her Daiquiri.

"What brings you to London's red light district?" says Violet.

"Soho? Is that still true?" Olivia pulls her eyebrows down.

"You can't hide sex away."

"Were you just passing this place?" says Olivia.

"A business meeting." Violet waves her hand vaguely over her shoulder.

Olivia doesn't want to explore any more details of what that meeting may involve. "Tell me about Jeremy," she says.

"What you want to know?"

"What's he like?"

"In the sack? Good, considering his wife isn't interested."

Olivia rides the wave of shock and awe. "What's he like as a man?" What makes him tick?"

"Thinking of trying to get into his bed, Olivia?"

"I'm going to have to work with him, insights about clients are always useful."

"Aren't they just," says Violet. "Well, he's sensitive, kind at times and likes simple pleasures – that's a reaction to his privileged childhood where they carted him off to boarding school too young. But on the other side of the scales, he's jealous, childish, and he can be cruel."

"Who's he jealous of?"

"Greer mostly," she says. "And anyone with a better lifestyle then him, and for some sad reason he constantly seeks out people like that for companionship, then doesn't understand why he gets frustrated at their shows of wealth."

"Why is he jealous of Greer?"

"She's more intelligent than he is, has more friends. People like her, not many people like Jeremy for who he is, they mostly want to know him for the size of his wallet."

"Does that include you?"

Violet smiles. "Sleeping with men for a living gives you a certain power, Olivia. But only as long as they're interested. The art is to get out before they lose interest." She sips her drink. "What do *you* want from him?"

"Honesty."

"Then, I fear you are going to be disappointed."

"He's just someone who is part of the landscape of people I have to deal with in this job," says Olivia. "He's important to other people, so he's a person of interest for me."

Violet stops and watches Olivia. "Maybe we can help each other," she says.

"Maybe."

Violet looks at her watch. "I need to go. My handsome princes await. Cheerio." She raises her glass as she turns to leave and walks across to a group of men at the bar.

CHAPTER SEVEN

The queue is short at the St Stephen's Entrance to the Houses of Parliament. The security team inspect Jeremy's bag and scan his clothing, and one of them nearly salutes as he walks through the gates and into the guts of the Palace of Westminster. This building always makes him feel slightly depressed with its dark wood panelling and careworn pale green carpet near the Commons Chamber. He arrives at the Members' Dining Room and can see his father waiting at a table in the centre. His father's three-piece suit is a size too big for him, which is something that Jeremy remembers from his childhood. His greying hair, that was once black, is cut short back and sides by the same barber who has done it for thirty years. Sir Bruce Alpin displays a red nose and saggy face from decades of smoozing, but his small brown eyes still show lively attention to detail.

"Hello, Dad."

"Jeremy!" He raises his hand to shake but doesn't stand.

A bottle of Domaine de la Genillotte Chablis is already open on the table and Jeremy pours himself a glass before the waiter can get to them.

"Are you still allowed in here, Dad?"

"I have my contacts." Sir Bruce winks at his son. "Tell me what's going on with you, my boy."

"Work, mostly."

"What's happening on this communications bid for Heather Wells?" says Sir Bruce.

"She's dragging her feet."

"Want me to have a word?"

"You don't work here anymore, Dad."

"The only important thing in this place," he says, waving his glass around to indicate the Palace. "Is who you know. Once you've been here, you never really leave."

"I've got a couple of people working on the inside to ensure I get it."

"Civil Servants?" says Sir Bruce.

"We all have our private networks." A waitress approaches to take their order.

After their food, the dining room has started to empty.

"I wanted to talk to you about a little deal I'm putting together," says Sir Bruce. His son looks up at him. "There's some land that I have had my eye on in Docklands. Derelict site now, it was warehousing fifty years ago. Prime for development."

"What's the plan?"

"Food processing plant."

"Isn't it all residential or retail out there?" says Jeremy.

"This land *is* earmarked for residential in the local plan," says Sir Bruce. "However, I have some friends on the Planning Committee."

"And they can get it through?"

"With sufficient incentive, yes." Sir Bruce's eyes twinkle.

"I know what your incentives are like, Dad."

"Wondered if you wanted in?"

"How much?"

"We're looking for ten million capital."

"I'm probably good for a million," says Jeremy. "I have a condition, though."

His father waits.

"My involvement is anonymous."

"Why?"

"I have to manage my PR these days," says Jeremy. "There are a few things going on that I want to keep close to my chest, so this project is fine, but any implication of under-hand practices, I can't afford to be seen to be involved."

"Then you have my word," says Sir Bruce. "Your investment will be confidential."

*

The Eve Bar on Southampton Street in Soho is half full and the barman is coping efficiently with the volume of drinks orders. As the place promotes cocktails, he has mastered the art of mixing quickly and memorising all fifty four of the drinks on the menu. Poppy walks out of the ladies bathroom and back to the table that she and Marianne have been at for two hours.

"Another?" says Marianne, pointing at the empty martini glasses in front of them.

A man in his twenties has been sitting on one of the bar stools and walks over. "Can I buy you ladies some drinks?"

"You American?" He nods. The women looks at each other and smile, then accept his offer.

Half an hour later, the three of them are laughing at a story about when the man was at Glastonbury last summer as they have discovered a joint love of music festivals.

"What do you do?" says Marianne.

"Writer," he says.

"What sort of stuff?"

"All sorts, news websites, a few profile pieces."

"What about?" says Poppy.

"Mostly political," he says. "And politicians' sordid lives."

"Tell us more," says Marianne her eyes lighting up. "What gossip you got?"

"They're all fiddling something," he says.

"I bet."

"D'you only do US stuff, though?"

"No," he says. "England too. That's why I'm here."

"Come on, spill," says Marianne. "Who are you looking into over here, then?"

"I can't say."

The women turns their noses up in disappointment. "You're no fun," says Marianne, finishing her cocktail in one gulp.

"Alright." He laughs. "There was that guy who died a few days ago, you see it?" The women look blank. "Anyway, he was working with another guy who has been covering stuff up for years."

"And he had him killed?" says Poppy, getting more interested. She puts her hand on his leg.

"That's what I gotta find out."

"Why did they kill him?" says Poppy.

"Dunno," he says. "I'm researching all the details, what happened, what he was doing to get himself killed."

"They could go to prison, couldn't they?"

"Sure."

"The big question," says Poppy. "Is… are you buying another round?" The man reaches for his wallet and the woman smile at each other in victory.

"We don't even know your bloody name," says Marianne.

"Ethan," he says.

*

Olivia can't get a number of questions she has out of her mind. When she gets home, she rifles through her sideboard drawers and pulls out a pack of sticky notes. She grabs a marker pen then walks to the big window that leads out to the balcony and writes, 'Stephen' on a note then sticks it high up in the middle of the glass.

She writes on more notes then sticks, 'Alpins', 'Claire', 'Harwells', and 'Work' across the pane.

"Now, what are the major questions for each group?" she says out loud to herself.

She thinks about the Alpins. They have power undoubtedly and where there is power, there is instability, in Olivia's experience. From her very brief conversation at the party and having overheard the argument, Greer is in control of that relationship. Jeremy seems to be influential, but he is also very careful about his public image, and only people with something to hide have to manage their public image. He seems untrustworthy, certainly. His veneer of charm in only that, she can tell. The party, and many like it before no doubt, are only about bringing people into his web.

Greer is a different matter. A rich girl from her father's wealth, but hasn't yet done much of consequence with her life, or she's been careful not to get much captured online. There are no pictures of her on holiday islands with yachts, there are no pictures of her coming out of nightclubs. There doesn't seem to be a public image for her to care about, or not a bad one to cover up. The woman remains a mystery.

And then there's the brother. A lobbyist now, so instantly untrustworthy - a salesman, supporting whichever piper is paying him to dance.

Under the Alpins column, she sticks some notes.

'How would Stephen's death benefit Jeremy or Greer?'

'What was the relationship between Stephen and Evan?'

Now, Claire Boyd. She played the grieving widow the other night, but her lawyer's cynicism makes Olivia question whether that is the whole truth and nothing but the truth.

There's no doubt Stephen married well. Claire had a top-drawer education and childhood. Olivia finds pictures from Facebook when it was at its height. The Maldives, Cyprus, Malta; long sunny days and family meals from restaurants up in the hills with views of verdant valleys and shining seas.

After university, where she had met Ellen, Claire seems to have become a freelance designer and set up a workshop in a converted warehouse in the East End of London. Six or seven artists and creatives had shared the space. She had done graphic work, much of it digital, but some physical arty pieces, maybe under the influence of the painters and potters in the studios around her. There's no evidence of boyfriends in this stage of her life on her social media despite what Ellen had said about there having been many. When Stephen appears, the coverage of her life online distinctly changes. Suddenly, the images Claire shared were more cultured, more serious. Opera, quiet weekends in Hastings, farmers markets; the creative Claire all but disappeared.

Olivia guesses that, like many couples, they were changing to find common ground, and that necessitated losing some parts of her passions. Olivia also knows that this change can be a root of discontent sometimes, and wonders if they were happy together.

Under the Claire sticky note, she adds the questions in her mind.

'How did Stephen end up marrying a well-connected heiress?'

'What did Claire really know about Stephen's activities?'

'Who sent the letter?'

Claire's parents are another area that Olivia needs more information about. The only reason that there's a column for them on the window at all is due to Ellen's ideas that there may be more to Gerald and Patricia Harwell than meets the eye.

Under the Harwells sticky note, she adds:

'What companies is Gerald Harwell involved with?'

'What issues is he pushing in the Lords?'

'What cases is Patricia Harwell is presiding over?'

Olivia stares at the Work note, thinks for a second then rips off two blanks and writes.

'Who is bidding for the big contract apart from GreenLink?'

'Had Stephen created any enemies inside Government?'

She stands back to admire her handiwork. This is a lot of work, she knows. But she can't resist a chance to dig out the truth. At first, she had accepted that Stephen's death was an unfortunate accident, but the thing that told her that may not be the case was the warning from Lord Harwell via Heather. You only get warnings when there's something to hide, it's a clear indication that Stephen's death isn't all it seems.

She considers where to begin, and suspects that Evan Rice is critical to the whole set of relationships, so decides to start there. While Olivia doesn't like pretence, in her gut she feels that Evan will give more away if he considers there's something in it for him. She walks to the window and looks out at London's bustle and movement. From her vantage point, she can see Tower Bridge and the buildings on the north bank rising up from the river, their lights bouncing up from the rippling water, and slowly a plan comes into her head.

*

Cold rain has started to fall on Jermyn Street as the cab pulls up outside the Cavendish Hotel. Jeremy pays off the driver and jumps out. Stanley, on the door, tips his hat to Jeremy.

"Good night for it, sir."

"It's always a good night for it, Stan." Jeremy shakes the man's hand, leaving a ten pound note in his fingers.

"Anything you need, sir, I'm your man."

"Thank you, Stan."

Jeremy ascends to the seventh floor and knocks on Room 701. There's no answer so he turns the handle and goes inside.

"Darling?" Violet calls from the bathroom. Jeremy appears at the door to the room. Violet is in the bath, she stands up in the tub. "Help me out will you?" He offers his hand and she steps out. Jeremy offers her a towel. "No, come here," she says and grabs his hand then pulls her towards him and kisses him. He lifts her up and carries her to the bed.

Violet leans over and checks the time on her phone by the bedside, then turns back to Jeremy and lays an arm across his chest.

"That suit's bloody ruined," he says.

"That's the price you have to pay for having me in your life, Jeremy." They both smile and he kisses her.

"The price I have to pay," he repeats, almost to himself.

"When we live together, darling," she says. "I'll buy you much better suits than that one." He looks at her but stays silent.

"Are you frightened?"

"Of what?"

"Letting go of her," says Violet.

He thinks about a suitable response. "It's just timing, you know?" he says.

"Timing of what?"

"A couple of deals I have going on; and Dad's just invited me into some land development in Docklands."

"What's that got to do with you starting the divorce?"

"All these things take time, they take *my* time," says Jeremy. "I can't give my full attention to business if Greer kicks up all sort of fuss."

"Will she?"

"You know she will." He kisses her again. "It'll be a roller-coaster for us. She'll want to take me for all she can."

"I'll be here for you."

"I know, my darling."

CHAPTER EIGHT

Olivia, Tom and Ellen spend all morning in the conference room sorting out the paperwork for the contract which have all been printed off by Gia for a reason that escapes Olivia. This stage is only a vetting process to ensure only viable companies go to the next round – which is when they submit their bids.

There are three companies who have applied: GreenLink, Salango, and Mercantile-Lindle. She hasn't heard of the other two but they have all sent in details of their directors and partnerships, and Olivia makes a mental note to go through those sections later to glean any insights about links to Stephen Boyd or the Harwells.

Ellen goes off to lunch with a friend and Olivia invites Tom to the staff canteen on the third floor. They queue for quiche and shepherd's pie under garish lights, then sit on orange, moulded seats at a table with a yellow top.

"How long have you worked here, Tom?"

"Ten years."

"Bored yet? Being in the same place, I mean."

"Sometimes."

"Why don't you do something about it?" She looks at his slightly down-turned eyes. "You ever looked outside?"

"I'm happy here," he says.

"What did you want to do when you were a kid?"

"Artist," he says without discomfort.

"Painter?"

"Yup, oils. Portraits."

"You still do it?" she says.

"Not for years," says Tom. "I had a girlfriend, Kate. We spent all our time together when I wasn't at work, and before I could look round it was seven years later. One day, I was looking through a cupboard and found my old stuff, but it was all dried up."

"What happened to Kate?"

"She died."

"I'm sorry." He doesn't respond and Olivia can't tell if he is still affected by her death.

"You should paint again," says Olivia.

"I need someone to paint, I only do portraits."

"Why don't you ask Ellen?" The words come out before she has thought them. There's an embarrassed pause. "She could do with something new in her life," she adds. Olivia smiles at him and he does a little smile in return.

Her phone hums on the table. She reads the message from Claire which tells her the name of the courier company who had delivered the letter to the Boyd's home.

"We've got nothing big on this afternoon, have we?" she says to Tom, who shakes his head between mouthfuls of food. "In that case, I'll take a half day."

*

TrustEZE Couriers are based along Ashwin Street in Dalston. She catches the District Line then the Overground to reach the place. At the corner she turns down the street. It turns a dog-leg half way down to reveal a large red sign with the company name on, sitting over a small, dismal shop unit. Olivia pushes the half open aluminium door in the centre of the shop front and goes inside. A tall desk stands across the whole room with shelving behind stuffed with packages. There are piles of damaged boxes in one corner awaiting someone's attention. Two men move around the shelves picking up boxes in the body of the room, and three motorbike-helmeted people stand at the far left hand side, all staring at their phones as they wait for pickups.

"Yes, love?" One of the men walks over to her on the other side of the desk.

"I had a parcel delivered," she says. "But there was no sender's name."

"Right," says the man as he types into a keyboard. "Taz!" he shouts towards the helmeted waiters, one of whom walks over and takes the parcel on the counter in front of the man. "Camden, and don't fucking leave it without a photo again." Taz doesn't reply but walks out. "Wrongly delivered, love?" the man says to Olivia.

"No, I wanted to know who sent it."

"Can't tell you that," he says. "Data Protection, you know?"

"But it was sent to me."

"Not much I can do, darlin', don't want to break the law," he goes back to looking at his computer screen.

"Ali!" Another of the waiting couriers walks over. "Highgate." He turns back to Olivia. "Anyway, sorry, love. Anything else I can do for you?"

"You know you said about not breaking the law."

The man stops and looks at her. "What about it?"

"All your drivers got insurance for their bikes?"

"You a copper?" he says.

"Just asking," she says. "Wouldn't want you to break the law."

The man sucks on a blue pen for a second. "What's the name?"

"Claire Boyd, Well Walk, Hampstead."

"Date?"

"Twenty-ninth."

"It'll only be the pick-up address," he says without looking at her. He types and reads off the screen, then takes a square of paper from a stack next to his machine. He writes on the paper then folds it and pushes it over the counter to her. "You didn't get this from me."

"Thank you," she says and walks back outside. She unfolds the paper. On it are written five words, 'Houses of Parliament Postal Despatch.'

*

The knock on Claire's door is not unexpected as it's about the time that post is delivered, and her design work means that she is often at home when that happens. The courier on her doorstep gives her a large envelope and is gone before she can say anything. She walks back slowly to the lounge and rips open one end of the manila package.

Inside, is another single piece of paper, the same as the note she received the day after Stephen's death. On the page are typed two sentences. 'We want twenty thousand pounds for us to stop going to the papers about your husband's criminal past.' Then further down the sheet, 'We'll send details of where to drop the money in a few days, get it ready. Old bills, tens and twenties only.'

Her eyebrows drop into a frown as she reads the lettering four times. She holds the paper in one hand and walks around the room in a large, absentminded circle. She stands and watches the few flakes of snow riding on the breeze and catching on the branches of the trees outside. She takes a deep breath out and reaches for her mobile in the back pocket of her jeans.

She dials a number from her contacts and waits while the call connects. "Can we meet?" she says without formality. "I need to talk." She waits while the person on the other end of the call says something. "No, we can't. Meet me later, the usual place. Nine?"

Claire ends the call and pushes the phone against her closed lips, her mind awash with ideas, only some of which upset her.

*

The first floor dining room of The Bistro restaurant on Buckingham Gate is doing a steady trade with a few members of the House and political newspaper hacks discretely discussing the going on in the village of Westminster. They chatter in quiet but infinite detail about the bubble that they care passionately about, but no one outside their world really understands.

Sir Bruce Alpin and his daughter-in-law meet outside as their taxis arrive simultaneously. The maitre d'hotel knows Sir Bruce and the couple get a good table by the window overlooking the street.

"I find this is a good place for quiet conversations," he says as they look through their menus. "Slightly out of the main flow around Parliament."

They order a bottle of Le Serre Nuove dell'Ornellaia and a shared starter of meats and cheese.

"How is Jeremy?" he says.

"I'm worried about him, Bruce."

"Tell me."

"He's made some mistakes recently," says Greer. "In his business decisions."

"With consequences?" says Sir Bruce.

"I managed to cover his arse," she says. "Or we would have paid a heavy price."

"What happened?"

"I won't give you all the details, but he made the wrong call on a contract for Germany. Agreed terms that were poor and gave the Germans a distinct advantage; all the risk was with us."

"You're a non-exec of his companies aren't you, Greer?"

She nods as she drinks her wine.

"Are you in a position to steer him clear of these mishaps?" he says.

"Only because I'm his wife," she says. "Officially, I have no power over him on business dealings apart from discussions at the board, that's one of the reasons I wanted to have lunch."

"What are you thinking?"

"That I am given an executive position," says Greer. "You're Chairman of the companies, you could get it through the Board."

"Why do you think he's making these mistakes?" says Sir Bruce.

"His mind is not on the work, he has…, shall we say, other things to occupy his attention."

"I know about his companion, Greer. I had the same at his age."

Greer doesn't give away any trace of her feelings towards the acceptance of a mistress as just part of the trappings of being a male Alpin. She considers taking her father-in-law to task over his Victorian values, but she knows that if she is to get anywhere in politics, she can't let her true feelings show.

"He needs more support on the Board, Bruce," she says. "I'm sure you can see your way to convincing him to find a role for me."

After the main course, they take coffee and move to some soft seating at the far end of the restaurant.

"Let's discuss your candidacy," says Sir Bruce, sitting down on one of two blue chairs around a square table. "I have spoken to old Mikey Chambers and he was thinking of retiring anyway at the next general election. He's more than happy to go early and trigger a by-election."

"What about the constituency party?" says Greer, stirring sugar into her drink.

"I can control them," he says. "At the next meeting Mike will tell them he's going. I'll say there's an excellent candidate and mention your name. Then you'll visit month after next. A few drinks, a meal in the local pub and you'll charm them."

"Easy as that?" she says.

"I have known most of them for forty years from when I was their MP. Not many of them have any political nous, all they're interested in is guarantees about not building new roads near their houses."

"Will I have to live there?" she says.

"I still have a cottage in the constituency, we can register that as your address."

"I do want to make a difference, Bruce," she says. "Create something good."

"We all do when we join parliament, my dear."

*

The wind is stronger now it's dark. Claire fastens the top button up on her coat to try and keep warm. The road curves alongside the railway viaduct that towers above her and the houses opposite. Properties are squeezed into all the available land in this area of London after the Victorian's carved up the suburbs with criss-crossing train tracks. She stops at one of the railway arches, almost all now filled in with offices or warehouses despite the regular rumble of engines and carriages a few feet above people's heads.

He's there, on the corner, just like always. The first sign of him in the winter air is the end of his cigarette, glowing orange in the coldness. The smoke curls up from his mouth and above his hat that is pulled down low against the weather. He doesn't frighten her anymore; he did once, before she understood what made his mind tick, before he had told her about his plans. Only when she is ten feet from him does he finally turn towards her, his coat is unbuttoned, even in this weather. He doesn't lean in to kiss her. No greeting is necessary, they always know if the other one is OK.

She tells him about the blackmail note. "What did the note say?" His voice is raspy tonight, he's been drinking she guesses.

"Threatening to go to the press."

"How much are they asking?"

"Twenty grand."

He whistles low and it cuts across the coldness to her ears then seems to bounce off the viaduct and out across the houses in the roads around them. Their conversation is cut short by a goods train trundling across the tracks above. It seems to go on forever, she thinks, and turns away to let the clackety-clacks finish before turning back to him.

"What can I do?" she says.

He shakes his head. "You got that cash?"

"Yup."

"I could stop them in other ways."

"I don't want violence," she says, grasping his hand.

"Persuasion, that's all."

"Promise me you'll not hurt them?"

"If it takes that to stop them!" His anger starts to spiral.

"No!" She nearly shouts. She grips his hand harder.

"Get off me," he says. "I'm just looking after you!" He tears his hand away but she clings on. She won't let go, he pulls his hand away but she is still attached. "Fucks sake." He slaps her across the face, only then does her grip loosen and her hand go up to her cheek.

She bows her head and holds her hand to her face. They stand together in silence.

After a minute he says. "I didn't mean to..." She doesn't reply. Claire raises her gaze to his face. There are no tears but her eyes are red around the edges, and she turns to walk away.

"Claire?" he calls. "I'll sort it."

"Don't!" she calls back to him. She walks off along the curve of the viaduct and out of sight through one of the empty archways.

CHAPTER NINE

The offices of Anstone Lobby Partners occupy the corner building where Barton and Cowley Streets meet. A quiet backstreet but only eight minutes' walk to the Houses of Parliament. Olivia turns the street corner and stops for a few seconds to take in the area. Expensive undoubtedly - Anstone had not skimped when they acquired this house for their base.

She read up on Anstone earlier this morning over an Americano and almond croissant in a café next to her block of flats. James Anstone had been a member of parliament in the seventies and set up the company when he retired in the early eighties. The company quietly built relationships with civil servants and parliamentarians on behalf of their clients for a decade. The clients had not been contentious; mostly manufacturers and trading companies from the north west of England, where James had been an MP.

'The old man', as they called him, had retired in 2000 and from that date, Anstone Lobby Partners had taken on a different trajectory. The client base shifted to more risky sectors such as genetically modified agriculture, oil derivatives and companies who were heavy polluters. As Olivia read the press coverage of those years, it was obvious that Anstone had purposely chosen difficult clients to work with. The new CEO then was a young Irishman called Gavin Delaney who built his own profile in the media defending his clients. He was brusque, but even his enemies admitted that he was an excellent lobbyist and had managed to get the clauses he wanted into the new laws being created in parliament. Delaney had been headhunted to America in the early 2010s and Anstone had shifted again. The company hardly appeared in the media from the day he left. Whether they were still successful was hard to judge, but their income has trebled in the years since Delaney, so they're doing something that clients are willing to pay for. This is the version of Anstone that still exists today, and the one that Olivia needs to know more about.

She pushes down on the handle set in a green front door and walks in to what had been the hallway of a middle-class domestic house when it was built. A woman in her thirties sits behind a dark oak desk. Her hair is highlighted blonde and with her jacket off, she reminds Olivia of an air hostess. Olivia confirms that she has an appointment with Mr Rice under the name Rebecca Delaney and she is told to wait on the upright leather two-seater sofa opposite the receptionist.

Five minutes later, a tall man comes down the stairs at the far end of a corridor that runs through the heart of the house. He has dark blonde hair and blue eyes that look intensely at Olivia as he approaches. His handshake is firm but not hard and his skin is soft. They walk to a meeting room towards the centre of the building after the receptionist promises coffees.

In the room, he takes off his grey jacket and hangs it on a coat hook by the door. He sits next to Olivia at a conference table built for eight, and turns his chair to face her. She explains that she is a freelance lawyer, working for a client who wants to remain anonymous at this stage of the discussions. Her client's products are electronic devices and software that are yet to be fully approved in the UK and her client is interested in getting their message to members of parliament to ensure that the products can be approved and sold.

"Can I ask, Ms Delaney," he says. "Why did you choose Anstone?"

"You're known for handling challenging circumstances on behalf of your clients, Mr Rice."

He nods sagely. "Tell me a bit more about the products."

"Here's a list of the technologies," she says, placing a sheet of paper on the table that she had copied from a site on the internet earlier today.

"I'm not familiar," he says. "Which are not approved yet?"

She points to three of the lines on the paper. "They're looking for you to press for approval quickly," she says.

"There's a new Telecommunications Bill in draft currently that should go to the Commons in the New Year, so that could get Royal Assent by March," says Evan. "We have another client in the sector and we already have excellent relations inside the relevant ministry."

"Let me be clear, Mr Rice." She can feel her heart speed up. "My client is prepared to be very generous to ensure the approvals go through." Evan looks directly at her, sizing up what to say. "This conversation is in strictest confidence," she says.

"Of course."

"If you need to persuade people, then, that's something you can do is it?" she continues. "People who may be reluctant."

Their eyes watch each other across the five feet between them.

"I'm sure Anstone Lobby Partners can meet all of your needs, Ms Delaney."

She makes the smallest of smiles.

"I will send you some documents," she says. "Here's my business card. You can find background about my practice on the website." She feels a flip of pride after asking Trevor, her IT friend, to create a site only twelve hours ago. "Why don't we meet again next week, Mr Rice, and you can tell me your plans? Do you know Sartoria, the restaurant?" He nods. "You can take me there. Shall we say, eight o'clock on Monday?"

*

The editorial room of Newsource is as busy as it gets. Adrian Gilbraith is sitting with his feet on his desk, reviewing a story that has just been written by one of his staffers.

"Layla!" he calls. A woman in her twenties looks up at him from across the room. "More personal stuff on this actress, darling. Less of the boring detail about her childhood." He doesn't look for a response from Layla, but moves on to another article that needs his review.

The door at the far end of the room opens and Ethan Poole walks in. No one greets him as they are all on the telephone or typing onto keyboards. He makes his way through the maze of people and hub-bub and stands in front of Adrian's desk. After a few moments, Adrian becomes aware of someone standing there and flicks his eyes up.

"Ethan."

"Hello, Adrian."

"Take a seat, love."

Adrian picks up two opened boxes of leaflets on the only chair near Adrian and looks for somewhere to put them. Finding nowhere clear, he dumps them on the floor and sits down.

"Hold on," says Adrian, as he reads. "Dan, this piece on the cabinet minister and his ex-girlfriend is fine to go up." A man raises his hand in acknowledgement by the window. Adrian turns to Ethan. "What you got for me?"

"You know that civil servant who died last week?"

"We didn't run it," says Adrian. "Bit dull to be honest."

"I've got something that links that death to Members of Parliament and a high-court judge."

Adrian widens his eyes. "You saying the chap was murdered?" Ethan nods slowly. "That might be of interest to us. What state's your story in?"

"Two weeks," says Ethan. "I know who did what but I need some more evidence to prove it."

"Tell me the outline. An MP had the civil servant killed and got the judge to cover for him?"

"More complicated than that. The guy was killed, and it links back to private deals he had been doing outside his civil service job."

"Working with the MP?"

"I don't know yet."

"What about the judge?"

"She is the mother of the dead guy's widow."

"Corrupt?"

"I'm still collecting the information."

"With the greatest respect, Ethan, darling, you haven't got much apart from your hunch that something dodgy went on," says Adrian. "Come back to me when you have hard evidence of a crime, and I'll look at it. Some vague accusations would expose Newsource too much."

"I'll get the evidence."

"I need colour too," says Adrian. "Hookers, drugs, intrigue! The more of that stuff you can get the nearer the home page of the app we'll put you."

"I know," says Ethan. "I'll get you something."

*

A dark blue Bentley Mulsanne pulls up at the kerb outside the Royal Courts of Justice as a woman shelters from a cold drizzle that has rolled in across London after the early dusk. She has grey hair, fashioned in a curly perm, her face is younger than her years with pale, oval eyes and a small nose. She pulls on gloves over long fingers, draws her coat around her, and puts up a red umbrella then walks the ten yards from the courthouse to the car. In the meantime, the chauffeur of the Bentley has stepped out into the streaming traffic and has walked around to open the door for her. She manages to hold on to her briefcase and hand him her umbrella in the few seconds that he stands there waiting for her to get in. Then he closes her door, before walking round and dropping into the driver's seat.

"Bloody weather!" she says to the man next to her. "Good day, darling?" She turns to him as he reads a copy of the Financial Times in front of him.

"Oh, you know," says Gerald.

Patricia looks at him. His hair is cut short and his round face is framed with large glasses which she has never liked. He turns to her and his brown eyes smile gently.

"What?" she says.

"Bit of a mixed bag. Good lunch with Kelsey, but two committees in the afternoon got nowhere."

"You worried about something?" she says, her eyes narrowing.

"Claire."

"Ah, yes." She breathes in and out deeply. "I spoke to her yesterday," she says. "Seems to be coping."

"She called in to see me at the House."

"Oh? Today?"

"Mmm," he says. "She looked tired. We should do something."

"Why don't we invite her down for the weekend?" says Patricia. "Invite some friends. Make a fuss of her."

"Good idea."

"Who would you invite?"

"You're better at that than I am, darling," he says.

"Let me think," she says, turning to watch the traffic and the rain outside. He returns to reading. "Alice and Avery, The Deelands, Teresa who she knew at school, who has a new man, whose name I have forgotten. Them anyway, and Lawrence of course."

"Her ex-boyfriend!" he says. "Hardly appropriate, her husband's not yet in the ground."

"Alright." She puts her hand on his. "Who else?"

"I wouldn't mind inviting the Alpins."

"Really? I don't really know them," says Patricia. "Why them?"

"She wants to stand as an MP." He looks across at his wife for reaction. Her eyebrows raise.

"Does she have any political experience?"

"No."

"But you're considering her?"

"Mike Chambers wants to retire," he says. "She'd bring in new blood, younger, female, be good for the party."

"I see now," says Patricia. "That's Bruce Alpin's old constituency isn't it? North Sussex. You think you can shoe-horn her in on the basis of old memories of her father-in-law?"

Gerald says nothing and pretends to read his paper. Patricia returns to watching the traffic as they pass Clapham South tube station and turn onto the B237.

"OK," she says after ten minutes. "I take it that you'll invite the Alpins, I'll do the rest?"

"Righto, my darling," he says without looking up.

CHAPTER TEN

Poppy is late for lunch. Olivia flashes a look at the clock on the wall of the pizza restaurant on Northumberland Avenue where she's been sitting for twenty minutes. Poppy has always been late, throughout her childhood, and now she's eighteen, she's no different. Olivia thinks about the time when she was a baby, before the girl's father Ludo and Olivia had split. Then her mind skims across the years as her daughter grew up and lived mostly with Ludo as Olivia was travelling somewhere with work.

"You day-dreaming, Mum?" Her daughter's voice runs in from the real world. The girl is standing there. Olivia stands to hug her. "What were you thinking about?"

"You, actually."

"How amazing I am?"

Olivia smiles at her. "Yes." Poppy gives thumbs up as she reads the menu. A waiter approaches and they order. "How are you?" says Olivia.

"Good," says her daughter. "Met a bloke."

"Yeah? What's he like?"

"Gentle." She checks her mother's face to reaction and smiles. "American guy."

"What's he do?"

"Journo."

"Where's he work?"

"Stop doing your courtroom cross-examination stuff, Mum."

"I'm interested."

"He's freelance, anyway. Writes about politicians' dirty laundry." Their pizzas and drinks arrive. Poppy sucks on the straw of her Diet Coke.

"Is he hoping for a big story?" says Olivia.

"He's had a load of stories published."

"He's done well if he's just starting out."

Poppy's voice rises. "He's not just starting out, he's well-known in the US."

Olivia pauses for a second as her mind jumps to a question. "How old is he, Poppy?"

"Don't know."

"Not your age then?"

"Stop being ageist, mum." Olivia eats a mouthful of pizza. "What are *you* doing, anyway? This new job?"

"Working in Government," says Olivia. "A bit dull, really."

"Any gossip from 10, Downing Street?" says Poppy.

"I'm not working there, and I couldn't tell you anyway. I signed the Official Secrets Act."

"Interesting!" says Poppy. "They must have something to hide if they're muzzling you."

"Everyone signs it in Government."

"I rest my case, your worship."

"Your honour, it is."

"You know what I mean." Poppy lifts her pizza to her mouth and takes a bite from it. Olivia does her unimpressed face but Poppy ignores it.

"How's Dad?" says Olivia.

"Tabatha's still about. They're serious, I reckon."

"Good," says Olivia. "He needs stability."

"You got a new man, Mum?"

"I don't need them, you know that."

"You could do with stability too, Mum. You're not getting any younger." Her daughter smiles cheekily.

"Who's being ageist now?" says Olivia and they laugh.

On her walk back to the office, Olivia scrolls through her phone contacts and selects Inspector Savage's number then dials it. The call is answered, but he doesn't say anything, and there's silence on the line. Then after two seconds his voice comes on.

"Savage."

"Inspector, it's Olivia Streete," she says. "I gave a statement on the Stephen Boyd case?" She regrets the rising of her voice at the end of the sentence, a habit she picked up from her time in New York.

"Hello, Ms Streete."

"I was wondering if there had been any progress on the case, Inspector. I am meeting Mrs Boyd later so wanted to be prepared."

"Can I ask why you're meeting her, Ms Streete?"

"We've become friends, Inspector."

There's a slight pause as Savage assimilates this new information. "My official answer is that our investigations continue."

"Is there any new evidence?"

"Ms Streete, as I'm sure you know, I can't…"

"I'm not asking you to break the rules, Inspector. I'm just looking after my friend."

"I appreciate that," he says. "If there's anything significant that we can talk about then you'll be the second person to know, after Mrs Boyd."

"Thank you."

"My pleasure, Ms Streete."

She ends the call and turns into the reception area of her building on Whitehall Court.

*

"Greer not in, Jeremy?" says Sir Bruce Alpin as he steps over the threshold to the house in Hereford Square.

"Out at some committee meeting," says his son. "One of her pet charity things."

They walk through to the sitting room and Jeremy pours them two large whiskies before they sit in deep-red leather armchairs towards the garden end of the room.

They have had three drinks each by the time Sir Bruce feels the time is right to have the conversation that he came for.

"How are the businesses?" he says, watching his son and comparing his facial expression to his mental library of Jeremy's reactions over the years.

"You're the Chairman, Dad."

"I mean details, not strategy."

Jeremy genuinely stops to think. "Good on the whole," he says. "Very good on the trading partners, volumes are up."

"And less good where?"

"The land deals are not hitting the mark yet," says Jeremy. "But they're long-term, you know? They'll get there."

"How are you coping?" says Sir Bruce.

"Meaning, what?"

"Saw a couple of decisions from you recently that didn't work out for us."

"You've lost me." Jeremy takes a large gulp of whisky.

"Greer was saying…"

"Greer?" Jeremy nearly shouts the word. "My wife has been saying what?"

"That perhaps you need more bodies on the Board who can support you."

"And let me guess, Dad?" he says. "She has suggested that she is exactly the right person to be on the Board to provide that support?"

"I think she'd be good in an executive role."

Jeremy stands and laughs. He walks to the window.

"Don't you see what she's trying to do, Dad?" says Jeremy. "She's pulling the wool right over your eyes, planting little stories about my inability, wheedling her way in to the company."

"You *are* married, she's not wheedling anywhere. She's already part of the family."

Jeremy turns to his father and stands over him. His voice slows so he can spell out to his idiot father exactly what he needs to hear. "Over my dead fucking body, Dad, will Greer ever be an executive in our family businesses." Jeremy turns back to look out at the rain.

"I'm sorry you feel that way, Jeremy, but as Chairman, I think we need to take this to the whole Board for a discussion."

Jeremy says nothing but swigs back the last of his drink and can feel anger rise inside his body.

*

As she walks towards the restaurant that Claire has booked in Primrose Hill, Olivia turns over in her mind the information she knows about the recent widow of Stephen Boyd. Some of the things she has learnt have been positive and some less so. From her experience of building files on someone's background for court cases, guilty people are either mostly good and made a mistake, or they're mostly bad. She smiles at the idea and how, as a newly qualified solicitor, she had insisted on not categorising people but had always tried to keep an open mind. It's true that no one is a hundred percent good or bad, but she gets a feeling about some people, about their potential to commit crime. But Claire is different. Ellen said that she 'wouldn't trust her' and yet Ellen also was very negative about Claire's parents, so could just have it in for the family. On the other hand, Olivia had been watching Claire when she was telling her about the letter and she seemed frightened, and more importantly, innocent. Maybe Olivia is letting the fact that she likes Claire get in the way of her judgement.

La Collina is nestled in a row of Victorian houses near the Regent's Canal. As Olivia walks through the gentrified streets the only sounds are occasional dogs barking at other passing dogs as their owners walk them at the end of the day. There's the merest hint of snow in the air as she turns into the restaurant and sees Claire at a table near the window.

Olivia can't help assessing how people are as they talk to her, a practice she adopted from her legal training. As they begin to chat, Olivia watches as much as listens to this woman who seems to be central to solving the puzzle of her husband's death. She's sophisticated in her manner, more intelligent than she wants to show. The key to understanding a personality is to start at the beginning and Olivia steers the conversation towards Claire's childhood.

She was sent away to boarding school at seven. The school was set thirty acres of Dorsetshire countryside. She hadn't liked it at first and missed her parents but after she moved to the upper school, she gradually grew more confident and by the sixth form she had discovered boys. Local boys from the towns and villages around the school had always been present when the girls were allowed out to shop or sneak out to the local pub when they got older, and Claire had been in her element. Olivia can see that Claire is looking back with happy memories at this stage in her life as she talks. During university and in her early twenties, she carried on focusing on men as the part of her life to give her excitement and escape. What she was escaping from isn't clear to Olivia, but she gets the impression that there's a whole part of Claire's life story that she's holding back.

"I meant to tell you," says Claire, as they near the end of their main course. "There's been a second note."

"What did it say?"

"Asking for money. Money we don't have." Olivia doesn't ask about who the 'we' is.

"You've still no idea who might be sending them?" says Olivia. "No enemies? People who you or Stephen may have annoyed?"

"No, none that I can think of."

"I followed up on the delivery of the first note," says Olivia. Claire says nothing but Olivia can tell she's on tenterhooks. "I found out where it was sent from."

"And?"

She lights the fuse and stands well back. "The Houses of Parliament."

Olivia has seen people change mood dozens of times in court and when giving witness statements, but rarely has she seen such a reaction. Claire has been generally relaxed for the whole of the meal, not buoyant or bubbly but not unhappy either. Now, Olivia watches two waves of emotion cross the woman's face. Firstly, bewilderment, but behind that Claire's brain working at top speed, thinking through, Olivia guesses, who she knows there. The more important piece of evidence though is that this information is news to Claire. Secondly, fear rolls across her features. That only makes sense if Claire has thought who the culprit might be. Someone to be frightened of. But Olivia knows that, whatever is now in Claire's mind, she's not going to share it.

Claire shakes her head. "Very odd," she says, but her demeanour is utterly changed.

"No ideas who it might be now?"

"I haven't."

"What do you plan to do if you can't afford the money they're asking for?"

"I don't know."

"Could they be violent?"

The woman starts to get frustrated. "Olivia, I know you're trying to help."

"You asked me to help, Claire."

"Yes, I know."

Olivia knows it's time to address the elephant in the room and uses Claire elevated emotional state in that instant to press her. "What do you really want?" says Olivia, directly but calmly. "You asked me to help but then told your father that I was annoying you, and now you don't seem to want to know any more. I can help but you have to be part of this. Is there something you're not telling me?"

Claire's eyes water but she doesn't cry. The waitress approaches them and Olivia orders coffees for them without asking Claire. After the girl has gone, Claire takes a mouthful of wine.

"I know, I'm sorry. I'll talk to Dad."

"What are you hiding, Claire?"

"Nothing, I don't know any more than is in those emails."

They drink their coffees and pay the bill, but Olivia learns nothing more from Claire. She concludes that it'll take more time for her to be open.

As they walk back towards the Chalk Farm tube station, Claire takes out her phone and reads the screen. "Oh God."

"Bad news?"

"Mum is inviting me to theirs this weekend," says Claire. "I could do without two days of being patronised."

"They're just trying to help."

"I can't face it."

"Maybe it would do you good?" says Olivia.

"The two of them, and their friends probably, all against me. A bloody weekend of saying how lovely Stephen was and how dreadful it all is."

"Will it be that bad?"

They walk in silence in silence and Claire takes a deep breath out.

"I've had an idea, Olivia," says Claire. She turns to her. "Why don't you come with me?"

"To your parents?"

"Yes," says Claire. "We can chat more and you being there will deflect them from me."

"I…"

"Please," says Claire.

Olivia mind has not enough time to think of pros and cons but she knows her answer before any thought. "OK," she says.

CHAPTER ELEVEN

Surridge Place sits on a rise in the land within the valley of the River Kird in West Sussex. Claire turns off the road between Billingshurst and Petworth and along an unnamed lane then right until they arrive at a large gateway with tall, sandstone pillars supporting ten-foot high iron gates.

"There's a gate thingy," says Claire to Olivia in the passenger seat next to her. "In the glove box. You know, opener."

Olivia finds a small black plastic case with a button on it, which she presses. Nothing happens for two seconds, then a large clunk signals the start of the very slow opening process of the gates. The women sit there watching the iron swing aside then Claire drives in. The driveway runs along between an avenue of beech trees and curves round to the right. Once passed the trees, Olivia can see Surridge Place for the first time. An enormous central doorway dominates this side of the house with two balanced wings either side that form a vast Victorian frontage. Beyond the house, she can see lawns sweeping down into the valley for a hundred yards before the grass disappears into a woodland. Claire stops the Volvo in front of the door and they clamber out. Large grey clouds sit in the sky and a soft breeze blows up the valley and moves their hair. No one comes out to meet them and Claire beckons Olivia to follow. They walk inside and across a high-ceiled hallway with dark panelling before going through double doors and into a long lounge that looks like something owned by the National Trust, Olivia thinks. Claire's parents are there at the end of the room and introductions are made. Olivia doesn't sense any notion of disquiet in the couple despite this being the first time they have met her. An inquisition will come, she has no doubt, sometime over the weekend.

The other guests are not due until tomorrow, so the four of them have dinner in a conservatory attached to the lounge which is colder than Olivia would have liked but Claire and her parents don't seem to mind. Dinner is served by a young blonde woman who says nothing, her long hair tied back in a ponytail.

"Have you both lived here long?" says Olivia switching her gaze between the parents.

"Four or five years," says Patricia. "Gerald's aunt lived her before that and it goes back five or six generations in Gerald's family."

"Claire said you have a place in Mayfair too?" says Olivia.

"I don't think I did tell you," says Claire. "We did have one. Dad sold it."

Olivia can sense discomfort for the first time with this group.

"We wanted to focus on Sussex," says Gerald. "It's beautiful here."

An obvious lie, Olivia can tell from his body language, and a clear marker of something hidden that they want to forget, but why? She moves them on from that potential minefield but notes it as part of the profile of this family.

They finish dinner and Claire and Patricia go off to sort out the rooms for the weekend, leaving Olivia with Gerald. He offers her whisky, which she declines, collects the wine bottle from the dinner table and empties the dregs into her glass. They sit on a sofa in front of an open coal fire which Gerald pokes with ironmongery before sitting down.

"Where was constituency, Gerald?" says Olivia after being told on arrival that she should call them by the first names and 'not bother with all the Lord and Lady business'.

"I had the honour to serve the good people of Devon South East for sixteen years."

"Do you miss it?"

"I keep myself busy," he says.

Olivia decides to use this opportunity to test an idea she has. "There's something I've never understood," she says. "How does lobbying work?"

He splays his hands either side of him to show openness. "People tell us what they need from the new laws, so we can be better informed and make better legislation."

"For the benefit of only those people who lobby, though?"

"Anyone can lobby their member of parliament."

"But not everyone does?"

Gerald nods. "Of course."

I met a lobbyist the other day."

"Who was that?" he says.

Her eyes lock onto his face. "Evan Rice." Gerald's face is a master class in control. It is only Olivia's experience that allows her to see the tiniest muscle movement in his jawline. "Do you know him?" she says.

"Can't say I do," says Gerald. 'Gotcha' she thinks to herself.

*

Breakfast the next morning is an elaborate affair, worthy of a five star hotel. Porridge, smoked salmon, full English and fruit with large coffee and tea pots provided on an enormous dark-wood sideboard in the dining room. The silent blonde girl moves without noise around the room, her eyes never looking at anyone, and Olivia can't stop her brain thinking that the girl could be a fascinating source of internal Surridge Place insider knowledge.

Claire suggests a walk after the food and she and Olivia walk down the valley, through the woods and out of the other side until they reach three or four houses that Claire says used to belong to the Surridge Estate but were sold to pay for death duties when her aunt died.

By lunchtime, the first guests arrive and Claire has briefed Olivia how bloody awful they are all going to be. The first to arrive is a couple called Frank and Loren Deeland, Patricia's oldest friends who have known Claire all her life. Frank is a large and loud man with a perfectly spherical head. His hair is grey but voluminous and his grey eyes have a constant glint in them. Loren is the opposite. She is slight and willowy but as tall as her husband with beautiful blue eyes and an aquiline nose. Frank tends to want people to listen to him, Olivia notices. He starts to talk about rugby to her and she can't escape for twenty minutes. Alice and

Avery Tilley, who live in the next large house up the valley, arrive half an hour later. They are in their seventies and Patricia insists on calling them, 'a lady couple' much to Olivia and Claire's amusement. Alice is dark and has a long face with close, enquiring eyes. Avery is a red-head with small, circular glasses and a bandage on her left hand. Teresa York, the expected school friend of Claire's has sent a message, Patricia announces, to say she won't be able to make it as her father has been taken in to hospital, leaving only the Alpins to arrive.

Alice and Avery seem to only deal in gossip and relate various stories about people they know but Olivia doesn't, making the gravitas of the tales much less impactful. The three of them all accept glasses of Prosecco from the silent girl and step out to a terrace that sits outside a pair of French windows on the side of the sitting room.

"Do you know about previous generations of the Harwells, ladies?"

"Poor dear Annabel died four years ago," says Alice.

"Did she live here alone?"

"Oh yes, Annabel wasn't one for marriage," says Avery.

"How did she end up in the house?" says Olivia.

"She was Gerald's sister but their father didn't like Gerald," says Alice. "When he got the Barony after losing his seat in the House, their father more or less cut him off. Couldn't face his son being a Lord when he was just a commoner."

"Despite the Harwells having had money for centuries, they never had a title," says Avery.

"He cut Gerald out of the will, leaving it all to Annabel," says Alice. "By the time she died, both the parents had gone too, so it only left Gerald to inherit."

Avery leans in towards Olivia. "He was strapped for cash at that time. Had to sell the house in Chesterfield Gardens in town, and those houses in the hamlet further down the valley here. Death duties you know? He only inherited property and no money so something had to go."

The Alpins have still not arrived by the time lunch is served, and the silent maid is joined by an even younger girl, who must be about the same age as Poppy, Olivia thinks. The meal is mostly a match between Frank and Alice on who can hold the attention of the group for the longest. Half way through the starters, the sound of a car engine pulling up outside can be heard and Patricia gets up and walks out to greet their guests. Five minutes later, Greer and Jeremy follow Patricia into the dining room and everyone is introduced.

When Patricia gets to Olivia's introduction, Jeremy announces that he has already met her, and Greer says so too, causing raised eyebrows around the table including Patricia. "I am working in Heather Well's department," says Olivia, which seems to elevate her status in Gerald's eyes, but not Patricia's.

After lunch, Alice suggests they walk to an old church across in the next valley and everyone congregates in the hallway before Alice leads them off like schoolchildren on a geography field project. The party wind their way along footpaths by the side of empty fields waiting for the spring. The wind has died down so the air is still, but the sky has taken on a languid battleship grey colour.

When they are nearly at the old church, Jeremy catches up to Olivia and walks beside her. "So, you're a friend of Claire's?" he says. "Is that how you got the gig in the department?"

Olivia turns to him showing her best calm face. "No, Jeremy, it's not. I was recommended to Heather."

"Oh," he says quietly. They walk on in silence for a while. "How is Claire she coping with it all?"

"She's sad," says Olivia. "It's only been ten days."

"You're providing support though, eh?"

"I am."

"Terrible accident," says Jeremy.

Olivia turns her head to him as she needs to see his reaction to her next words. "If it was an accident."

He laughs. "What do you mean?"

"The police aren't clear."

"Really?" She can tell his mind is running at speed.

"Yes, really," she says.

"What else could it be?" says Jeremy.

"Oh, maybe someone killed him?" She opens her eyes wide to give him the option to read her words as not serious, but he doesn't take the bait.

"Well, I don't know," he says quietly, and drops back to talk to his wife who is the next one behind Olivia on the path.

They walk to the church then up a local hill and are making their way back to the house as dusk starts to fall. Patricia announces that there will be drinks at six and people start to dissolve away to their rooms.

Olivia is the second one to arrive in the lounge later. Greer is already there with a gin and tonic in her hand, looking at shadows that outline the gardens and the river. "Want one?" she says raising her glass to Olivia.

Olivia accepts and Greer pours at least a double into a cut-glass tumbler, opens an individual bottle of Fever Tree and hands them both to the lawyer.

"We didn't get the chance for a proper chat at the party the other week," says Greer.

"My first day on the job."

"Second, surely?" says Greer. "The first was the day Stephen died."

Olivia is taken aback by the woman's ability to recall a detail like that concerning someone else's life. She pretends to think back and work out the dates. "You're right." She makes the words sound casual. "Good memory."

"I've always had it. The ability to recall little things people think have been forgotten," she says. "Details that people might want to be lost over time."

Olivia decides to ignore the tone of her words as she can't imagine what the woman means, but it feels like the start of a duel.

"I hear you are standing as the local MP?" says Olivia. Greer's professional mask can't cover her surprise.

"I didn't think that was out in the open yet."

"It's not," says Olivia, playing the woman at her own game. "Gerald was telling me." Olivia can see Greer wasn't expecting the conversation to go like this.

"You've known Gerald and Patricia long?"

"Claire's a friend." Olivia is enjoying the game.

"I hadn't heard of you until Jeremy mentioned your name as he'd invited you to the drinks party."

"Tell me about Jeremy," says Olivia.

"What do you want to know?"

"Can I trust him?"

"To do what?" says Greer.

"To mean what he says."

"That depends on what he says."

"I take that as a no, then?"

Gerald and Patricia walk into the room at that moment and the conversation jumps to more mundane topics about the area. Greer's gaze lingers on Olivia for a few seconds as the four of them chat, leaving Olivia with the impression that conversation with Greer is not over.

By the end of dinner it is passed nine o'clock. Claire and Olivia go out onto the patio with the remains of their wine. Just inside the door, blankets have been piled and they take one each to pull around themselves in the night air.

"How's it been?" says Olivia.

"Not as bad as I thought," says Claire. "Mum and Dad have been surprisingly chilled about it. They haven't once told me that 'there's more to life' or 'we've all had difficult times'." They smile at the idea.

"I'm glad."

They both take a gulp of wine and stand in silence for a few seconds.

"What do you think happened to him?" says Claire. "Do you think it was an accident and I'm just wasting my time?"

"That doesn't explain the notes."

"Maybe someone is just trying it on when they saw he'd died," says Claire.

"How did you and Stephen meet?" says Olivia, moving Claire on to an area that is still unclear, from one of the sticky note questions. "He doesn't seem like…"

"What?"

"He doesn't seem like the kind of man that your parents thought you'd marry."

Claire turns to Olivia and pulls her blanket further up around her neck.

"What kind of man would that be?" Claire's face breaks into a smile.

"You know, daughter of a Baron, private education, a pony for your tenth birthday," says Olivia.

"So my husband was supposed to be called Toby and own an Aston Martin?"

They laugh again. "So how did you meet?"

"A friend introduced us."

"Ellen Hill, wasn't it?" says Olivia.

"It was," says Claire, her eyes narrowing.

"She mentioned it to me, that's all," says Olivia. "You know she works in the Department?"

"Ellen Hill works in the Department?" Claire repeats.

"Yes, you knew surely?"

"I didn't."

"Is that significant?" says Olivia.

Claire takes a deep breath out. "We're not friends anymore. We had a big bust up before the wedding."

"What about?"

Claire waits. "They had a relationship," she says eventually.

"Ellen and Stephen?" Claire nods. "What is serious?"

Claire doesn't look at Olivia. "Yup."

"How long ago?"

"Four years maybe."

"So, before you met Stephen?"

"Yes, but she never told me," says Claire. "And why would you introduce your ex-boyfriend to your friend? A bit weird if you ask me."

"But it didn't put you off getting married?"

Claire's mood visibly shifts with those words. "I don't need you to stick your nose into my life, I just want to know what happened to my husband, that's all!"

Olivia doesn't respond, not knowing quiet what to say.

"I'm getting cold," says Claire more quietly. "I'm going in."

*

Olivia is the first to arrive for breakfast. In the dining room, the silent girl is putting the finishing touches to the food laid out on the sideboard, but slips away before Olivia gets a chance to speak to her. Within a minute, Greer appears in the doorway and walks over.

"Enjoying the weekend, Olivia?"

"Lovely, the Harwells are gracious hosts after all the confusion over Stephen," she says. "And it's been good to spend more time with Jeremy."

Greer stops adding eggs to her plate and looks at Olivia. For the second time this weekend she has felt the woman's penetrative gaze.

"What's your game?" says Greer.

"Game?"

"Why are you constantly prodding away at things?" says Greer. "What are you after?"

"I don't understand."

"By 'all the confusion' I presume you're still trying to push this agenda that the police think there was foul play?"

"Suspicious, don't you think?" says Olivia. She can see Greer starting to simmer inside, but not yet boil. "Why would someone want to hurt Stephen?"

"I didn't know him," says Greer.

In Olivia's mind, now she's gone this far to antagonise, she may as well go full throttle. "Oh? I thought you may have met him through your bother."

The corners of Greer's eyes turn up into a dismissive smile. "If I didn't know better, I'd think you were a journalist."

"Just chatting," says Olivia. "Someone targeted him, we both know that."

"Olivia," she says, holding her now full plate of food in front of her. "I have learnt that one does need to be discrete sometimes. One never knows what damage can occur."

"You don't want to talk about it?"

"I suggest you get back to your work as a minor lawyer in the Department."

Patricia and Claire walk in through the double doors at that moment.

"Gorgeous food, Patricia," says Greer, calling out. "Olivia and I were just saying how you always know what is right, no matter what the situation."

The Harwell's have arranged clay pigeon shooting for everyone before the final lunch and departure. Gerald announces this over breakfast and they all gather on the lower lawn in the middle of the morning. A man who knows what he's doing has been hired and he tells them about the launcher which is called the trap, Frank tells everyone, just before the man does. Then each of the guests have a turn. Alice is surprisingly good and puts it down to her father having guns when she was a girl. Frank is keen to fire the gun, but misses every clay much to everyone's private amusement. Greer goes next and, unsurprisingly for Olivia, the woman hits every clay. Olivia takes a turn and is better than she thought. After everyone else had shot, Claire is left. The hired man explains the routine and she listens carefully to the instruction. The man stands next to the trap and awaits the command.

"Pull!" says Claire.

A near miss. "Keep going," calls Alice.

"Pull!"

A direct hit. Claire turns to the group and allows herself a small smile as they cheer.

"Pull!"

Everyone's eyes turn to watch the clay glide through the sky. In the one second of time between the clay leaving the trap and the expected explosion in the air, a large bang sounds and the clay sails on. All eyes turn back to Claire. She is lying motionless on the ground with blood across her face.

CHAPTER TWELVE

Olivia catches the train back into London after staying with Claire in the Princess Royal Hospital in Haywards Heath where she had been taken after the accident. Claire had remained unconscious throughout the ambulance journey from Surridge Place and all her time in the hospital. The doctor on duty had put her into intensive care and had only allowed Olivia to go in to stand beside her bed after Claire had stabilised to some extent and even then only for five minutes. She remained unconscious, so there was no chance to say anything. The prognosis was 'open' according to the doctor, which is code for, 'we don't know yet'.

As the train sweeps into London Bridge Station, the same thoughts are going around in Olivia's head that have been there since leaving Surridge Place. This can't have been an accident. This has to be related to Stephen's death, even though the link seems tenuous at best. Was the gun supposed to kill Claire or just be a warning? The expert man had been very apologetic afterwards and had said he had checked all of the guns immediately before the session. He also added that there is insurance to cover him for just such an occurrence.

Was the expert man involved? Could he have tampered with the gun? Olivia is annoyed that she wasn't watching closely enough to see if the man gave Claire a different gun to everyone else. The other aspect that doesn't fit with the blackmail notes, is that if the blackmailer is the one who had tried to injure Claire, then they are premature. There have been two notes, but no instructions about where to leave the money. Attacking your victim before they drop the money seems illogical. The one thing about criminals, Olivia knows, is they are logical, even if their frame of reference is distorted - things makes sense within their own world. The blackmailer as the culprit doesn't make sense. But two other things could be true - the gun accident really was an accident, or someone other than the blackmailer tried to injure Claire, or worse, tried to kill her.

When Olivia arrives home, there's a note pushed under the door that looks like it's been pulled off a note pad. She unfolds it and reads the pencil scrawl. Inspector Savage would like to meet her as there have been 'new developments'. Olivia enjoys the standard police vocabulary they're taught to use like 'proceeding' instead of walking and 'in the vicinity' instead of in the area. There's a mobile phone number at the end of the note and she dials it. This isn't the number on Savage's business card and she guesses that, as it's the weekend, he's using his personal phone. They chat for a minute and she suggests they meet in an hour at St Catherine's Dock.

It is passed five o'clock when Olivia walks over Tower Bridge and turns into the docks where twenty super yachts lay at their moorings and bob on the waves. A cold but persistent breeze blows in from the river and cuts across her cheek.

The Dicken's Inn is a black and brown pub by the water with flowers across its frontage. Olivia walks in and sees Savage straight away at a table in one corner nursing a pint of beer. They shake hands and he offers to buy her a drink then goes to the bar and returns with a gin and tonic.

"Miss Streete…" he begins.

"Olivia."

He stops.

"In that case, I'm Jack."

"You said on the phone that there has been a development?" she says.

"I'll come to that. Let me just tell you, in confidence, where we have got to."

"OK."

"The deceased was found on the tracks outside Clapham Junction." She nods. "He was, as I think I said to you, not in a great state. He hadn't just fallen onto the tracks."

"You said before that his face was unrecognisable."

"Quite," says Savage. "So, we've interviewed family, friends, enemies and colleagues - anyone who knew him or had contact with him in the last few weeks."

"And?"

"Nothing." Savage flicks his eyes up to her. "Everyone who might have been a likely suspect has a solid alibi."

He stops talking, his eyes locked onto hers.

"And then, there's you," he says. "You appear in his life, two days later he's dead. The day after that you become best friends with his widow to the extent that she invites you to meet her parents at their country house. The wife is an heiress to a multi-million pound estate and you start asking questions of people connected to the death of her husband. No one saw you at the time he died as you were apparcntly alone in your flat. I have been in touch with my colleagues in the Italian police and they tell me you were mixed up with a murder in Venice six months ago, and now I hear that there's been a near-fatal gun accident and you're there."

Olivia is frowning but says nothing.

"Opportunity, motive, expertise."

"Is this why you called me, Inspector?" she says. "This is all circumstantial, you have no evidence because it's all categorically untrue."

"I'm just trying to piece together the events that led to Stephen Boyd's death."

"I didn't know him, I have had no dealing with him." She can feel her anger in her throat. "His widow asked me to help her find out what happened."

"That's my job."

"She doesn't want a scandal," says Olivia. "Her parents are in important public roles."

"And she doesn't want my size tens all over her family?"

"Inspector…" says Olivia, then pauses. "Jack, I think there *were* people in Stephen Boyd's life who wanted him dead." She stops and looks at him directly. "But it wasn't me. I am on your side."

"Who are these people? We've found nothing."

Olivia breaths out. "He seems to have been involved with some sort of deals that involved people who could be dangerous."

"And you know that – how?" His eyes are blazing with a mixture of frustration and disbelief.

"Claire has received threatening notes."

"Now she tells us!"

"Mrs Boyd swore me to secrecy, I am breaking a promise by telling you this, Jack," says Olivia. "She doesn't want the police to know."

Inspector Savage pulls his hand through his hair and takes a swig of his beer. He puts the glass back down on the table and watches the bubbles rising to the surface of the golden liquid.

"I'm not your suspect, Jack, but I can help you."

"How?"

"Anything I find out, I'll share with you."

"That's not your choice anyway," he says. "You have an obligation to tell me anything of relevance that connects to an investigation."

"I know." She is calm, and puts her palm down on the table. "Claire is not going to tell you anything, but she will tell me."

Olivia stands up and offers to buy another round which he accepts and she goes to the bar then returns five minutes later with the drinks.

"Two things, Olivia," he says as she drops into the seat opposite him. She looks expectant. "Firstly, what I said earlier about you." He pauses, thinking about the best way to say what he wanted to tell her. "The guvnor told me to look into you and your background."

"Who is he?"

"The Superintendent."

"Your boss's boss told you to investigate me as a possible suspect?" Her pacing stresses each word to show her disbelief and he raises his eyebrows as confirmation. "Can I ask his name?"

"Ralph Peters."

She shakes her head. "Means nothing."

"Why would it?"

"I mean, I haven't heard the name," she says. "Is he an honest copper?"

"Of course, he's the Super."

She doesn't continue the line of questioning as she can tell that Savage won't be objective enough.

"You said there were two things you wanted to tell me," she says.

"I wasn't going to tell you this if you had reacted a different way to being investigated."

"Did I pass the test?" she says.

He smiles. "A new piece of evidence has come to light."

"Go on."

"Someone was seen near the body."

She lets her brain spin across the questions this raises. Did Savage already know this when she made her statement? Is it true or another part of his plan to investigate her?

"No ID, I guess?" she says. "Any description?"

"Male, short, dark eyes" says Jack. "Wearing a padded jacket and a woolen hat."

"Like a thousand men in London in December."

"Alright, hang on, there's more." She puts up her hands in apology. "A woman saw him walking up from the track to the platform and he had difficulty getting up the slope. Not a limp, the woman said, but one leg seemed damaged."

"He could have injured his leg attacking Boyd?"

Savage nods slowly and watches her.

"Did you do an artist's impression?"

"Yup."

"Can you…?"

"Yup."

"What do you want me to do?" she says.

"Tell me everything that you find out," he says. "Doesn't matter if it seems irrelevant."

"I know how to collect evidence, Jack. Every case in my job demands rigorous research, just like your job."

"One thing I'd add, though."

"What?"

"Be careful."

"Of what?"

"The Super didn't randomly suggest we look into you. That had to come from somewhere."

"What do you mean?"

"Someone with influence must have got in touch with him," says Savage. "He didn't say as much, but bosses only know what they told by stuff coming up from below or coming down from on high. I'm just saying be careful. They're all connected and there are plenty of important people who link back in some way to Stephen Boyd."

"I'll be careful."

"Also, I was wondering," he says. She looks at him. "Can I take you to in dinner?"

CHAPTER THIRTEEN

Olivia books a meeting room on the top floor of the building on Whitehall Court the next lunchtime, intentionally away from other people in her team and far enough from Heather Wells' office to feel isolated from prying eyes. She locks the door and immediately starts to write on the white board that is fixed to the far end of the room. Two large windows let the winter sun cascade in, creating shadow windows on the opposite wall.

She reads from her notebook and faithfully recreates the questions on the board from the sticky notes she wrote in her flat. Once she has finished, Olivia surveys the landscape of words sketched out in front of her to allow her brain to take in the information and turn the points over in her mind.

The first box on the board that has not been addressed is, 'How would Stephen's death benefit Jeremy or Greer?' What new evidence has come to light about this question? Greer had reacted to the conversation on Sunday in Sussex more aggressively than Olivia would have predicated. That indicates a hidden truth, the woman is protecting something, or someone. Could she possibly have had anything to do with Stephen's death or knows someone who did? That seems implausible, but it would explain her reaction.

On the questions about the Harwells, after weekend chats, she now knows that Gerald is involved in planning laws in the Lords. He had told her a long and unstimulating tale about how he was keen to 'release the value in brownfield sites' during which he spoke more about the value for developers than people buying the houses. Does that help her? She's not sure.

Next, 'Had Stephen made enemies inside Government?' is on the board. She needs more on this and suspects that Ellen will be a good source given that she now knows the woman is an ex-girlfriend of the dead man. Another thing she needs to know is what stopped Ellen telling her that Stephen had been her boyfriend.

She moves on to thinking about what new questions she has. From the weekend she writes down, 'Who tampered with the gun?', and 'Was it a murder attempt on Claire or someone else?'

Finally, she writes a statement that she believes is true, 'There is a link between the gun accident and Stephen's death, but what?'

Olivia takes photos of the board with the new questions, wipes it all clean and walks back to her desk on the first floor.

*

A taxi pulls up on the corner of Vane Street and Vincent Square in Westminster. Greer pays the driver cash, steps out and disappears through a large portico that leads to the flats above.

"How are you, sis?" says Evan as she pushes open the door to his apartment that he left ajar after he buzzed her in on the entry phone downstairs. They kiss cheeks and she dumps her tan cashmere coat on the sofa.

"What's this about you standing for parliament?" he says.

"North Sussex, if we can convince the locals to rubber-stamp me as their candidate for next time."

"Mike Chambers stepping down?" Evan takes a bottle of Prosecco from the fridge and starts to open it.

"You heard it here first."

"Good; the man's an idiot," says Evan. "We tried to lobby him on food packaging regulations and he was having none of it." He pours out two glasses of wine.

"You mean he has principles." Greer's eyes shine as she grins at her brother.

"I'll be lobbying *you*, sis, when you get in."

"Cross my hand with silver and I might just listen," she says.

"It's a deal," he says quietly and offers her a wine glass, which she takes, and they chink a toast.

As they finish a lunch of seafood that Evan had prepared, Greer changes the subject from family and Westminster gossip. "I need your help, darling," she says.

"What?"

"You've got research people in your company haven't you?"

"Of course," he says.

"I need to know about the local party committee in North Sussex, their background, any skeletons, you know?"

"We call that a dirt trawl in the lobbying business." His face is dead-pan. "Is that what you want? Dirt?"

"Well, leverage, let's say."

"You never bloody change," he says. "Always digging around in the shit, ever since you were a girl. Like a truffle pig."

"Takes one to know one, Ev." She opens her eyes wide.

"I'll see what I can do," he says and forks the last mouthful of food into his mouth.

*

In the early afternoon, Ellen appears in the office and sits at her desk at the far end away from Olivia. They only say hello to each other before Ellen busies herself with a large spreadsheet of detail about the contract that is being tendered. They barely talk as the time ticks on. Olivia makes coffee and gives Ellen one but the woman's only response is a curt thanks before she returns to her work. No one else is in the office all afternoon and not until after five does Ellen seem to finish the work.

"Fancy a drink?" says Olivia. Ellen looks at her for a second then accepts. They walk to The Red Lion pub, five minutes from Downing Street. The place is packed full of parliamentarians and journalists trying to get value from each other. One side wanting information, the other publicity; a mutually-dependent but flawed relationship. They buy gin and tonics, find a tall table to one side of the main bar and squeeze onto stools between suits standing inches away.

"How are you?" says Olivia. "You looked busy today."

"I have to finish my schedules for that telecoms contract by tomorrow, so I had to keep my nose to the grindstone," says Ellen. "It goes live on the website in three days and it has to be approved by Heather before then. Then the fun starts."

"Why do you say 'the fun'?"

"Once it is live, the bidders can't lobby Heather in theory, so it all goes underground."

"What do you mean?" says Olivia.

"If the contract isn't live, Heather and the team can talk to anyone, there's no risk of favouritism," says Ellen. "But after that, all contacts have to be registered and all communications have to be recorded and available for anyone to see on the public site."

"And that isn't what happens?"

"The exact opposite. Once there's a live contract in play, the big lobbying starts," says Ellen. "Lunch invitations, days out at the races, dinner speaking offers. All seems innocent and those are all recorded." She takes a gulp of her drink and puts it back down on the table.

"So, what's the problem?" says Olivia.

"Those events only exist to provide opportunities for off-the-record conversations. You scratch my back sort-of-stuff."

It reminds Olivia to research the bidders. GreenLink, she knows something about, but she has no idea who is in charge of Salango or Mercantile-Lindle.

"What do you think of Heather?" says Olivia.

"I've been in this job for four years," says Ellen. "In that time we've had three ministers and they all have similarities. Anyone who makes it to this level in politics has two things about their personality – ambition and ego."

"Like any director in a company, surely?" says Olivia.

"More than that. Politicians all have an unnerving belief that they're right," says Ellen. "But also, critically, they believe that they can't be wrong, which is different. That's when they start behaving to save their own skin to cover up their errors. It should all be brought out in the open so people can see it."

Olivia can see that the woman is not just passionate about this topic, there's something else in the way she is talking. This is personal for her. She's not just driven by professional ethics, it sounds more like a vendetta.

"Why d'you stay if you hate it?"

"What else would I do? This is the type of job that people are willing to pay me for, and I've got a mortgage."

Ellen takes another mouthful of drink. "What about you?" she says. "You enjoying this job?"

"The work's fine, bog-standard contractual documents," says Olivia. "Not ground-breaking."

"That's what you like, is it?" says Ellen. "Ground-breaking?"

"Something to make my brain work, sure. But it's not the contract work that makes this job interesting, it's the Stephen thing."

"What do you mean?" Ellen screws up her nose.

Olivia doesn't hesitate to push a line of questioning that she planned earlier in the day. "I talked to Claire."

Ellen turns her eyes to Olivia, her demeanour is more engaged than a moment before. "And?"

"Stephen was an ex of yours."

"Yup."

"You didn't say."

"Didn't seem relevant."

"And you and Claire don't speak now."

"She couldn't cope with me being his ex."

"But didn't you introduce them?"

"Well, they met first when I was there, I wouldn't say I introduced them exactly."

Shifting narrative, noted. "Why did you and Stephen split?"

Ellen takes a deep breath and shakes her head. "Just drifted apart, I think." Olivia notices Ellen has stopped making eye contact so much.

"Claire didn't know you worked in the Department," says Olivia.

"He didn't when Stephen and I were..." The word describing the exact nature of what was between them drifts away, unspoken.

"Do you think he made enemies in his job?" says Olivia, keeping on track to find out more.

"You mean people who have the capacity to kill?" Ellen's eyes are watery.

"I didn't say that."

"He was good at all the diplomacy stuff, not upsetting people, but you never know what's going on in the background, do you?" says Ellen.

"He had some private businesses, outside of his government work, did he?" Olivia knows the answer to this from Claire, albeit vaguely.

"He had a couple of businesses."

"Doing what?"

"Trading is all he ever used to say," says Ellen. "Buying and selling stuff."

"But you don't know what he was buying and selling?"

Ellen shakes her head. "I saw some documents when I stayed with him in the flat he had before they bought in Hampstead."

"See anything?"

"Yes, but not what the actual goods were, just delivery dates; can't remember much else." She screws up her eyes trying to recall.

"Any names of people he dealt with?"

"Ralph something? There were messages from a Ralph on Stephen's phone that used to come in when he was in the shower a couple of times."

Olivia lets the woman turn over the memories inside her head.

"It's sad, thinking about him," says Ellen.

"Have you thought of talking to Claire?" says Olivia, testing her knowledge of the accident.

"God, no! Why would I?"

"You're both mourning."

Ellen's wet eyes smile. "I don't think that's going to happen."

*

The waiter shows Olivia to a table in the window of the Sartoria restaurant in the maze of streets behind Regent Street and near Saville Row. Evan Rice arrives within a minute of her sitting down. They shake hands and he makes a fuss of ordering wine immediately.

They choose polpo grigliato starter, then risotto allo zafferano and rombo chiodato for mains. She notes that he asks her to choose, then orders the same.

After the starters and chat about the state of the country and Westminster, Evan directs them towards the work that she needs.

"As I said when we met last week," she says. "My client is keen to ensure that the legislation meets their needs. Did you see the papers I sent to you?"

"I did," he says. "And I can guarantee that we can deliver those changes for your clients."

"Guarantee?" she repeats. "You can *guarantee* it?"

"Yes, it's not difficult," he says. "Our network of contacts is second-to-none in Whitehall."

"There's something else. My clients have some key competitors who we'd like to know about." She picks up her phone from the table and pretends to look through some screens before apparently finding what she needs. "GreenLink Industries is one."

"We know them," he says immediately.

"What do you know about them?"

"That's protected through client confidentiality, Ms Delaney."

"Then I'm not sure you're the lobby partner for us in that case, Mr Rice. We want people who have the relationships and the information that they can readily share. My client doesn't like to be told about confidentiality clauses. This contract with my clients would be big for you, I checked. We're talking a quarter of your annual income, guaranteed."

Evan is getting frustrated, she can tell. "We can *find* the information," he says. "But I'm sure you wouldn't want us divulging your plans to them. It goes both ways."

She sits back, taking a mouthful of wine.

"What *can* you share on GreenLink?" she says after leaving a gap of silence to continue the pressure on him.

"What do you need?"

"Who they know in government, and what they have paid to whom." Her eyes are locked onto his. "Not the stuff on their website, the stuff they don't want people knowing about."

Evan turns the stem of his wineglass and drops his eyes to the tablecloth. A waitress brings their mains, giving them some breathing space to think. Olivia waits to see if her bear trap will spring.

"We may be able to help you," he says eventually.

"I'm glad to hear it."

"I'll ask some contacts," he says. "But what about the larger lobbying work we discussed last week?"

"Let's do this GreenLink research first, then my client can assess how good Anstone really is. We'll use your efficiency on this small job as a test for the high value stuff."

"This has to be confidential between us," he says.

"You need to stop saying confidential, Mr Rice. As I said, my clients don't like..."

"It's too big a risk unless we are water-tight," he interrupts.

She stops to consider, acting out looking serious. She takes a bite of food and takes her time to eat it.

"Alright, I can agree to only share the information with my client." He raises his arm and offers his hand to shake which she does. As they do so, she's thinking that he doesn't know that her client, for the purposes of this discussion, is the British Transport Police.

CHAPTER FOURTEEN

When Jeremy arrives back at their house in Hereford Square, Greer has been drinking since five o'clock.

"Good day, darling?" he says.

"Been on the bloody phone all day to various people in North Sussex. I asked Evan to send me background on the locals and he has come up trumps."

Jeremy is listening intently, which, she thinks, is a refreshing difference to his normal behaviour.

"The local party chairwoman invested in a company with links to man who was subsequently convicted of fraud," she says triumphantly. Jeremy nods in approval. "And one of the committee who vote for the parliamentary candidate was caught drink driving a few years ago but didn't lose his licence despite being three times over the limit."

"Dirty buggers," says her husband. He pours a whisky and tops up her wine.

Over dinner, they talk about their respective days, and again, she is surprised at this change in him.

"I was talking to that girl," says Greer.

"Which girl?"

"The lawyer," she says. "At the weekend."

"Olivia?"

"I think she's up to something," says Greer. "She asked me if there's a link between Stephen Boyd and Evan."

"What did she say?"

"Just asking me about it - nosey, you know?"

"What did you say?"

"Gave her the brush off," says Greer. "I'm not sure what she was getting at, but I didn't like her tone."

"Like that thing she was saying about the police considering Boyd's death maybe wasn't an accident," says Jeremy. "There's no substance to it. He just had a few too many and slipped onto the tracks. Could happen to anyone."

"Even so," says Greer. "We should put a stop to that sort of conjecture, I've got this selection coming up in my constituency; it could cut across my press coverage."

"*Your* constituency?" says Jeremy. "That's a bit premature, darling, even for you."

"You know what I mean."

"Did you talk about it to Gerald at the weekend?" he says.

"Yes, he doesn't see any problems. Your father is pushing too. They still love him there from when he was the MP."

"Be careful with Dad."

"What do you mean?" says Greer.

"He always has his own agenda."

"And what's his agenda when supporting my candidacy?"

"He'll want to call in the debt at some stage," says Jeremy. "Once you're an MP."

Greer considers his words for a second.

"What about this lawyer girl?" she says. "We should stop her."

"I can talk to Heather," says Jeremy. "I'll tell her she's prying into our lives unnecessarily."

*

After she arrives home and eats, Olivia checks her emails and there's one from Inspector Savage with the photo-fit of the man seen around the area the night Stephen died and a message saying, 'lovely meal the other night.'

She ignores the message and pulls the photo-fit up on the laptop screen to look at the face. She doesn't recognise him. He has large bushy eyebrows over deep set eyes. His nose is squat and round at the end. The picture shows him in a woollen hat, so no hair is visible. As she looks at the eyes, she traces her memories. Has she seen this man? There are options without a hat, but they're more guesswork, designed to give some idea of what he might look like hatless. Olivia photographs the images onto her phone and stores them away in case she needs them in the future.

Olivia tries to watch a film but her mind keeps turning over more questions after the Ellen conversation. Why is the woman so upset now if they split up four years ago? Maybe Olivia's own attitude towards relationships is colouring her judgement, but four years seems enough time to get over a break-up.

Maybe it's not the break-up that is upsetting her. Is there something that Olivia is missing about Ellen? She knows that Stephen and Ellen had planned to meet on the night he died, but then Stephen invited Olivia along too. That doesn't make sense. Were they only meeting up for a social chat? Olivia remembers distinctly that Ellen wasn't put out despite Olivia turning up unannounced. She's sure there's something glaringly obvious that she has missed.

When she starts asking questions Olivia finds it fairly easy to tell the liars from the truth-tellers. Some people have no problem lying, and in fact are very accomplished at it. Based on the evidence so far, Ellen may be slipping into the liar's camp.

*

Ethan watches the shadows of the city play across the hotel room ceiling. He strokes Poppy's back as she lies half on top of him after they have made love. He had wanted to sleep with her from the first time they met but he is pleased that he didn't rush it. He considers if she is too young for him. Eighteen is young, but he reassures himself that's there's only a few years between them.

They sleep for a few hours then she gets up to go to the bathroom. She clambers back under the covers as the heating is on low and the December air tugs at her warm body as she crosses the room. He kisses her as she snuggles into him. They lay there for several minutes but don't fall back to sleep.

"What do you want to do after school?" he says.

"Uni, English," she says. "Bath if I get the grades."

"Why English?"

"I want to be a journalist." There is surprise in her voice at the question.

"Do you?"

"I told you."

"You also told me you want to walk to Great Wall of China, motorbike across the Sahara and swim naked in a coral sea." They laugh.

"If I can find someone to pay me to do those, I'd do those for a living!" She climbs on top of him so all her weight is on his body, resting her chin on his chest. "Did you always want to be a journo?"

"Yup. My Dad was one."

"Was?"

"Died."

"Sorry."

"It was years ago."

"What happened?" she says.

"Accident," says Ethan. "He was doing a big piece on politicians here in Westminster, but he crashed his car before he could publish it. We were living in England for a year while he wrote it. But my mum took me and my sister back to New York after he died."

"So, he never finished it?"

"I have the last version he wrote, but the same people that he was investigating have kept on doing it since so it's out-of-date now."

"It sounds much more interesting than your boring politics thing you're doing," says Poppy.

Ethan smiles. "It's the same piece," he says. "That's why I'm back here, to update it. This time, I'm gonna catch 'em."

Silence marks out a minute in the room as their hearts beat against each other.

"Dad was writing about a man called Bruce Alpin, he says."

"Never heard of him." She sits up to see his face more clearly. Ethan looks at her, his eyes exploring her face, which she notices. "What are you thinking about?" she says.

"You've not heard of Bruce Alpin and his son, Jeremy?" he says.

"Some boring old politicians, why would I?"

"Your mom has."

"What are you talking about?" She screws up her nose.

"She knows Jeremy Alpin."

"I don't get it," says Poppy. "How do you know anything about what my mum knows?"

"Her name came up, that's all." He looks away but she keeps looking at him, trying to work out what he means.

"Came up, where?"

"She works for the Government and she's dealing with a contract that Alpin is bidding for." He sounds reluctant to tell her, she thinks. "Insider knowledge, it's always useful."

Poppy looks serious, waits for a second, then climbs off him and goes to the window. She looks out at the traffic droning passed the hotel.

"Are you fucking me because of my mum?" she says.

"Don't be crazy, Poppy."

"Are you?"

"Of course not. I love you. Adult relationships are like this."

"Like what?" Her voice has anger in it.

"You help me, I help you - it's a partnership."

She is quiet and sullen. Poppy can't think what to say.

"Look, if you're not up for it," he says. "I get it, you're young."

"I'm not."

He shrugs. "Then prove it."

"What? You want to see my birth certificate?" She's angry now. He climbs out of bed and puts his arms around her. She fights him off but he holds her tightly.

"Hey," he says. "It's nothing, forget it." She relaxes into his hug after five seconds. "It's you I want."

*

The waiter takes away the starters from the table in the River Restaurant in the Houses of Parliament and Sir Bruce Alpin pours out two more glasses of Chateau Fourcas Dupré for himself and Gerald Harwell.

"How's Claire doing?" says Sir Bruce.

"Patricia's been on the phone to them three times a day, but not much to report."

"What happened exactly?"

"Bloody gun went off in her face," says Gerald. "I've used that man at least four times before so it was just unfortunate."

"An accident, then?" says Sir Bruce.

Gerald looks at his friend and momentarily pinches his eyebrows together. "I've heard to rumours, Bruce, the bars are all full of it."

"What are they saying?" says Sir Bruce.

"Nothing really, just stupid gossip about how odd it is to have that accident right after her husband's death."

"Are they saying there may be more to it?" says Sir Bruce.

"I'm not party to that, if they are." Gerald is reassuring in his tone. He smiles.

"Do you think Stephen's death was all above board?"

"The police don't know," says Gerald. "Some chap was seen near the body apparently."

"Oh?" Sir Bruce's brain is ticking through the facts and the consequences. "What else did they say?"

"Hard going, apparently," says Gerald. "Not much evidence." He raises his eyebrows.

"Accident then?" says Sir Bruce. "Plain and simple, that's obviously what happened. Terrible thing."

As cheese and brandy is served to the two parliamentarians an hour later, Sir Bruce has successfully steered the conversation away from the death of Stephen Boyd.

"Gerald, this Development Bill that you're pushing through."

"What of it?"

"I have some interest groups who have been lobbying me."

"Oh yes?"

"In the Docklands," says Sir Bruce. "The local plan doesn't have enough land allocated to industry, and there's no power to review those local plans after the councils have voted on them."

"That's the whole idea, local councils shape the local community."

"Docklands is different, they're suggesting a carve-out for brownfield sites in London."

"To what end?" says Gerald.

"To balance the needs of local businesses and the community, after all, the businesses create the jobs for local people."

Gerald pauses. "Send me the stuff, Bruce," he says after a few moments. "I'll have a look and ask the civil servants to draft up amendments."

"Thanks, old man," says Sir Bruce. "Appreciated."

CHAPTER FIFTEEN

The sky over London is surprisingly bright and sunshine splays down and across Heather Wells' office as Olivia arrives and takes a seat.

"We spoke before," says Heather. "After Stephen Boyd's father-in-law had raised a concern to me." Olivia waits and can see the woman is balancing risks as she speaks, treading a fine line. "Now, I've had another message."

"From the Harwells?"

"No, Jeremy Alpin."

"Interesting," says Olivia.

"Why do you say that?"

"Minister, you and I both have to deal with people on a daily basis and assess how much of what we're being told in true. A solicitor is continually faced with people who are selective in what they reveal." Heather doesn't react and Olivia hadn't expected it from a seasoned politician. "I was invited to the Harwells for the weekend. Claire invited me as her companion to support her from the onslaught of her family asking about her late husband. The Alpins were there too and Claire was injured when her clay gun mis-fired."

Heather watches Olivia.

"During the weekend, there was a good opportunity to further the discussions that you and I spoke about ten days ago surrounding the death of Stephen Boyd. I pushed some buttons to see what happened. And, evidently, we got a result."

"You think the Alpins are involved in something?"

"I don't know yet," says Olivia. "I do know that both Jeremy and Greer are hiding something, but it could be nothing to do with Stephen."

Heather stands up and walks to a tray with a thermos jug of coffee that Millie has placed on a side table. She holds up the jug to Olivia who shakes her head, then she pours herself a cup and sits back down.

"We need to be careful, Olivia," she says eventually, after her mind has weighed up the consequences of what Olivia has said. "You said before that the police have some suspicions about Stephen committing suicide?"

"That's changed a bit now, a man was spotted near the scene, so it could be murder."

Heather takes a long, slow, quiet breath through her nose and makes the smallest shake of her head. "What did you say to the Alpins at the weekend?"

"That the police have suspicions about Stephen's death." She leaves a gap to let the words sink in, then says. "Those tiny suggestions were enough to generate a complaint to you. You're the one person they perceive could stop me asking questions."

"I've been making some of my own enquiries," says Heather. She pauses, thinking about the right form of words. "Olivia, I've only been here for just under eighteen months. Stephen Boyd had been in this Department for much longer. After you prompted me to think there may be something odd about his death, I started asking some people around here about him."

"And what did you find?"

"That he was not as popular as I had first thought. That the people who had all told me a year ago that he was a good egg, that he could be trusted, had all changed their tune. All of them. All of them have told me in the last week that he was less than trustworthy What do you make of that?"

"That they've all agreed to say the same thing," says Olivia.

"That's what I thought too."

"And two more observations, minister. Firstly, that they're all aware of something that we aren't".

"And?"

"They're covering something up."

The two women sit in silence for a moment. Olivia knows that when words have been said out loud, they take on more meaning and seem more real than compared to mere thoughts inside your head.

"If this is some sort of widespread corruption," says Heather. "Then we need to tread extremely carefully."

"Who did you talk to?"

"One Head of Department, another senior civil servant, and two of my junior ministers," says Heather.

Olivia turns her eyes to the window, thinking. "The key to all this is Stephen Boyd and what he was up to," she says. "They want me to stop asking my questions, so I must be getting somewhere."

"Also," says Heather. "I need to be seen to be doing something to respond to the complaints. It's what politics is about - what you're seen to be doing is more important than what you actually do."

"I get that," says Olivia. "Tell the Alpins you have given me a final warning; that any more funny business and I'll be out. Let that be known to your senior team too."

"Meanwhile, what?"

"I'll be more careful. I want to find the truth about Stephen, and you want to limit anything hitting the fan, I imagine."

Heather nods.

"Can I ask you one other thing, minister?"

"Of course."

"Will Jeremy get the contract that we're just about to advertise?"

"GreenLink are one of three bidders, so there's thirty three percent chance of it."

"And it's all above board is it? The process?" says Olivia.

"As far as I have been told, yes," says Heather. "I know it can look all chummy between me and the bidders, but I'm not interested in lining my nest."

"An honest politician?" says Olivia. "Surely, that's an oxymoron?"

"You do me a disservice, Olivia." They smile at each other, neither knowing how much the other has said is true.

*

It's five o'clock when Adrian arrives at the American Bar in the Savoy Hotel which is only just starting to get busy for the evening. He finds a table tucked away from the vast, mirrored bar and orders two Margaritas. They know him here and the waiter serves him within a few minutes, he likes the traditional feel and invisible service of the place. When Violet arrives, he sees her immediately. She is wearing a short, purple dress and barely any makeup, her hair loose on her shoulders. He stands and raises his hand to catch her eye and she walks over, raises a long arm to shake his hand and sits slowly opposite him before turning her eyes to his face and smiling.

"I got us cocktails," he says. She turns her head and raises barely raises her fingers before a waiter is by her side.

"The usual, Miss Violet?"

"Please, Jonathan, thank you."

"Is the gentleman alright with his Margaritas?"

"I think he is," she says.

Adrian's journalistic experience enables him to take all of this in and not be swayed by her show of power.

"I can see they know you here," he says.

She smiles. "Now, tell me about you, Mr Gilbraith."

He talks about Newsource and what he is trying to do with it, using his favourite phrase, 'mixing serious news in an accessible format'. She asks him insightful questions about who owns the company, how it works, and what have been his biggest successes to date. He only realises how penetrative she has been as she comes to an end of her scrutiny.

"What do you want with me?" Her eyes are wide.

"I know that you are on good terms with many people who are powerful and influential," he says.

"I am."

"I'm interested in understanding what those people are really like, the public are interested in the lives of the rich and famous."

"My friends are rich but not many are famous."

"It's how much power they have, that's the real interest for me," he says.

"Do you have anyone in mind?"

"I'm thinking that we could do a series on a number of men." Their eyes gently blaze across the table, his more than hers. She picks up her cocktail and curls her lips around the straw. "There's one we could start with, who would make a big splash."

"And who's that?" she says.

"Stephen Boyd."

Her eyebrows move minutely to register that she has heard. "My business, Mr Gilbraith, is about reality. The reality that exists beneath the veneers that successful people put up to protect themselves. To strip that protection away would be damaging for their families, no doubt. But equally, it would damage me. My success is based on discretion, they come to me for comfort, away from the prying eyes of others."

"Are you saying that you're not interested in talking to me?"

"I'm saying that you probably can't afford me, Adrian."

*

The Prince Albert pub next to Battersea Park is warm and inviting as Ellen pushes the door through into the place. Brown square tables and red upholstered benches running across the front of the building make it feel modern and traditional simultaneously and she wonders if Tom chose this place as a guess as to what she might like. He is sitting at the last table in the corner, with a pint of lager in front of him, reading a book.

"What's the book?" she says as she approaches, before sitting down. He looks up and gives the most genuine smile she has seen in a while.

"Art," is all he says, and shows her the front cover.

"Want another drink?"

"I'm fine." She walks to the bar and gets herself a red wine.

"Thanks for inviting me," she says as she sits next to him on the bench. He's nervous and two fingers on one of his hand are shaking. "Is this your local?"

"Yes. I live five minutes away."

"Tell me about your painting, Tom."

The question unleashes something in him and he starts to tell her about his pictures, how he started, how it was difficult at first, and how time just disappears when he's painting. There's nothing else he has ever found that does that.

"Why aren't you an artist, for God's sake?" she says.

"I just paint what I like, not what people want."

"Isn't that what all artists do?"

"You have to make a living," he says. "I was brought up to get a steady job."

"That's so fucking damaging!" Her words echo her own experience. "We have to do whatever we want to."

"Are you doing that?" he says, and turns to look at her, then waits as she has to think about the answer.

"No," she murmurs eventually. "I'm not."

"What would it be?" he says. She is finding his simple openness disarming. She is more used to bullish, confident men who want something from her, but who aren't really interested in getting to know her first.

"I don't know." She says eventually. "Travel, maybe?"

"You've never thought about it?" he says.

She drinks some wine to give her brain time to give an answer that doesn't make her sound like a complete idiot. "Maybe I need to discover it," she says. "Maybe, I've never had the time or a reason to find out."

"Why?"

Half of her wishes he's stop this line of questioning, but the other half of her likes that someone actually cares enough to ask. She drinks more wine, pauses, then starts to talk in a way she never has before, not even inside her own head. "I've surrounded myself with people who don't really care about me." He looks quizzical. "Don't ask me why, they're just the ones who've been there. I almost didn't choose them, they chose me. But they didn't treat me very well, they didn't listen to me, and they didn't..." She stops but she doesn't know why. "Didn't love me." Her last words are barely audible.

They have more drinks and the conversation is easy. Later, she ventures a question. "You been single long, Tom?"

"Five years."

"You told me she died." He nods and looks glum. "You want to talk about it?"

"I've never told anyone," he says.

"I'm interested."

She waits. He stops for a few seconds and looks at her. "Her name was Kate," he begins. "We'd been together for a few years. We spent all the time we could together. We both had jobs but every evening and all weekend we travelled all over, we went to shows, or just hung out. Time went by so quickly when I was with her."

"Did you live together?"

"In the end, yes, but not for a year and a bit. She's the only other thing apart from painting that has ever made me feel happy." She smiles at his honesty. "She worked in a bar in Victoria, cocktails and stuff. They used to get big groups of guys from Westminster though and they were always rowdy and treated her like shit."

"Did she leave?"

"She wanted to, but the pay was good and she got loads of tips so it would've been hard to find another job like that, and she put up with it. It went on for a while, a year maybe, and it was really getting to her, she started hating it. One night this big group of men started touching her arse and generally being wankers, and she told them to fuck off. They complained, she was fired. She didn't come home. The police found her at six o'clock the next morning, in the alley next to the bar. Head smashed in."

He stops and Ellen watches the remains of the memories pass through his mind.

"They arrest anyone?" she says. He takes a deep breath and shakes his head. "What never?"

"Nope," he says. "No evidence. Her mum and dad kept asking but the police gave up after a few months. Couldn't find anything."

"I'm sorry," says Ellen. "It's horrible."

"I asked around a bit," he says. "Went to the bar, and sat and watched who came in."

"Find anything?"

"Not yet."

"You still go there?"

"Sometimes," he says. "Is it weird?" He looks at her eyes to check what she really thinks.

"I get it, you loved her," says Ellen. "Moving on is hard, I can never do it. My last boyfriend was four years ago and I'm still..." She stops herself.

"In love with him?" says Tom.

"He didn't listen like you do." She smiles. "Anyway, you getting me another drink?"

"You're not getting away that easily," he says. He stands up and picks up their glasses.

She touches his hand. "Thank you for telling me about Kate."

"Can I ask you something?" he says.

"Sure."

"Can I paint you?"

Her face smiles without her thinking about it first. "Yes, of course you can."

CHAPTER SIXTEEN

In the middle of the afternoon, a message buzzes into Olivia's phone. She's is the middle of a meeting with one of the junior ministers in Heather's department, David Masters. He is bouncy and enthusiastic, wanting to get things done. He is in his forties, fair haired with a handsome face which may have got him more votes, she thinks in passing. There are two civil servants in the meeting and one of them is droning on about a tiny detail so Olivia looks at the incoming message. It's from Evan Rice, asking to meet this evening. He has some information along the lines they had discussed, but he would rather talk face to face than write anything down.

"Are you with us, Olivia?" The minister's voice cracks through her focus on Evan.

"Yes, David." She gives him a particularly big smiles, knowing that he is vain enough to be affected by that. He smiles back.

They discuss the issues further for another hour and Masters asks Olivia to stay for a couple of minutes to agree the list of priority actions. The two others slope off and close the door.

"Good meeting," says David. He raises his eyebrows and looks across at her.

"We certainly went through all of the detail."

He smiles. "Are we public servants too slow for you?" he says.

"I'm sure you all enjoy talking." She gives a big smile this time and he lets out a short laugh.

"Priorities," he says. "Here's my list." He hands her a single sheet of paper with his narrow, scrawled handwriting on.

She reads his notes and nods. "Yup, looks good. There's a load to do now, and we only have a few people."

He looks wistful for a fleeting second. "I think we're all missing Stephen."

There's the slightest pause between them.

"Did you know him well?" she says.

"Yes, I did," says David. "I've been in this job for a year and he was my main contact on a daily basis."

"Did you like him?"

The natural politician in him hesitates for a moment. "Yes, of course, he was a great guy."

She starts her questioning strategy. "I bet he was a great drinking buddy, then?" she says.

"Well, yes…, we had a few evenings in the Red Lion."

"He liked the ladies, I hear." She pairs this potentially barbed comment with a flirty smile.

"Erm, yup…" The minister is uncomfortable, but that makes him vulnerable.

"Do you think he was trustworthy? He was married to Claire only a couple of years ago but he played the field, I hear." She stands and walks to the window, not looking at David, to give him a social breathing space.

"Some chaps are like that," he says.

"What? Unfaithful?"

"They find it difficult not to get involved, you know?"

She keeps her back to him. "Did he have enemies in here because of that, do you think?"

"There were people who didn't get on with him, sure," says David. "What are you getting at?"

"Claire is a friend of mine and she's trying to sort out in her mind just what happened."

"A tragedy just slipping onto the track like that," says David.

"She doesn't believe that," says Olivia. "And neither to the police." She turns to look at him.

"I didn't know," he says. "What, they think someone bumped him off?"

"Possibly." She watches him for signs of nervousness, but he displays none. "Did you witness anything over the last weeks or months when Stephen riled someone?"

"Apart from the thing last Christmas, nothing, no."

"What happened last Christmas?" says Olivia, feeling a scent in the air.

"Some chap threatened him at the Christmas do," says David. "We'd hired a room above The Barley Mow on Horseferry Road, you know it?" She shake her head. "The party was in full swing and this man arrives who seemed worse for drink to be honest, and proceeded to mouth off loudly to Stephen."

"What happened?"

"He stood right next to him and was shouting, so three or four of us bundled the bloke out, told him to piss off."

"And he did?" she says.

"Seems so, I didn't see him again."

"Did anyone explain it later?"

"No one mentioned it," says David.

Olivia pulls out her phone and finds the photo-fit picture of the man that Savage sent to her. "Was it this man?" She holds the phone up for David to see.

"No, he had fair hair, eyes too close together," says David. "Who's that chap?" He nods at her phone.

"He was seen near Stephen's body on the night he died."

"You think this photo-fit guy was involved?" David's eyes look afraid suddenly.

She nods. "The police do."

David is uncharacteristically quiet; his mind chasing through whether all of this is damaging for his public image.

"Is there anything else the drunk man said at that party? Anything at all?" says Olivia.

"Raving about some deal they had as far as I remember. Stephen had reneged on it and the chap had got into debt as a result."

"And no one there knew him? No one recognised him?"

"Oh yes, someone did," says David. "That young girl… you know, works in your team, doesn't she? Blonde."

"Ellen is the only blonde in my team."

"That's her", says David. "Ellen Hill. She knew the drunk. In fact, she tried to talk to him. Young Ellen tried to get the guy to leave, and said something along the lines of, 'we can talk later', but he took no notice. Just before we threw him out it was."

At last, for the first time, Olivia gets the feeling that the wall of silence around the death of Stephen Boyd is starting to break.

*

"Any news, darling?" says Gerald.

Patricia plonks herself down on the bench-seat next to her husband in the bar of the Cavendish London Hotel. Gerald raises his hand and says, "Tony?" no louder than normal. He makes a circular motion with his fingers. The barman across the room acknowledges the drink order for Lord and Lady Harwell with a subtle head nod.

"I have called that hospital four times today, always a different doctor answers."

"They're on shift, I imagine."

"But no one knows about her case in any detail," says Patricia. "*I* could read off a bloody chart." The drinks arrive and the Harwells wait until the waiter has walked away again before continuing their conversation.

"What did they say?" says Gerald.

"She is still unconscious. It's medically induced to help her recover, so she's not out of the woods. All they can do is monitor her vitals until they wake her up."

"How bad is it?" says Gerald. He puts his hand on Patricia's and gives a mild squeeze. He notices that her eyes are watery. "Don't worry, darling. They can do marvels these days."

She takes a large gulp of gin and tonic and places the cut-glass tumbler back down on to the glass table.

"We should talk about what happens." She pauses. "If she doesn't make it."

He shakes his head. "It's not that serious."

"You don't know that!" Their eyes stay locked together. "If she dies, we lose the house, it's in her name and it'll go to creditors."

"I know the arrangements, Pat." He enunciates each syllable.

"We should change the arrangements then," she says.

Gerald takes a deep breath and takes a slug of his whisky. "I'll talk to Kenyon, see what he thinks."

"He's our solicitor, Gerald; Kenyon does what we say, not the other way around."

"Of course, but he knows his stuff," says Gerald.

"Does he? Is he always looking after our best interests? Half the time he seems to put in place things that provide him with a nice income and leave us at risk."

"I'm not changing him."

"I'd like a second opinion on our options. I'm going to contact Mr Harrell, my family's lawyer."

"As you wish."

"You seem very relaxed at all this, Gerald," she says. "That house is all the capital we have now."

His anger is palpable, but his voice is quiet. "And as you know, Pat, we would be bankrupt today if we hadn't put those arrangements in place. It was the only way our creditors couldn't get to the assets."

They raise their drinks simultaneously but without speaking. They are both hot with anger inside as the ice clinks against the cut-glass.

*

The place that Evan Rice has chosen for their meeting is The Mayfair Bar on Berkeley Street. Olivia arrives just after six o'clock and sees him as she walks in. He is sitting on a u-shaped sofa in one corner, well away from the main part of the room. She is led over to the table by a waitress who takes her order then leaves.

"You said you had some news?" she says.

He stirs his Margarita. "Mmm."

"And?"

"Sensitive stuff, Ms Delaney." He doesn't say any more.

"Mr Rice, I'm a busy woman, can we get to it." The words are not posed as a question.

He finishes his drink as a waiter brings Olivia's wine and Evan orders another round without asking her.

"Mr Rice?"

"OK," he says, looking up at her. "Gerald Harwell. You've heard of him?"

"Don't patronise me," she says.

"We've found some information."

"About Harwell?"

Evan's hands are shaking, she notices. "And Sir Bruce Alpin. It's damaging information."

"Mr Rice, before you continue, I should tell you that I am aware of your family's connections to these men. Harwell is a good friend of Sir Bruce who is your sister's father-in-law." Evan looks at her, his mind trying to catch up. "Are you willing to share damaging information about a company connected to your family?"

"Anstone provides information irrespective of personal connections," he says coldly. They pause for a second, both wondering if this is a point of no return.

"What have you found?" she says eventually.

"Harwell and Alpin have been using GreenLink as a front."

"For?"

"There's evidence about bribes on land deals, but there's probably more activity hidden away," says Evan. "They pay politicians to get the laws they want, and then pay local planners to approve their schemes."

"Where's the money come from?"

"City of London, private high net worth individuals, the usual sources. All untraceable. There's big money in land development."

"What about the mobile contracts that GreenLink runs?" she says.

"Sub-contracted out. They take a cut, the sub-contractor actually does the work. GreenLink own no assets, it's smoke and mirrors."

"This is very useful information," she says. "My clients..."

"You can't use this," he says bluntly. "It's strictly confidential."

"I said to you last time that I would need to tell my clients."

"But they can't use it for any action, only their background information."

"I'll have to think about it."

"No!" He nearly shouts the word and she can feel his breath on her face. "You can't think about it. They're dangerous people."

"What do you mean?" she says.

Evan is sweating now along his hairline. "I found out this information two weeks ago, before you asked me. I was planning to go the police with it."

"Why didn't you?"

"I needed to know the consequences of doing that," he says. "There's only one other person I told it to. His name was Stephen Boyd. You know him?"

Olivia nods.

"He and I knew each other from way back, when I found out about GreenLink, I called him because I needed to tell someone I trusted and talk about what to do. He was in a bar somewhere. Four hours later he was dead. They did it, Ms Delaney. GreenLink killed Stephen Boyd."

After telling Olivia about GreenLink, Evan gets increasingly drunk and she has to call him a taxi in the end and pay the driver to take him home. She takes a cab herself and it drops her outside her block of flats. The doorman is his usual monosyllabic self as she passes him and presses the button for the lift. She turns the key in her front door and walks in. She hears someone there immediately. She doesn't turn on the lights and lets her irises get used to the level of darkness. There is no sound now but she's sure she heard someone.

Slowly, through the darkness, she lifts one foot and places it noiselessly in front of her. Then she moves her other foot and places that equally gently on the floor. She stops and listens like a cat. She takes another four steps. She's near the sitting room door now, she can't see detail but she can see the room is in a mess, cupboard contents thrown across the floor. She turns to the kitchen, walks five paces. The light from the river casts deep shadows across the work surfaces, a few cupboards have been opened and packets are on the floor. She waits. As a minute ticks by, her brain starts to say that she was mistaken and whoever has done this has long gone. She can feel her muscles start to relax and she allows herself a long, but silent, breath out.

She doesn't see the fist before it is six inches from her face, out of nowhere. Then the force against her skin, hard and powerful. Her body is thrown backwards, the area around the punch starts to hurt. She's on the floor, the intruder moves toward the door but she reaches out and gets her fingers around his ankle. He tries to shake her off, she hangs on but he doesn't fall. He leans over and hits her again, this time her head bangs against the floor and pain shoot across her skull. She doesn't know where she is for a second, she feels lightheaded; her emotions rise through her body, nearly unbearable. Her breath goes from her lungs, she struggles for air. Olivia brings her hands up to her face, waiting for the next impact. Through her closes eyes, she hears his footsteps on the floor. She needs to defend herself, kick him, punch him; anything to stop him. She hears him walk, she hears the front door open. Then it closes and he has gone.

Blood from her nose seeps down her cheek and drops silently onto the wooden floor. She can feel it, but doesn't stop it at first. Her nose and cheek pound with pain. She eventually holds her nose to stop the flow. Then she just lies there, the throbbing becomes aching; her rasping breath becomes a silent rising of her chest. The blood from her nose dries on her skin. Only then does she cry.

Olivia doesn't know how long she has been lying on the floor before she moves her legs and pulls herself up to a sitting position. She feels her cheek, which has a deep cut on it, and wonders if her nose is broken. She stands, walks to the sitting room and pours out a brandy, then throws the papers that have been discarded on her chair by the window and sits down hard into the leather. She knocks back the whole glass of brandy and rests her head back against the cushion. Her eyes close. Just before she falls asleep, her brain connects something. There was a second when the man who attacked her had stepped across a pool of light in the darkness. She has no doubt at all that he was the man in Inspector Savage's photo-fit.

CHAPTER SEVENTEEN

She can hear her phone ringing in the distance. For a second as she wakes, there is no pain in her head, then it pours into her consciousness like a waterfall. The ringing stops and she keeps her eyes shut. As well as head wounds, Olivia's whole body feels battered. She doesn't know what time it was when the man attacked her, nor how long she's been asleep. She tries to stand, stops and sways as she gets used to being vertical. She finds her phone and flicks through the notifications. Four calls from Gia in the office at half hourly intervals, plus numerous other messages. She checks the time, it's half eleven. She calls Gia's number which fortunately goes to voicemail, clears her throat and leaves a message to say she's unwell and has only just woken up. She'll be off today and back on Monday. Then she showers, clinging on the tiled wall to steady herself. She cleans up her nose and the cut on her cheek in the bathroom mirror, then walks to the bedroom and goes to bed.

It is nearly five o'clock when Olivia wakes again. She feels distinctly better as she lays there but her nose still hurts. She goes into the sitting room, picks up her belonging scattered by the intruder and shoves them unceremoniously back into cupboards. She looks at her phone messages, one from Poppy says she is calling in to see her after school today, which will be anytime now. Ellen has left a message asking if she's free and does she want to meet up? Olivia replies telling Ellen to come over but later on.

The sound of the front door banging announces her daughter's arrival. Poppy rolls in, dumps her backpack and sits in a chair opposite her mother. "You look like shit, mum. Been in the wars?"

"A burglar, last night."

"Oh God, you OK? Did he give you that black eye?"

Olivia goes to the long mirror on the lounge wall to inspect the latest on her face.

"Did he take anything?"

"I haven't checked to be honest."

"I've only got half an hour," says Poppy. "I'm going for drinks with the girls then seeing my new man."

"Oh, yes?" says Olivia. "How's that going?"

"Good. I'll make you tea." This is the first time Olivia can remember her daughter doing that without being asked.

"How's the job going?"

"Still dull, but they pay well because I could do it at short notice."

"Tell me about it, I've always been interested in that Whitehall stuff," says Poppy to Olivia's surprise. "Who's involved? Anyone I've heard of? We did a politics stream in my A levels. This woman called Heather Wells came in to talk to us a couple of months ago about being a woman in Westminster."

"She's my boss!"

"She mentioned some woman who wants to be an MP," says Poppy. "Greta Alpin?"

"Greer," says Olivia. "I've met her too. You know I was away last weekend? She was there."

"Do you know anything more about Greer Alpin?" says Poppy.

"Successful and rich," says Olivia.

"But what's she *like*? Is she a mad control freak or nice to your face then bitch you off when you've left the room?"

Olivia laughs. Her daughter looks across at her. "You know, I think she could be both of those." They smile at each other.

"D'you reckon she's corrupt?"

"I have no evidence, but she could be," says Olivia. "She and her husband could even be linked to the death of a guy in the office who died."

"Fuck! That bloke you said died on your first day?" Olivia nods. "What was his name again?"

*

By the time Ellen arrives, Olivia is another step along the recovery path. They cook pasta and sit by the window watching the few boats on the Thames at this time of year chug passed. Ellen drinks wine but Olivia sticks to tonic with ice.

"How was the weekend in Sussex?" says Ellen.

"You know about Claire?" Ellen nods. "Apart from that, what struck me was how everyone had something to hide."

"Such as?"

"Greer Alpin tried to shut me down when I asked about Stephen. Wouldn't talk about it. That makes me suspicious. Then her brother told me that GreenLink or Jeremy killed him."

"Christ, what a family," says Ellen. "I can't bear corruption, people like that get away with murder, in this case, literally."

"We don't know that."

"You defending them?"

"Nothing likc that," says Olivia. "I mean we've got no evidence which is what we need to go to the police. I can't use the Evan accusation, he won't talk on the record. But there was something else you said."

"What?"

"When we met early on you said that you knew Claire in her twenties, and that her parents seemed to be hiding things too. I saw that again at the weekend. They were all very nice and pleasant, and they're experts at avoiding what they don't want to talk about. They just wanted to give the idea that everything was under control. It just didn't seem real. They lost their Mayfair house, did you know?"

"What happened?"

"Gerald was disinherited by his father and his sister lived in the house in Sussex until she died, but there was a big inheritance tax bill to pay, so big that they had to sell their London house. But they want that all hidden, they made up some story about wanting to live in Sussex."

"You know Gerald he was mixed up in a fraud case when he was an MP? Some girl died too. Sir Bruce was part of it, you know, Jeremy's father? It links the two families."

"Who was the girl?"

"No idea. It was in the papers briefly then nothing, they probably suppressed it."

"That reminds me, I wanted to show you something," says Olivia. "I got a photo-fit from the police." She picks up her phone, scrolls through to the photos and shows Ellen the picture.

"Know him?"

Ellen stares at the screen. "You know, maybe, I *have* seen him."

"Where?"

"At Claire's parents' place," says Ellen. "Not recently, years ago, when he was younger."

"Who was he?"

"Don't know, he was at some party she had when her folks were away. I remember he kept coming in and out, and whispered in Claire's ear a few times, and she looked annoyed each time. I said something to her about him but she didn't tell me who he was."

*

On her way back home, Greer's phone chimes in her hand. She checks the name of the caller and answers.

"Heather, what a lovely surprise."

"Thought I'd just update you, Greer, on the girl in my department who you and Jeremy were finding intrusive."

"Oh yes?"

"I just called Jeremy but there was no answer, so thought I'd try you," says Heather. "I spoke to the girl and left in no doubt that she is on a final warning."

"Thank you."

"She seems to have a bit of an ego, and I mentioned about professionalism, particularly when meeting senior figures."

"It *has* been worrying me," says Greer. "I'm standing in the by-election for Sussex North, and I didn't want her silly questions to cause unnecessary disquiet."

"I didn't know you were standing," says Heather. "I heard Mike was retiring. Well done. Are you selected yet by the local committee?"

"Next month, but should all go well. Sir Bruce is lobbying for me down there."

"How's Jeremy?"

"Fine, why do you ask?" says Greer.

"I haven't seen him for a week or so, he seemed out of sorts last time," says Heather. "He was asking about my chap who died, Boyd, and about the police investigation."

"What did you say?"

"Only that they are damnably slow about the whole thing. It seems cut and dry, but they're dragging their feet."

"Why do you say that?" says Greer.

"There's a witness now, I think. Saw someone, I'm not entirely clear."

"Witness to what?"

"Someone was there at the time of death, on the tracks," says Heather. "They need to trace him to clear him or arrest him."

"Are you in a position to bend their ear over putting the whole thing to bed?" says Greer. "I could do with it being all sorted before voting starts."

"I know the Superintendent there," says Heather. "I can have a word."

"I won't forget your help, Heather."

"Talk later."

Greer has reached her front door as she ends the call and turns her key in the lock.

*

The front door to the Bluebird Bar can only be accessed down a side alley from Buckingham Palace Road. There's no large sign shouting the name of the place as the clientele prefer to think that they are members of an exclusive group who uniquely know where the place is.

They know Tom here. He's the lonely bloke who arrives on his own, doesn't talk to anyone, drinks three drinks over the course of two hours and reads a book on art, then leaves. Marie, who has worked behind the bar for many years knew Kate and only she knows why he turns up. Tonight, Tom has been here for nearly an hour when there's a lull in the flow of patrons. Marie tells Freddy that she'll take a break, pours two glasses of Sauvignon and walks over to where Tom is sitting.

"Thought you could do with another, Tom." She puts one glass on the table in front of him and sits down next to him on the banquette.

"Thanks." Marie is used to his brevity.

"You should move on," she says after a minute. "She ain't coming back."

"I know." She can't tell his mood from so few words.

"Why d'you keep coming here then?"

"To find him."

"The guy who did it?" Tom nods. "He's long gone, Tom. Whoever he was, blokes come in here sometimes for one evening, get pissed, wake up somewhere and can't remember what happened the next day, then never return."

"It's all I have, Marie."

"Whoever did it is hardly going to come back is he?" she says. "Hardly going to have another pissed-up evening in a bar where he beat a girl to death?"

Tom is unflinching as she refers to the events of the night that Kate died.

"You're a good looking bloke," she says. "You should get another girl, fall in love, get Kate out of your head. Even I'd shag you, there's an offer!" He turns his head and he smiles at her. "That's better, a bit more cheerful. You're too young to become an old duffer. We all have shit days, we all have things happen to us that we want to forget. I've had fucking awful blokes in my life, but I got over them; saw they were bad for me. It's not worth spending your days moping over stuff that doesn't go your way."

She raises her drink to him and they chink glasses. She takes a mouthful of wine and looks across as a group of men arrive at the bar. "I'd better get back." She kisses him on the cheek. "I'll hold you to that shag!" She winks and points at him then walks back to the bar.

Tom continues to read his book, not noticing anything around him. After a half an hour, he looks up and surveys the people in the bar. He doesn't know what he's looking for. He wasn't in the bar the night Kate died, it could be anyone. He watches the faces of the men, trying to imagine if each in turn could be a killer. One face looks familiar to him and his mind scans through when he has seen him before. Not work, not college, not near where he lives. Who is that guy? His brain flicks through his life and the people he has met, or at least the one that he can remember meeting. It's the eyes that he has seen before. Then he remembers his face from one of the drinks parties at the Alpins house. The man drinking and loudly laughing at some joke or other is Sir Bruce Alpin.

CHAPTER EIGHTEEN

The brasserie opposite Olivia's flat is packed full of people having breakfast when she arrives a little after ten the next day. A few people give her sidelong glances given her black eye and she finds a table in the back corner which is warm and away from the winter. She orders a basket full of pastries as she feels she needs to build up her energy to help her recover. The coffee is strong and black in her cup. Olivia opens her notebook and looks back at the pages she has written since the day they found Stephen Boyd dead on the tracks outside Clapham Junction. She reads through her previous questions and crosses out those she has answered or are that are no longer relevant.

She starts a fresh double page and writes the big questions in her mind along the top of the book.

Was the gun supposed to kill Claire or only injure her? The method seems wildly unreliable as a way of killing someone, so it was designed to injure and scare. Logically the follow-on question is, 'who would want to scare Claire?' The blackmailer is the obvious answer, but are there others? Olivia can't think of anything else she knows about Claire that would drive someone to frighten her like that apart from whoever sent the blackmail notes.

What does she know about the notes? They were threatening to reveal information about Stephen, not about Claire; and they came from the Houses of

Parliament. So, someone in Parliament sent them or someone who can access Parliament; and the sender has insider information about Stephen's activities that were in some way scandalous or illegal.

What is the motive? What was Stephen doing that caused the blackmail? Evan had suggested that GreenLink killed him to stop their corruption being made public. But Evan knows the information as well and he is alive and well. Why kill Stephen when he only received the information second-hand?

Olivia moves on to a new section and entitles it, 'Greer'. She stops and wonders why she has written that rather than 'Jeremy', or 'The Alpins'. It is now clear to Olivia that Greer is the one who is the driving force in that couple, particularly when it comes to potential links to Stephen's death if there are any. What is the evidence? Greer had been highly motivated to suppress Olivia's questions in Sussex, and, Olivia suspects that it was Greer who instigated the second complaint to Heather, not Jeremy. During the weekend in Surridge Place, Jeremy's reaction to Olivia's planted questions had been to quietly withdraw or change the conversation. Greer, on the other hand, had met the issues head on and tried to stop them. The pitch that Olivia made that got the biggest reaction had been to suggest that the police thought Stephen's death was something other than an accident. The two options of suicide and murder both seemed to scare Greer. What is she hiding? Olivia cannot get the sixty thousand dollar question out of her mind despite little evidence – did Greer pay for Stephen to be killed?

Olivia stops and thinks about Greer's personality. Would that woman really be involved with people who kill? It's possible, of course, but it still seems at stretch. But, if Olivia rejects this particular explanation for Stephen's death, there are few other credible explanations.

Suicide needs to be considered. What would be the scenario? A successful and powerful man, driven to kill himself over the humiliation of some sort of corruption being made public. That goes back to the type of corruption – something scary enough to make Stephen feel he had no other options but to end it all. Drugs? Handling stolen goods? Maybe those, but Stephen had not seemed the type. Olivia has met many criminals who have been the most charming people at first. White collar criminals particularly are more often than not very easy to get along with and easy to chat to.

What about motive for him to get into crime? What hadn't Stephen had in his life when he left education that drove his aspirations? Her mind clicks through the common motivations of people and she writes, 'money' and 'status' on her book. How had he met those needs in his life? A senior job in the civil service, for sure. What else? Marrying into a rich family too. Was that enough to meet his aspirations? If not, that would have driven his lust for more.

It all comes back to GreenLink. A shell organisation according to Evan Rice; but she needs evidence of their operations. The emails from Claire gave hardly anything new, but the Evan conversations have to be one of two things: either two innocent people considering going to the police with information about crimes; or in Evan's innocence, he contacted the very man who was involved with the crimes that had been uncovered. Whether Stephen had any role in GreenLink is one of the next key questions she needs to answer.

How can she get into the records of GreenLink Industries? She sips her coffee, and a possible route to get the information starts to unfold inside her head.

*

The evening has closed-in on a freezing London. The sky is a solid grey mass as her cab takes her across the river, and there is signs of snow floating above her head gently falling one minute then being picked up as bursts of cold air bowling down Frith Street in Soho as the taxi draws up outside the Sussex Bar & Restaurant.

She opens the restaurant door and the warmth envelops her. The waitress takes her coat and leads Olivia to a circular, wooden table in one corner set between two long, light-blue benches along the walls. Jack stands as she approaches and after the smallest hesitation as they try to decide what the right form of greeting. He opts for a kiss on one cheek and they sit down.

After ordering drinks and food, they chat casually and the conversation flows. Before their starters arrive, Olivia wants to talk about the case.

"You know what Evan Rice told me?" she says. Jack's eyes flick across to hers full of expectation. "He thinks someone in GreenLink killed Stephen Boyd."

"Who in GreenLink?"

"He doesn't know that."

"Does he know this or is it just a guess?" says Jack.

"He can potentially show that it's used as a shell company for illegal activity."

"*Potentially* won't convince a judge," he says and smiles at her.

"He has evidence." She sounds more decisive that she meant, as Evan didn't talk about evidence at all.

"What would be their motive for murder?"

"Boyd knew about their practices and was going to go to the police." Jack looks unimpressed. "I know it's a bit tenuous," she says. "But it's all we have really. I haven't found any other evidence. Plenty of sensitivities and the need to cover things up, but nothing more. I need to see some documents inside GreenLink next."

"Breaking and entering?" he says. They both smile.

"You know what I mean."

"I'm not sure I do." His eyes still hold the remains of the smile.

"Look, shut up a minute," she says. "I mean, how can I get to see them? Legally?"

"Maybe the Super was right and you're the main suspect." They continue to laugh all the way through their starters.

"There was a fraud case," says Olivia as the coffees arrive. "Seventeen years ago, Sir Bruce Alpin and Gerald Harwell."

"I know, I was a junior officer in the Met on it."

"Can we get to see those case files?" says Olivia.

Jack breathes out slowly through his nostrils, takes a swig of his beer and looks at her for ten seconds without saying anything. "What are you looking for?"

"Connections to activities still going on today."

"You suggesting they didn't stop after the investigation?" says Jack.

"Mm-hmm."

Then he nods. "OK. I'll try to get them dug out."

"Something else," she says. "Was Superintendent Peters connected to the fraud investigation?"

"He was," says Jack. "Peters was the lead officer on it, we were both in the Met then."

"And Sir Bruce and Gerald Harwell weren't prosecuted, were they?"

"Insufficient evidence."

At ten thirty, Olivia and Jack step out of the restaurant and start to walk along the street then up through Soho Square. The place is bursting full of people in winter coats, their breath in clouds ahead of them. The two of them arrive at the junction with Tottenham Court Road and she stops.

"I'm going to get a cab," she says punching details into a phone app to call a car.

He turns to her. "Thank you for saying yes to dinner again."

"My pleasure." The car draws up beside them. "This is me." She nods at the waiting Toyota. Jack leans in and kisses her on the lips. She smiles and makes a tiny wave before stepping across the pavement to the waiting taxi. Only then does he notice it's started to snow again.

*

The restaurant in White's Club is full. Tables with mostly two people at them have hushed conversations over exquisite food and wine. Sir Bruce Alpin has been a member here from the day he became a member of parliament, introduced by other MPs to this exclusive place. Jeremy is late. Sir Bruce had specified eight o'clock but his son had failed to show on time and it is now nearly half past. Sir Bruce is half way through his starter of scallops as Jeremy is shown to his table.

"Sorry, Dad."

"You'll never get anywhere if you're late all the time."

"Good to see you too."

"No need for sarcasm, Jeremy."

The waiter takes a bottle of Smith Haut Lafitte 2013 from the ice-bucket next to the table and pours Jeremy a glass. He orders the same starter and main as his father as he can tell that the old man is not in a great mood.

"What's the matter, Dad?"

"Nothing, boy."

"Don't give me that, I'm not ten years old anymore, you know," says Jeremy. "Come on, has something happened?"

Sir Bruce takes a large mouthful of wine and places the glass carefully down on the cloth, his face portraying a man deep in thought.

"Someone is asking questions about GreenLink," says Sir Bruce eventually.

"Who?"

"I don't know."

Jeremy's eyebrows knit together. "So, how do you know someone's asking questions?"

"Two friends of mine have told me that they've been approached and asked about GreenLink."

"Do they know who asked them?" says Jeremy, still confused.

"Both of them were bought drinks in bars around Westminster by a women they didn't know. The woman gave them a business card and said she was interested in investing in land development, she'd heard about GreenLink and could they get her an introduction."

"And?" says Jeremy.

"When they followed up and checked out the business card, the companies didn't exist."

"And what did your friends tell the women?"

"The conversations went on for some time and they can't recall everything they talked about, but both came to me after they had discovered the business cards were fiction. The stranger was very interested in the land deals we're doing."

"Could have been anything, Dad," says Jeremy. "Aren't people asking about investments all the time?"

"This was different, I can feel it," says Sir Bruce. "The woman was specifically targeting information about us."

"Can we do anything to find out more?"

"I can't think what, we have no names. My two friends can't recall anything particularly distinctive about what she looked like. What can we do?"

"I don't know then," says Jeremy. "We have nothing to hide anyway."

Sir Bruce doesn't continue to conversation and the waiter arrives to remove the starter plates.

"Gerald Harwell was telling me that Greer's campaign on the local politicos in Sussex is coming on well," says Sir Bruce.

"I'm sure she is giving it her all."

"You should support her more, Jeremy. She'll be useful for us when she's an MP."

"Dad," says Jeremy. "I'm going to divorce her."

Exactly at that moment the mains arrive and there is enough tension around the table to cut it with a knife.

"Did you hear me, Dad?" Jeremy says when the waiter has gone.

"That's not a good idea, my boy. I can't let that happen."

Jeremy scoffs. "Well..., not really anything to do with you, is it?"

"It's not going to happen, Jeremy."

"I'm sure you're shocked, but it's been coming for some time."

Sir Bruce shakes his head and he raises a fork of lamb to his mouth.

"Are you doing this now, intentionally?" says Sir Bruce after taking a long time to chew and swallow his food.

Jeremy watches his father across the table. There was a time when he would have been worried about the old man's reaction, but not now. This old dog hasn't learned any new tricks, his time has come and gone. Now is the new era when the son will take over and send the old boy off to graze in the countryside somewhere. He's waited for too long to start being his own man, start making his own decisions. But now, it's different. The first thing had been the death of Boyd, now the divorce. He's taking control, at last.

"It's of no concern to me what you think," says Jeremy.

"Then, why are you telling me at all?"

"Out of past respect."

"Your mother would have been sad to witness your behaviour."

"She not here to witness anything, Dad," says Jeremy. "Mum covered up for your crassness and your selfishness for too long."

"Don't talk about your mother like that."

"You always treated her badly."

"Rubbish!"

"She hated you, Dad," says Jeremy. "Didn't you know? Maybe not at first, but in those final years. She used to tell me all the time, she wanted to get away, but she had nothing except the lifestyle you funded."

"You don't know what you're talking about, boy."

"I'm not taking your bullshit any longer, Dad," says Jeremy. "I've asked the GreenLink Board to vote you out as Chairman. They were unanimous. We'll formalise it at the next Board meeting."

"I don't recommend you do that, Jeremy."

Jeremy eats his food in silence.

"You see, GreenLink is involved with other matters, areas that you know nothing about."

"What do you mean?" says Jeremy.

"If you remove me, it will all come out; and you, as CEO, will be liable for any risks we incur."

"You've lost me."

"Let's just say, not all of the GreenLink activities would be welcomed in the public eye," says Sir Bruce. Jeremy is quiet, watching his father's face. "You get rid of me, and it all comes out."

"What have you done, Dad?"

"Protected us as a family," says Sir Bruce.

"What activities are you involved in?"

"What activities are *we* involved in, you mean?"

"If any of this is criminal, I'll go to the police," says Jeremy.

"Your name is on every document."

"I'll deny it."

"I have friends in the court system will see to it that you are sent down," says Sir Bruce. "You don't want that." He pauses, enjoying the power of the moment. "Alternatively, you can stay quiet, and we can carry on as before. You stay with Greer and we all get rich. That's not too much to ask is it?"

CHAPTER NINETEEN

The snow from the previous evening has not thawed and the pavements around Chelsea hide areas that can suddenly be slippery when you least expect it.

Violet has only let Jeremy stay at her Chelsea flat twice before. Once when she broke her leg and needed help getting about, and once when his mother died. She likes to keep this flat as her own space, where she can just be herself - no makeup, no cocktail dresses, no smiling for another man who buys her dinner. But after Jeremy called her last night in such an angry state, she had agreed he could stay.

The red numbers on her bedside clock say 0704 and she knows it's half an hour until sunrise. She knows that because she's always up early, no matter what time she has arrived home. Sometimes, if clients keep her up all night, she takes a taxi back to Chelsea in the early hours and only slides into her own bed and sleeps for an hour or two before waking up. Then she makes tea and sits out on her tiny balcony overlooking the King's Road to watch the world come to life. She likes the night time, but she loves the dawn.

She finishes her drink and turns her head to look inside her bedroom. Jeremy is sleeping on his back. He had tried to say what had got him so angry last night when he arrived, but eventually he said he'd talk to her in the morning. They hadn't had sex and they'd fallen asleep together.

He makes a faint grunting noise just before he opens his eyes and looks around the room. She walks back inside, sits on the edge of the bed, and smiles at him.

"Sleep well?" she says.

"Mmm. I always do here."

"How do you feel? You were in a state last night."

He takes a big breath out. "It's Dad."

"What about him?"

"He's blackmailing me," says Jeremy.

She frowns. "Over what?"

"The company."

"What about the company?"

He sits up. "Got any more tea?"

"Two secs." She walks off to the kitchen. He follows her and she makes mugs for them both and they sit at her kitchen table. "Come on then, get it off your chest."

"This is confidential, right?"

"OK."

"I got the company directors to agree to vote Dad out of his job as Chairman. I told him that last night. I need to get control of the company and grow it, there's big potential but Dad always votes to keep it small. The other directors have said they're frustrated too."

"And he got angry, I guess?" says Violet.

"No," says Jeremy. "That's just it. He didn't at all. He said that it isn't going to happen and that the company is actually involved with more than I know, illegal stuff, and if he goes, then all that gets publicised with me in the frame."

"What sort of illegal?"

"He didn't say. I'm guessing white collar stuff, he was involved with a case a few years ago when he was accused but nothing happened in the end."

"What are you going to do?" she says.

"I want to go to the police," says Jeremy. "If I go to them and say Dad is trying to frame me, then I can help bring him down and avoid getting convicted."

"Or you can do nothing?"

"That's what he said. Keep quiet and we all benefit. But that's not the worst thing," he says. She looks at one of his eyes then the other, scanning his emotions and waiting for more. "He won't let me divorce."

"What do you mean? It's got nothing to do with him!" Her raised voice echoes around the room.

"He'd cut me off."

"That fucking little man!" She hits the table with her hand and the mugs jump up then clatter back down. "We should ruin him."

"What?"

"Go to the papers," says Violet. "Tell all. Take the fight to him. I've got a tame journo I can use."

"He'd say that I'm the one who's been breaking the law."

"But your not are you?" she says. "He'd have to produce evidence to back up his fantasies."

"He says my name is on all of the documentation."

"Then we'll be selective about what we share. Tell the police the parts that will sink the bastard," she says. "And go to the press at the same time."

Violet opens her eyes wide and smiles at him. "It's the only option we've got, darling," she says.

*

Ethan is reading a newspaper when Poppy arrives at the café in Covent Garden at ten thirty. "I don't think I've ever seen someone read an actual paper newspaper," she says, and kisses him on the lips. He has the remains of pancakes in front of him.

"I'm a bloody dinosaur at twenty-five, then," he says.

She orders a bacon sandwich and tea, and more coffee for him.

"I managed to get some intel from my Mum for your article."

"*Intel*? Who are you? Jane Bond?"

She narrows her eyes comedically. "Fuck off then, I'll take my intel somewhere else!"

"Tell me your intel, Poppy," he says. "You know you look beautiful today?"

"Slimy toad!" she says. "Anyway, that couple you mentioned, the Alpins?"

"Yup."

"Mum reckons that they could be involved with the murder of some guy in the civil service. He died on her first day in the office."

Ethan stops with his coffee cup half way between mouth and table.

"Does she now?"

"Mmm-hm." Poppy has her mouth full of bacon.

"Any details?"

"Nah."

"This is Stephen Boyd we're talking about?"

"That's him," says Poppy. "She said he was a nice guy and they're trying to cover up his death as an accident, but it could be suicide or murder and maybe the Alpins drove him to end it all or put a contract out on him?"

"You're cute when you're excited."

"Stop with your sexist bollocks for a second," she says. "I'm serious, this is big stuff."

"I know," he says. "I can use it. I'll go talk to the police, they always give away what's really happening. I've got contacts there."

*

The voicemail on Olivia's phone from the hospital in Sussex explains that Claire is out of intensive care and is now conscious and eating again. The nurse, who left the message, says that Mrs Boyd would be grateful if Olivia will come and visit her.

Sunday visiting hours start in the early afternoon, so Olivia drives down from London. The snow has melted from the previous evening and the sky is the lightest blue with high cloud marking the horizon. As she walks into the ward, Claire is sitting up in bed. The mostly white room has space for ten and a waft of antiseptic hits her nostrils as she enters. Claire turns her head and smiles. The cuts on her face have healed over leaving a cloud of red under her skin.

"Did you have to fight to get in?" says Claire.

"This black eye? I know its shit."

"What happened?"

"Nothing important," says Olivia. "What about you?"

Claire relates what the doctors and nurses have done and said. "They reckon a couple more days, then I'll be out as long as I can rest at home."

They talk on for a few minutes about the whole set of events in Sussex and about the accident. "As well as all that," says Claire, making a distinct break in the flow of the chat. "Can you do something for me?"

"Of course, whatever you need," says Olivia.

"You may say no in a second." She leans over to her handbag and pulls out her phone. "I got an email." She turns the phone around and gives it to Olivia.

Olivia reads from the screen. "You've been warned. Any funny business and next time it'll be more serious. Leave the money in a black backpack at this grid reference, 1am on Tuesday. This is your only chance."

"The grid reference is Primrose Hill Park," says Claire.

"I'm guessing you want me to go?" says Olivia.

"Will you? I can't get out of here. The money's in the safe at home, I'll give you the keys."

"We don't know who this guy is, do we?" says Olivia. "Or whether he'll be violent?"

"Sorry, no ideas at all."

Olivia looks out of the window beside Claire and thinks through the risks and the best way she could do the drop. If she arrives early and is long gone before the guy turns up, it should be safe enough.

"OK," she says. "I'll do it."

*

The door to access the flats that sit on a layer above the shops is between a glossy estate agents and a coffee shop selling gluten-free croissants. Ellen buys drinks and some things to eat, then turns a sharp left out of the café and presses the bell to Flat 4. A buzzer sounds and she pushes the door into a hallway with a steep staircase rising in front of her. She climbs the stairs and knocks on a door with a plastic number 4 held on by only one remaining screw, but still vertical. The door opens.

"Hi," she and Tom say simultaneously.

"I bought Danish." She holds up the bag in her hand and he invites her inside. The flat is an enormous room with kitchen units crammed into one corner, a double bed to one side and a single door leading to a bathroom at the far end. Two large windows in the sloping ceiling throw light across the floor giving the room a feeling of space and brightness. The walls are mostly bare, but there are two large framed pictures on one wall, tastefully positioned to show their grandeur. "Those are good," she says holding up the coffees in the direction of the two paintings.

"A Van Gogh self-portrait," says Tom. "And that's called Head of a Young Woman by Degas."

"Why do you like them?" she says, handing him one of the cups.

"Honesty," he says. She waits. "They break down the pretence of everyday life and tell you something you don't know."

They talk on about the pictures and art in general, about what she likes and why, about how she has no artistic talent but hasn't tried to do it since school. He listens, mostly, and watches her.

"Where do you want me to sit?" she says eventually.

"Here." Tom picks up a stool that has been under a table near the front door and places it in the centre of the whole space. Ellen takes off her coat and sits, drinking her coffee while she watches him unpack his easel, brushes and paints.

"Why do use oils?" she says after he has sorted out his equipment and sat on a chair, with only the easel between them.

"Because you can keep on going over them again and again," he says. "Your first attempt doesn't have to be right, unlike life."

Ellen wonders if she should continue the conversation on the lines that he has mentioned but decides not to, as it feels vaguely depressing and she feels happy. The winter sun fills the room with light and this whole idea of her portrait excites her.

By one o'clock, Ellen is getting hungry and suggests they go to the café downstairs. They have chilli con carne and large mugs of builders' tea and relax a bit more in each other's company. He's not used to talking about himself so much, she thinks, and she enjoys hearing her own voice talking about her own life up to this point.

Tom is keen to not lose the light and they go back for another session. He won't show her the painting until it is finished, he says.

She talks about Stephen without saying his name. This is the first time she has gone through all of it, out loud. It feels cathartic. Ellen checks to see if Tom is still listening, and he is.

"I've never had an ex who died though," she says. "I don't know how you've coped." He doesn't say anything, but she doesn't mind. "Do you miss her still?"

"Of course."

"What was she like?"

"Beautiful."

"I mean inside."

"Beautiful," he says again.

"Tell me about her," she says. "What did she talk about? What did she like doing?"

"I want to concentrate on the painting."

Ellen is silent for a few minutes.

"Did she decorate this place?"

"Look, shut up about her, will you?"

"Sorry, I…"

"She's ancient history, Ellen." His voice has a rising tide in it. "She was my world, now she's dead, that's it."

"I didn't mean to upset you. I want to get to know you and she was important to you, I can tell."

"For fuck's sake, I don't want to talk about her!" He throws a brush across the room, splatting crimson on the wall near the floor boards. After a minute, he mumbles. "The light's gone now, anyway."

"Yeah, I'd better be going, need to sort some stuff before tomorrow," she says, but they both know it's a lie.

After she has left, Tom looks at the picture he has painted. It looks like Ellen, he thinks, but there's too much of Kate in the eyes as well. He packs up his equipment and stores it all carefully away in the cupboard to give some space in the studio flat. He goes into the bathroom and undoes his belt then let's his jeans drop to the floor. He rubs his knee, his injury has been playing up in the cold weather, and after he just got angry, the joint is throbbing. He pulls back the Velcro tie on the strapping over the joint to relieve the pressure, then takes some pain killers from the cabinet by the mirror and washes them down with water from his cupped hand under the tap.

He walks back into the main room and sits with his leg stretched out, waiting for pain killers to work.

CHAPTER TWENTY

On the drive home from Claire's hospital, Olivia cannot stop her mind rolling over and over with the questions she cannot answer, so she uses a technique that has worked very well before to clear her mind. She pulls over to a lay-by and sets her phone on audio record before pulling out again to the sparse traffic flow heading back into London from the country on a Sunday evening.

"What did Claire really know about Stephen's activities?" she says out loud to the waiting phone. "Claire continues to deny any knowledge of anything untoward that her husband was involved with. Does this feel true? It doesn't. Claire patently imagined that Stephen could be having an affair and preferred to ignore it than confront him. She's an intelligent woman and it seems improbable that Claire would have been happy in the longer term to suspect something without confronting him or doing anything about it. Maybe it was just a matter of time before she would have done something." Olivia is already feeling the objectivity of talking to an imaginary third person even though it's only her phone.

"Next, how did Stephen end up marrying a well-connected heiress?" says Olivia. "Of course she had fallen in love with him, but she also had a long history of men in her twenties and surely would have fallen before, but doesn't appear to have done. Is that realistic? It could be. Stephen only moved in her social circles in her late twenties. Why had the party girl suddenly stopped? Was she bored of the lifestyle or was there something more compelling that forced her to be with Stephen Boyd? Her parents had been short of money at the time that Stephen first met Claire, and her father, Gerald Harwell had said that they had to sell the house in Mayfair to pay death duties. Did Stephen come along at just the right time, with money, and support his prospective parents-in-law? Gerald was also a named person in the fraud case fifteen years ago, was that connected to Stephen? It seems too early given he only met Claire four or five years ago. Was the marriage a reward by the Harwells for Stephen's help when they were strapped for cash? Claire may not even know that, even if it is true."

There's a service station up ahead and Olivia pulls off the road and fills up with fuel. She parks up at the back of the plot before going into a coffee shop next door to take a break. She puts in her headphones and listens to her own voice on the recording, as though she were both parties in a court of law, hearing the case for the defence or prosecution.

She gets back in the car and turns the recorder app back on, then starts the engine and returns to her journey home.

"What's the link between the gun accident and Stephen's death?" she says to the car's interior. "The blackmailer either caused the accident or has just leapt at an opportunity to apply more pressure to Claire. The expert clay pigeon man would have to have been involved with the crime if the accident was anything more than a coincidence." She stops and adds a side note on the tape to tell Jack about the expert man, telling the future Olivia to ask for the man to be checked out.

By the time she reaches New Cross Gate and turns north towards Bermondsey, she is on her final question of cross-examination of herself.

"The Alpins," she begins in her projected court-room voice. "Are they involved at all in Stephen's death or do they just behave in a suspicious way? Given their wealth and attitude, they may behave as though they think they can do and say anything they like. What's the evidence of criminality? Jeremy is a bit slimy, and well-in with Heather. Does that mean anything? Does that mean he would kill or order a murder to meet his own ends? We don't know. There is no third party who has said anything that supports the idea of Jeremy being involved with anything that links to Boyds' murder. Greer's involvement seems more likely given her frame of mind. She's more predisposed to hit out and stop things she doesn't like. What was she trying to stop happening if she did have a hand in the killing of Stephen? A crime of some sort. Were she and Stephen defrauding the government, with him as her man on the inside? She is a non-executive of GreenLink, so has access, and she is close to Jeremy's father, Sir Bruce Alpin, who has a history of fraud accusations."

The idea seems vaguely plausible and Olivia locks the scenario away in her brain as a possible explanation of the sequence of events that led to the death of Stephen Boyd.

She arrives at her block of flats and drives down into the underground car park, then takes the lift to her floor. There's a moment as she opens the front door to her flat when she stops and listens for anyone in there, then reprimands herself for being stupid and slips inside.

*

The Crabtree pub is somewhere that is vaguely familiar to Ethan. He can just remember his parents taking him here in the summer before his father died. Ethan thinks about what his father would think of him now as an adult. He would want him to be proud, he would want him to say that journalism runs in the family. He can't remember much about what his father was really like beyond him being his dad Ethan still has a ten-year-old's view of what the man was. He had only realised that his father had become his hero when he got to high school. He had been fourteen just before he started at New York Academia and when the boys asked about his parents and how come his dad was dead, Ethan fought for his father's glory and his good name. In the end, he'd convinced them that the topic of his dad was off limits unless they wanted a black eye.

"Are you Ethan?" The voice comes from behind him and he turns.

"Yup." They shake hands and he indicates the bench opposite him.

"Sorry I'm late, I normally work on the east side of town."

"No worries," says Ethan. "Thanks for coming."

Ethan goes to the bar and gets drinks then returns and puts two pints of lager down on the table.

"Can I call you, Jack? Inspector seems kinda formal," he says.

"Sure."

"I wanted to talk to you because you helped my dad back in the day."

Jack nods and smiles at the memory. "I was a detective constable in the Met then."

"He talked about you over supper at the end of the day with us kids," says Ethan. "He joked about your name being Savage but you're not."

"He was a great guy," says Jack. "I've met loads of journalists since then and your father is still one that sticks in my mind."

"How so?"

"I could trust him, I think." The smiles haven't left Jack's eyes since he started talking about him. "He asked straight questions, we gave him answers, and if we couldn't tell him something, he'd understand. We would read his articles in the Evening Standard and they'd ring true, you know?"

They both take a gulp of beer.

"It was a tragedy what happened, of course," says Jack. "We were all in shock. I was on shift that night. We were called out to an RTA."

"A what?"

"Road Traffic Accident. Down on the Embankment. Three cars, your father was in the middle one. The first guy braked hard, your dad hit him then the guy behind rammed your father's car." Jack looks up. "Sorry, I didn't mean to go into grizzly details."

"I know what happened, mom told us when we got to eighteen."

"He was the only one who died," says Jack. "The other men got away with scratches believe it or not."

"How d'you reckon that happened?" says Ethan.

"Do you really want to know?" Ethan nods. "He'd been drinking, we could smell it on him."

"He was teetotal," says Ethan. "Granddad died of cirrhosis of the liver when dad was a teen, so he never drank."

"He'd been drinking that night," says Jack.

"Do you believe it was an accident?"

"As opposed to what?"

"Do you think he was killed by the people he was investigating in the big article he was writing?" says Ethan.

"There was no evidence of foul play."

"But were you looking for it?"

"No. It was a straight DUI as you would call it," says Jack.

"I think he was killed."

"Got any evidence?"

"I mean to get me some."

"How?" says Jack, taking another swig of beer.

"Confession."

"From whom?"

"The same guys that were criminals back then are still criminals now," says Ethan. "I've been collecting information to prove it, and when I do, I'll give them the chance to make a statement on the record of their involvement back then."

"Who are we talking about?"

"A father and son, called Alpin and one of your Lords, Gerald Harwell," says Ethan. "A source of mine tells me that you are investigating a murder connected to those guys and you suspect they're involved."

"I don't know what you're talking about."

"I think you do, Jack. I think you know exactly what I'm talking about, and I think you are building evidence to prove the Alpins killed a guy called Stephen Boyd."

"Your source is wrong, Ethan," says Jack. "Boyd died in an accident at Clapham Junction. There is no evidence to say anything else happened."

"I aim to prove it."

Jack shrugs his shoulders. "OK, you do what you must do, but there's no evidence I've seen."

"You wouldn't be holding back on me would you, Jack?"

"Ethan, I believe in the press and their right to know, your dad taught me that."

"Because if it all comes out," says Ethan. "You may want to be on the right side of it all, you know? Both now and back then. If there was evidence back in the day and you guys covered it up, you need to be careful."

Jack's temper has risen in the last minute, and his voice tone shows the emotion now. "Firstly, Ethan, do not threaten a police officer, your dad would have been appalled by what you just said. Secondly, all evidence I have ever come across has been correctly recorded and fed into an appropriate investigation team to be considered. Thirdly, if you had hoped that coming here and issuing threats is an effective way to get inside knowledge about an investigation then you simply don't understand the first thing about policing. If you have diaries of your dad's, then go back and read them again. He was an honest, effective journalist who dealt straight. Your father would never have dreamed of threatening someone."

Jack stands up and finishes what remains of his beer.

"Regards to your mother, Ethan," he says, then walks off out of the pub to the road outside.

*

Olivia decides to drive to Claire's house the next evening to collect the money for the drop. She parks right outside the house, walks down the side alleyway and lets herself into the flat. She fumbles for a light switch and flicks the first one that her fingers reach. A set of ceiling lights fade up to give a soft glow to the hallway in front of her. She walks down to a doorway on the right and steps through into the master bedroom that looks out over the back garden. The safe is in one corner inside a cupboard, Olivia taps in the code that Claire insisted she memorise when they were sitting in the hospital yesterday. The light on the safe goes green and she turns the handle. Inside are bundles of bank notes. Olivia picks them up in turn and puts them in the black holdall until she has the right amount. She zips up the bag, relocks the safe, and makes her way back outside.

The air is heavy with expected snow. She looks up into the grey darkness and wonders if it will start to come down tonight. Olivia gets back into her car and drives down Haverstock Hill and through Camden Town before taking a right and turning into the Victorian streets of Primrose Hill. She parks away from the place that the blackmailer gave, punches in the grid reference to her phone's mapping app, gets out in the night air and starts to follow the glowing green arrow on her screen for the rest of the journey to leave the bag.

The route takes her to the park gates and up to the viewing point on the top of the hill. Her breath starts to come more often and harder as she climbs the slope with the bag over one shoulder. There's a couple at the summit when she arrives, but they walk off as she invades their private moment. Olivia checks her phone and zooms into to see the detail of the place to leave the bag and drops it under a large display map on legs that shows which buildings are which as people scan the horizon of London before them. She looks up and feels her eyes focus on the distant lights. She can see the London Eye, Canary Wharf, St Pauls; they're all there, like characters in a never-ending play. She watches the city for a minute, her gaze locked to the landscape beyond.

She breathes out and pushes the backpack under the legs holding up the map and starts to walk away. She has a choice now. Just leave and let the blackmailer have the money, or hide somewhere and see who collects the bag. She already knows which she's going to do before the thought has finished in her head.

Olivia walks back the way she came, then doubles back on a side road that tracks across between Primrose Hill Park and Regents Park. It brings her to the other side of the viewing hill. She walks just inside the park and along the boundary hedgerows, and ends up behind the mound but with a view of drop point, the map on legs stark against the night-time horizon. She checks her watch, 00:53, seven minutes until pick up. Olivia relaxes back into the trees that are partially hiding her from any prying eyes. The time moves slowly, she checks her watch again and it's only a minute later, she can feel her heart beating, suddenly more aware of her surroundings and any noises at all in the darkness.

One minute to go, she looks up to the mound, she can just see the outline of the backpack. There's no movement apart from her eyelids blinking. A bird of some sort hoots from trees down the hill, then the night returns to silence.

Her breaths are suddenly in her conscious mind, the air slides in and out through her nose. Her eyes blink again.

In the corner of her eye, a shadow starts to move. She tries not to blink so she doesn't miss anything and her corneas sting. A figure. A man? Looks like it. Maybe. He walks more slowly than she would have thought for someone picking up blackmail cash. He is at the display map now and goes down on his haunches by the bag. He unzips it and pushes his hand in, then brings out a bundle and flicks the edges of the notes. He zips the bag up again and lifts it to his shoulder. He doesn't turn back the way he came but turns and walks directly towards Olivia. She desperately pushes back into the trees, the branches give way and she sinks into the undergrowth. He is walking fast, she is holding her breath. He's there now, the other side of the branches. He stops. Cocks his head to one side, listening. He stands stock still for what seems like an hour but is less than a few seconds. Then he walks on.

After a moment, she moves out of her hideaway and into the moonlight. His shadow is still there in the distance. She follows. The man reaches the edge of the park, but he has no car there. He carries on walking along the road with large, expensive houses down either side. He gets to the junction and turns left towards St John's Wood and Olivia follows.

The man continues along the suburban road, walking fast but not speeding up. He doesn't look back. As he passes the gateway to one of the houses, Olivia sees another man step out from the shadows. The newcomer has something in his hand and brings it down hard on the man with the bag who falls down. The new man kicks him in the stomach, once, twice, three times – then he grabs the bag, wrenches it off his shoulder and runs to an old, small, blue car on the opposite side of the road. He jumps in and starts the engine. Olivia half-closes her eyes as the vehicle moves off. She can't quite read the number plate, was that ETN something? Was there 47 in it? The letters and numbers fade in her mind and into the night, and the car has gone.

Olivia runs to the man on the ground. He hasn't moved since the third kick to his stomach. She kneels down on the ground and feels for a pulse in his neck. It's there. She pulls out her phone and dials for an ambulance, then leans close in to see his face. She doesn't know him. He's young, in his twenties. She waits for the ambulance and explains that she saw him attacked, but nothing else about why she was in the area. They take the man away and Olivia walks back through the streets to collect her car.

CHAPTER TWENTY-ONE

"Ellen!" Olivia runs down the corridor when she sees the woman just after lunchtime. "We've missed each other the last few days. I wanted to ask you something."

"I'm just going for a coffee."

"I'll come with you."

They walk up to the canteen, buy machine coffees and sit by the window overlooking Whitehall.

"December last year," Olivia begins. "The office Christmas Lunch. You remember?"

"Sure, but you don't, you weren't there."

Olivia ignores the interjection. "There was a guy came in and started shouting." Ellen nods. "He shouted at Stephen mostly, I believe."

"I think so."

"Some of the blokes bundled him out," says Olivia. She waits for verbal or non-verbal responses, but none come. "Apparently you said you knew him and would talk to him later. Is that right?"

Ellen drinks her coffee. "Yes. That is what happened."

"Who was he?" says Olivia.

"Just a friend of a friend."

"And why was he shouting at Stephen?"

"I don't know, really," says Ellen. "He said some stuff about losing his job. I can't remember the detail, it's a while ago now."

"What was his name?"

"Len something, I don't remember," says Ellen. An obvious lie, but Olivia doesn't know why, or consider it worth asking.

"What did you say to him, on that day?"

"I just told him to go home and sober up and how he was lucky he hadn't got into more trouble."

"And he just went?" she says.

"Yes, he didn't come back."

There's a brief pause while Olivia wonders if there's any point going on when Ellen is not telling her the truth. Once a witness lies, they have to keep lying to cover themselves. They chat on for a few minutes then Olivia finishes her coffee and thanks Ellen for the drink before going back to her desk.

*

After work, Olivia walks to the centre of the city and the air is cold against her cheek. She calls the hospital where the man from last night was taken to ask how he is and find out if she can visit him to talk. The nurse who answers sounds annoyed when Olivia mentions the man, as he had caused trouble in Accident & Emergency. As soon as he was conscious, he was angry and violent, then he had disappeared before they had fully treated him, or even found out his name.

She arrives at Trafalgar Square where Jack had suggested they meet to make them feel Christmassy. In the centre of the square, the tree from Norway rises up into the dark amongst crowds of locals and tourists who have come to be part of London at this time of year. All of this reminds her that she hasn't bought any presents so they walk around some shops and she gets something for Poppy, and one for Olivia's father. Jack doesn't buy anything and doesn't talk about what presents he has to buy. They find a brasserie and a couple are just leaving as they arrive, so they get the table in the window. From their vantage point, they can see the roving, cheery mass of people outside, happy to be part of something. They order Prosecco and seafood, and the place feels cozy away from the coldness.

Later on they talk about the case. "I was threatened yesterday," says Jack. "By some journalist."

"Threatened?"

"Bloody cheek, some of them think they can push their weight around. I knew this guy's dad and I told him that his father would never have done that."

"What was he threatening you about?"

"The Boyd case," says Jack, looking at her with wide eyes. "Like you, he thinks the guy was murdered, but he accused us of having evidence and covering it up. Some anonymous source of his had got it in their head it was an unlawful killing. No evidence of course, just random accusations."

"I might have some evidence."

"Oh yes?"

"A car reg number of the man who's blackmailing Claire Boyd."

"How did you get it?" he says.

"I dropped off the cash last night and saw him pick it up."

Jack sighs. "That's fucking dangerous, Olivia. You should have told me."

"Claire asked me."

"Will you tell me if you decide to do something like that again?"

"Probably not," she says. "Don't be all miserable about it, I got a number. Can you trace the car?"

"Go on."

"It's not the whole plate but it has 47 ETN in it."

"Colour?"

"No idea, dark."

"OK. I'll run it." He makes a note.

Their main courses arrive and his frustration subsides as Olivia plays a game of 'things we don't know about each other'.

"My turn first," she says. "Where were you born?"

"Croydon."

"*Someone* has to be."

"Fuck off."

"What did you want to be when you were a kid?"

"It's boring."

"Doesn't matter as long as it's true!" she jokes.

"Copper." They laugh.

"Last one, then your turn," she says, "What's your middle name?"

"Oh shit, it's bad."

"Come on, come on!"

"Allendale"

She bursts out laughing and they laugh together.

*

The Savoy is busy tonight. Adrian arrives early to get a good seat while he waits for Violet. Her call had been a surprise this afternoon as he thought she had decided not to take him up on his offer. This time, he makes a point of asking what Miss Violet usually drinks and tells the waiter to have it ready as soon as he sees her arriving.

She is wearing a tan coat with an enormous collar as she makes an entrance which reminds him of old Hollywood. Violet waits for the waiter to take the coat from her shoulders and reveal a pink sheer dress bought for her by a Saudi businessman two days ago.

"Sorry I'm late," she says. "My chap at lunchtime wouldn't let me go. Charged him double though, so the drinks are on me." The waiter appears at that moment with two Mai Tai cocktails. She stops and smiles to herself then looks up at Adrian. "I do like a man who listens." They pick up the drinks and chink glasses then both take a sip.

"Now, to business Mr Gilbraith."

"You changed your mind, Violet?"

"No, an opportunity has come up, and I thought it would be fun to go ahead with your little idea."

"What sort of thing are we talking here?" says Adrian. "Sex? Drugs?"

"Firstly, I want to make a little change. It won't be about the man you mentioned."

"That's disappointing, he was high profile and a dead man can't sue me."

"A bigger fish though," she says. "Sir Bruce Alpin."

"He's a client?!"

"No, he's not." She smiles in a way that makes him understand her success with men. "He is, however, corrupt."

"And you have recordings? Or paperwork?"

"Both."

"What's he been up to?" he says.

"Bribery and fraud over many years," she says. "He's taken money from many people to vote in a certain way in the house when he was an MP, and since then, he's taken money and made payments to ensure votes and legislation goes in his paymasters' favour. He's also been dealing in various goods which he wouldn't want the public to know about."

"He hasn't been an MP for ten years though."

"The little shit has been doing it for nearly twenty years."

Adrian nods slowly. "Good." He smiles at her. "No drugs and sex is there?"

"You journalists and your one track minds."

"Two track, to be fair." He smiles and she echoes it.

*

Sir Bruce looks at the brandy in the glass and swirls it around. He remembers watching his own father doing that when he was a boy but young Bruce wasn't allowed to have alcohol until he was eighteen according, so he had had adopted stealth tactics, behaving one way but appearing to behave in another. Always keeping to the rules in public, but ignoring them in private. That glass of brandy that his father swirled had been the start of it, the first time that he remembers thinking that what people see and how you behave are two entirely different things. He raises his glass. "To fathers!" he says and Gerald repeats the line.

"You look tired, old man," says Gerald.

"Fighting fit, as ever. How's your leg these days?"

Gerald puts his hand on his left knee. "Mustn't grumble. Plays up in the cold sometimes."

"Maybe you should move to the Med, old boy? Mild winters."

Gerald laughs mildly. "I couldn't stand it there! All that bloody sun. Give me the British countryside and hazy light rain anytime."

Sir Bruce smiles at his friend and takes another swig of brandy. "Funny you said I was looking tired just now, actually I haven't been sleeping that well."

"Oh?"

"I'm concerned about people snooping around our land deals."

"That Docklands one you got me to buy shares in?"

"And the others," says Sir Bruce. "I have a few more, all through a GreenLink subsidiary."

"Who's snooping around?"

"That's what I don't know."

"Someone asking questions?" says Gerald.

"A chap who I know, a good friend, said that he'd been asked to provide documents about the company. Someone's looking for dirt."

"A competitor?"

"Smells like something more underhand, to be honest," says Sir Bruce. "Police maybe."

Gerald is taking a mouthful of brandy and stops, still holding the glass. "Nothing to worry about, though? The police have the right to search if they get information, but ninety percent of the time, it comes to nothing, just someone wanting to cause trouble."

"I hope you're right," says Sir Bruce.

There's a pause between the two men. Gerald watches Bruce's face. "There is nothing to worry about in that regard, is there, Bruce?"

"Of course not."

"Bruce? I may be an old duffer but I can tell when someone is lying. What's going on?"

Sir Bruce shifts in his seat and raises his hand to the waiter for more alcohol. "Some of the deals..." He pauses to shape his words. "Some of the deals could look unusual if one just saw paperwork about them."

"For God's sake!" Gerald wants to raise his voice but the clientele of White's Club would remember it for years to come if he did. "What on earth have you been doing?"

"Nothing to get heated about, Gerald. It's just that some of the investors, quite rightly, have wanted to keep their investments private."

"Meaning what, exactly?"

"Meaning that the can manage their portfolios without getting bombarded with unnecessary taxation."

Gerald has not felt this angry since he was a young man. "And by 'unnecessary', I assume you mean avoidance?"

"Let's not get carried away."

"I can't be part of this, Bruce. I need to withdraw my funds from your schemes. I can't be seen to be part of some offshore tax avoidance scam. I'll ask my finance chap to talk to you tomorrow."

"You didn't mind it fifteen years ago, Gerry. You didn't mind it when we made a few bob and managed to slip through the police net, then. We did it then, we can do it again, old man."

"Ancient history," says Gerald. "Long gone. Yes, we got away with it, but that girl didn't, did she? She's in some graveyard somewhere thanks to us."

"And now you're invested in my schemes again, so best not rock the boat."

Gerald breaths out and closes his eyes for a moment. Then he leans forward and stares at Bruce's face. When the words come, they are slow and deliberate. "I'm withdrawing my funds, Bruce. This conversation is over." He stands up and walks to the door of the lounge in White's Club and down the corridor to the front door.

*

There are only two street lights on the short road that stretches out ahead of Ethan. He sits in his car and watches for activity. The night is quiet. He checks his watch; it's just after one. The man he had contacted had been very specific about the timing needed to get into the place undetected. Ethan waits for another minute then pulls at the door handle and steps on to the pavement and closes the car door as quietly as he can. He is wearing all black, including a woollen hat and thin gloves. He walks ten yards and stops beside a doorway. He has memorised the door code and stabs at the buttons on a stainless steel panel to one side of the portico. There's a faint click as the door unlocks and he pushes on into the building. The entrance hall is narrow but has a place for a receptionist's desk to one side that would be manned during office hours. He treads lightly on the carpet and makes his way to the bottom of the stairs ahead, then noiselessly up two half-flights to the first floor. A single door sits on the landing with a plain sign simply with GreenLink Industries written in white on a blue background. He puts in the same code as the front door and vaguely smiles at the lack of sophisticated security.

Inside, there's a large room in darkness. Outlines of desks, screens and chairs are picked out by the shafts of light coming through windows dotted down the side wall. The room has enough room for twenty desks but there are only six, each with its own assistant's desk nearby to delineate a territory belonging to each occupant. At the far end are two offices which he guesses are for Sir Bruce and Jeremy.

He walks the length of the room and into offices. In the first there is a filing cabinet, this must be Sir Bruce's office, a man who still enjoys dealing in paper. Ethan tries the top drawer of the cabinet but it's locked. He pulls out two hook picks from his pocket and inserts them nimbly into the keyhole on the cabinet, after less than ten seconds, a clunk sounds as the long bolt drops. He opens the top drawer and starts to read the papers inside, then works his way down the cabinet, pulling out files of interest as he goes. He ends up with six that he thinks have some juicy evidence in them. There are no other items of interest in that office so he sweeps into the second room. No filing cabinet here, only a desktop computer. The same contact who provided the door code gave him the password to Jeremy's machine. He clicks through the screens and inserts a memory stick into one of the sockets. He works through the folders and reads as much as he needs to assess whether the files are valuable. There are audio files too and he copies all of those onto the stick, and dumps four other documents across as well which have potentially incriminating information in them. He closes everything down and walks back through the main office. As he reaches the door, he can see the flickering of a torch on the stairwell. He is calm, his experience of doing a break-in like this twice before has given him bravado. He ducks into a recess where the photocopier sits and waits. Ethan pushes close to the corner of the wall and looks out towards the doorway. A man with a torch is outside, looking in through the glass. His hand shading one side of his view to eliminate the glare from the stairwell lighting that he turned on before climbing the stairs. Ethan ducks back into the recess. He listens for movement, anything that might tell him what is happening. The man must have tried the door and found it open, and now he is stepping into the dark reception area within ten feet of Ethan's hiding place. He walks slowly around the room, bringing his torch to illuminate features of the room. The light cuts across the recess, just beyond Ethan's body. The man walks towards the recess, each step closer. He stops. The torchlight explores the walls then turns to the main room and he walks on. Ethan can hear the man getting further away. Slowly, his confidence rises about making his move and the route tracks out inside his head - through the reception, out of the door, down the stairs and out into the street. He makes a single step, then he's away. He walks out of the recess, the other man hears something and plays the torch back to the reception. He sees Ethan as he opens the main door and starts to give chase. Ethan takes the steps two at a time, his balance is slightly ahead of him and he crashes into the half landing wall with speed, ramming his shoulder into the exposed brickwork. The man is at the top of the stairs now. Ethan takes the last flight with more speed, he hits the ground floor and runs with all his strength for the door to the street. He hits it hard, pulls the vast glass door and is outside. The coldness hits him and he turns towards the car. The man is closing on him. Ethan is accelerating towards his car. He reaches it as the man appears from the doorway. Ethan throws his bag in first, sits down onto the leather of the driver's seat and turns the key. Nothing happens and he turns it again, the engine roars, he pushes the accelerator hard. A screech of wheel spin echoes between the walls of the houses, the car shifts off from stationery, he nearly hits a parked car opposite him. The man runs out into the street showing his security guard's uniform, he steps out into the path of Ethan's vehicle and Ethan pushes the pedal harder. The car steams passed the guard who only steps out of the way as the car is feet from him. Ethan reaches the end of the street, squeals around the corner and shouts a victory cry at the top of his voice.

On the laptop that Jeremy left in her flat, Violet picks up the mouse and clicks to stops the recording of the CCTV from the GreenLink offices and clicks again to download the copy of the video on to a USB stick.

CHAPTER TWENTY-TWO

The first time she sleeps with someone is always Olivia's favourite time. She's not built for relationships, she thinks. This first time is like a film, when the audience knows it won't happen again but the characters don't know that yet. She looks across at the light starting to bleed out from the edge of the curtains in Jack's bedroom. He is beside her, facing the other way, sleeping silently. She gets up and goes to the bathroom, then showers and return to the bedroom where he's still asleep. She pulls on the clothes from last night, which she always hates doing, and walks around to his side of the bed and sits down.

"Hey," she whispers. "I've gotta go."

Jack rubs his eyes and opens one of them to look at her, then coughs.

"Very sexy, I must say." She smiles at him.

He clears his throat. "What's the time?"

"Seven." He breathes out through his nose. "I've got to get back home then to the office," she says.

"Mmm, OK." She stands up. "Olivia?" She turns to him. "Thank you for a lovely evening."

"Thank *you,* Inspector." They smile.

She starts to move towards the door. "Oh, I nearly forgot. The fraud case papers. They're in a folder, in the kitchen, on the side. Take them with you but I need them back in two days max."

Olivia collects the folder and calls a taxi on her phone app. She walks down to ground level and the car pulls up as she walks out in to the biting morning air.

She sinks back into the Toyota, opens the folder and reads the story of the case from fifteen years ago.

Mr Bruce Alpin, as he was not a knight then, had been under surveillance by the Metropolitan Police for a couple of months before they arrested him on suspicion of fraud. He was the MP for North Sussex and so the arrest caused a huge media storm. Gerald Harwell was also arrested but three days after Alpin. The allegations centred on what the papers called dirty money from offshore accounts. The Daily Courier tabloid newspaper had run a huge article called, 'King Bruce and his Money Island' where they added a whole range of allegations about prostitution, money-laundering and wild drugs parties, but the police documents in the file tell a different story. The detectives who had been tracking him did have evidence of bribes being taken by Alpin, but they couldn't find any offshore accounts or evidence of wild parties. Gerald Harwell had accepted money to vote in a certain way in the House. The crimes were felt by the Met to be outside of their jurisdiction and handed over to the Speaker of the House to deal with. There is no more in the file about the payments, and Olivia guesses what is not written in the file, which is that the case was forgotten and no punishments were given out.

The more intriguing part of the case was not about the payments at all, but the death of a young woman in a bar where the money had been exchanged. There is no name given for the woman, but all references to her only use an allocated cover name - Miss J. The file has notes about the interviews with Alpin and Harwell and they were both asked about Miss J but denied any knowledge. Also absent in the file is any mention of who received or took money from the two MPs. Olivia is shocked by the wooliness of the papers as she reads them. If she had received these as part of a defence trial, she could run rings around the police's case, if they had gone on to prosecute.

She looks at the list of people on the team in the Met who worked on the case and there are copies of their personnel photos pasted onto a page. DC Jack Savage looking younger, and DI Peters, who looks hard and scary. Olivia turns the page. There is only one picture on this final team photo page, showing the lawyer appointed to the team – Patty Wells. "Well, I never," she says to herself. Looking back at Olivia from the page is a younger but relatively unchanged Patricia Harwell.

*

It is ten o'clock before Jack arrives at the British Transport Police Head Quarters in Camden Town, to the amusement of his team who all share a large, open plan office on the first floor of the building at the back, overlooking the Regent's Canal.

The team continue to joke and ask him about his evening and suggest funny ideas about why he would oversleep. Their conclusion after several minutes is that he's definitely got a woman.

He presses the buttons on the coffee machine and takes his plastic cup to his office in the corner of the room. Lois follows him in. "Got a break-in, guv, that links to one of our cases. The local Met boys rang it in to us when they saw the name."

"Go on."

"The offices of GreenLink Industries were done about one this morning. The security guard was off having a fag, which he can't do inside the offices, so he goes round the corner to an alley way. Anyway, he was there about ten minutes, he reckons. He comes back in and the door is unlocked. He goes up stairs and the door to GreenLink is open too so he goes in. The perp does a runner, but the guard didn't catch him. Drove off like crazy almost crashing."

"Description?"

"Wearing all black, average height and build, in his 30s the bloke reckoned."

"What was stolen?"

"They don't know," says Lois. "Break-ins aren't a priority and no one has searched the place. They tried to call you though."

"Call *me*?" says Jack.

"Yeah, when they logged the call, the name GreenLink came up with our live case with your name attached. They thought you might be interested, but you didn't answer."

"I was busy."

"Don't you leave your phone on, guv?" she says. "You told us to leave ours on even at weekends in case we get a shout."

"I switched it off."

"Why did you do that? Did that bird you were with tell you to turn it off? I bet she did or you wouldn't get any," says Lois. "That what my Steve says. He says, if that phone stays on, we're not going to…"

"Yeah, I get it, Lois. Thanks."

Lois leaves the report of the break-in on his desk and walks off in a slight huff.

Jack reads the report and thinks about the timing of his evening and the break-in. He doesn't want to think that Lois is right about what she said, but Olivia had asked him to turn off his phone when they arrived at his flat. They had kissed and his phone had sounded a notification. He had moved to look at the screen and he now can't get the words she said out of his head. "If you look at that screen, I'm out of here, Inspector. It's me or the phone, just for tonight."

He keeps pushing the idea out of his mind. It can't be right. Then he remembers something she said the other day about needing to get evidence about GreenLink to back up her crazy idea that Boyd's death hadn't been an accident.

"Shit," he says out loud.

*

The headlights of the car scan across the shrubbery that runs down the driveway to Surridge Place. It comes to a stand by the front door and the driver opens Patricia's door for her.

"Thanks you, Michael," she says. "I won't need the car tomorrow, but seven thirty the next day please."

"Ma'am."

She walks into the house, takes off her coat and hands it to the silent girl, then changes her footwear for suede house shoes. She walks into the lounge and Gerald is sitting at the far end, reading The Times.

"Hello, darling," she says, and pours herself a gin and tonic. She sits in an armchair near him and looks into the fire that has been burning since three as her husband has been at home all day today. "How was your day, Gerald?"

"I've been talking to Carl Forrester about pulling out of some of our investments."

"What on earth for?" she says.

"I wanted to wait and tell you until you got home," says Gerald. "But Bruce and I had a disagreement last night at White's."

"What about?"

"He revealed that some of the investments he had introduced me to are not all above board."

"Meaning what, exactly?" She takes a sip of gin.

"He wouldn't go into details," says Gerald. "But safe to say they wouldn't pass muster if someone came looking too closely."

"And have we lost money?"

"Some, my darling," he says. "But not like after my sister's death."

"I assume this has not come out in the open, Gerald?"

"No." He shifts uneasily in his seat as she displays her courtroom ability to question forensically.

"Did Carl manage to move the funds?"

"He's working with Bruce's finance chap."

"So, we're still exposed until that happens?" says Patricia. Her husband nods dolefully. "Do we need to do anything else?"

"Such as?"

"Manage any reputational risk. I can't be seen to be involved with something that borders on criminal, even if that's not strictly the case, it's what appears to be the case with journalists, as you know."

"I'm not sure what we can do, darling."

"Who knows about this?" says Patricia.

"Only Bruce."

"What about his finance chap?"

"He doesn't know where the funds come from or go to, Bruce does all of that through blind trusts."

"I take it that some of the funds are dirty money?" she says.

"I didn't ask, Patricia," he says. "Intentionally so - I thought that the less we know the better. I can deny we knew about the investments. Which is true until last night."

"They'll crucify us if this gets out," she says. "I may take some action, Gerald."

"What?"

"I'm not sure yet, but this could be devastating for us." Her eyes lock onto his to double the impact of her words. "My career, your reputation, Claire's inheritance, could all be at risk."

"What can we do?" he says.

"If only Bruce knows, then at least that narrows down the field of possibly ways this could ever leak out. He wouldn't talk would he, if he was in a tight spot?" she says.

"If the police got hold of this, you mean?"

"Mmm."

"No, he wouldn't name names," says Gerald. "I've known him for twenty years - we were in cabinet together."

"If you say that you trust him completely, Gerald, I may have to review my entire idea of your ability to understand people," says Patricia. "I've never liked the man and wouldn't trust him further than I can throw him."

Gerald is silent.

"Leave it with me, darling," she says. "If there's a way to stop this, I will find it."

*

Ellen had accepted the invitation to dinner from Tom earlier in the day despite her feeling slightly uncomfortable after his outburst at the weekend. He has booked Cacio & Pepe in Churton Street, Pimlico. They arrive together and are given a seat towards the back. The place has an air of romance, subtle lighting and peace and they order a bottle of Sauvignon while they choose their food.

"Before you wonder," says Tom as they sit reading the menus. "This is my treat."

"It does look expensive," she whispers.

"I got some money last week, unexpected. My gran died and she gave all the grandkids a bit each."

"Thank you," she says.

"I wanted to apologise too, for getting annoyed on Sunday."

"Forget it."

"It was a difficult time back then and I'm only just getting used to talking about it," he says.

"Forgotten," she says. She raises her glass. "Here's to your gran."

They make a toast then they order burrata con asparagi and polpo fritto starters, then both have sea bream but no puddings.

"This has been an amazing meal," she says after Tom has discretely gone away to pay the bill and walks back over to her as she finishes her wine.

"My pleasure," he says. They walk out to the street and along the pavement in the direction of Pimlico tube station. "I was thinking, do you fancy doing something on Saturday?"

"Sure," she says. "What are you thinking?"

"Hampstead Heath?" he says.

"I've never been."

"We could drive."

"You gotta car, then?"

"Little blue one," he says.

"Expensive restaurants and a car, impressive."

"It's only old," he says.

"As long as it works," she says.

"The Heath's great at this time of year," says Tom. "Hardly anyone's out there, it's a bit desolate."

"You could get lost out there and not be found for days!"

She laughs and he does too.

*

Evan opens the kitchen cupboard, pulls out a packet of basmati rice and pours some into the waiting pan of boiling water. He enjoys cooking and the odd evening alone in his flat more than he would admit to his drinking mates or his lobbyist colleagues, all of whom seems to survive without ever staying in, or so they say. He stirs the curry and thinks about the documents that he had seen today. He doesn't know where his contact got them from, but they are damning for Gerald Harwell who seems to be the centre of a crime syndicate using GreenLink as a way to pay politicians bribes and hide the money in offshore accounts. The contact had said that Evan can't have copies until he has the money, and that is why Evan had emailed Rebecca Delaney last thing before leaving the office this evening to say that he needs half of the money to pay for the information she wants on GreenLink.

He takes his plate to the sofa and watches a documentary about fish while he drinks four bottles of beer steadily over the next two hours. He feels drowsy, and tells himself that he should go to bed rather than fall asleep on the sofa and wake up a two in the morning, which he's done all too often. Despite his intent, his eyelids are heavy. He's still awake though, he'll just close them for a moment then he'll get up.

Through the haze of darkness, Evan is dreaming. He's in the woods, it is night time but he's kept a camp fire going and the orange sparks fly up into the air and through the trees. He likes being out in nature, away from it all. The wind blows the smoke in his direction and he coughs, then keeps coughing. The coughing wakes him back into the real world. The first thing that he notices is the smell, the smoke from the camp fire was real. He opens his eyes. Is someone having a BBQ? There are no gardens near his flat so it can't be that.

Someone smoking in the street? He's never smelled it before from up here. He is only half awake now and stands up, his eyes sting from being asleep and suddenly waking. He rubs them while walking around the sofa towards the door to the hallway. As he reaches the door, grabs the handle and pulls. Flames lick out from the doorway and he feels the heat on his face. He slams the door shut and turns to the windows. There's no other exit from the sitting room apart from through the hallway. He grabs the window latch and tugs at the handle, but it's stuck. Evan's fingers slip off the metal and he gouges a slice of skin from his forefinger. He can see smoke coming under the door now and he can feel a tide of panic rising inside him. He pulls the window latch again, it holds fast. He can't open it. He tries another latch, the same. They seem to be jammed. Evan turns back to the door, his only way out is through the flames. He opens the door again, the fire has taken control of the room ahead. He needs to run though and out of the front door. It's only twenty feet, easy. He takes a deep breath and runs out into the fire, the heat snatches at face and crawls over his body. He can feel his skin burning, he can smell his skin burning. He reaches the front door, pulls the handle. Nothing. It's locked. He panics, it can't be locked. It's never locked. The smoke travels down his throat and into his lungs, he can feel it choking him. He hammers on the door and shouts with all the voice he has. No one is coming. The heat is unbearable. He can see the hairs on his arms on fire. He turns back to the sitting room but stumbles and falls. His body hits the floor with a heavy thump. He can't stop his cough now. The flames creep up towards him until he can't keep his eyes open any longer.

The blackness fades away and the interior of an ambulance fades in. A paramedic is bending over him and he can hear the sound of a siren and see slight blue around the edges of the windows as they push on through the streets of the city. Her eyes look into his and she scans a light across his vision. She's saying something but he can't work out what the words are. All he knows apart from the pain invading his body is that her eyes are smiling. His eyes water and the view blurs. She selects a hypodermic needle and pushes it into Evan's arm. He watches her and the ceiling of the ambulance, trying to see more but failing. The light fades again and with it, the pain too.

CHAPTER TWENTY-THREE

A breeze with a wintery edge cuts across the doors to the foyer of Ethan's hotel as he arrives in the reception area from a trip out to get a sandwich. He doesn't notice the woman sitting on the slightly worn sofa to one side until she calls his name. He turns and looks at her. She looks out of place in a relatively cheap hotel near Angel.

"Can I help?" he says, walking over to her. She stands and extends her expensively-coated arm to him and they shake.

"Do you have a few minutes to talk, Mr Poole?" His journalist's nous can feel this is important.

"I think they do coffee in the bar during the day." He holds his arm up in that direction and they start walking together but without words. He picks a table that overlooks the Pentonville Road. Once elegant, now a route to get away from the heart of the city to a place that has more space and light.

"I think we can be of help to each other," she begins. He remains silent so as not to spoil her flow. "You have something I need, and I have something that is of significance to you."

She drops one hand into her Gucci Ophidia handbag that sits on the seat next to her and pulls out a photograph which she places on the table between them. The waitress brings coffees and there's a moment of confusion as the girl has to find a spare place to put the cups.

After she walks away, the woman says. "That's you, Mr Poole. In the offices of GreenLink Enterprises."

He picks up the photo. The image is clearly Ethan, looking directly at the CCTV camera in the main office of GreenLink.

"I don't know what you're talking about," he says placing the photo back down on the table.

She gives a slight smile and tilts her head minutely to one side. "Here's the deal, Mr Poole. You share the information that you stole, and I won't go to the police with this photo and a copy of the CCTV from the offices," she says.

"Do what you like. It's not me."

"You're sweet when you lie, Ethan. Do you know there's a tiny vein on your temple that beats under the skin when you're not telling the truth?"

He picks up his coffee cup and takes a sip.

"You can still use the information for whatever reason you were going to," she says. "Just let me have a copy."

There is a pause of several seconds as she waits and he thinks.

"If I did have information that you would be interested in," he says. "What are you going to do with it?"

"Go to the police, but not about you."

"It would have to be after anything was published," says Ethan.

"Of course."

"I'd need a payment."

"It doesn't work like that," she says. "This photo and the CCTV with you on it will be destroyed though, you have my word."

"That's blackmail."

"You're the one who has committed a crime, Mr Poole - breaking and entering is illegal." She stands and picks up her bag. "I'll give you twenty four hours. Here's an email address to send it to." She hands him a business card with only a single email address on it in black lettering.

"What do I call you?" he says.

She pauses for a moment. "You can call me Miss V."

*

The obvious thinness of the police file tells Olivia that it doesn't tell the whole story of the investigation, and the photograph of Patricia that's in it tells her that she doesn't know enough about that woman.

Another thing that stems from Patricia being Patty Wells and single only fifteen years ago, is that she can't be Claire's mother. She must be her step-mother, but who was Claire's birth mother and what had happened to her?

The last piece of new information is about Miss J – killed in a bar where Bruce and Gerald had been accused of meeting persons unknown to exchange cash to influence votes on the Houses of Parliament.

Olivia has the day off work today, booked a week ago to try and do Christmas shopping on a day other than the 24th December, which is her usual day for getting everything done. This year is no different though, over breakfast she decides that presents can wait and she needs to research Patty Wells and what really happened fifteen years ago. She makes more coffee and sets up her laptop on the small round table by the window. Outside, black Thames barges and white river buses make slow progress against a rising grey tide and biting wind.

Patricia Wells was born in Leeds, the daughter of a bookshop owner and a nurse. She went to Ripon Grammar School and was one of the top students. Olivia finds pictures of her as school captain and winning at more than one sport. She went to King's College in London University and came out with a first in law. She joined a chambers in her twenties and became a barrister specialising in business and corporate cases. Olivia finds a video of her being interviewed about being a young female barrister and talking about needing experience to be an effective judge, which was her ambition. She evidently took her own advice about experience and moved to work in corporate jobs for five years before she joined the Metropolitan Police as a lawyer.

This is where Patricia's career changes. There is no mention of her being involved with the Alpin fraud case online, but that's not unusual. But soon after that case concluded, within six months, she got a job as a judge in a Magistrates Court, and within seven years she was appointed to be a High Court Judge. That seems fast and Olivia wonders if she had helping hands along the way. Nothing wrong with networking of course, but Patty became Patricia Harwell, wife of an MP, within a year of the fraud case being dropped, and subsequently rose through the ranks of the legal system at break-neck speed.

The next topic for research is Gerald Harwell's first wife. Olivia searches for a long time before she even finds the woman's name anywhere. Eventually she does find an obscure reference to her when Gerald first started in parliament - her name had been Jennifer Peters. There's barely a mention of Jennifer online at all, unusually so. Olivia is used to doing profile searches like this and Jennifer Peters is firmly at the far end of the nearly anonymous scale. There is no mention of her parents, the date of the wedding, or an announcement about Claire being born.

The one thing that Olivia does find is the year of Jennifer's death - it was fifteen years ago. The same year as the fraud, and Gerald was re-married within twelve months to Patty. Claire would have been only eleven years old and away at school then, so all this would have gone on without her around in the house. The machinations of her father being arrested, her mother dying and then her gaining a step-mother would all have happened while Claire was away.

The thing that strikes Olivia as odd is why Claire didn't mention any of this in their various conversations over the last few weeks. It is understandable that she didn't talk about her mother's death to someone who is a relative stranger, but no reference to any of this traumatic period seems odd. Maybe those events going on back home explain Claire seeking comfort in boys and then men when she was younger.

There's also not enough other evidence online for Olivia to paint a complete picture of the fraud case or the consequences for the Harwell family. She thinks about other sources of information. There is one place that might give her more details, Claire's flat, which is still empty, and to which Olivia has the key.

She parks in the next street to Well Walk so as not to raise any suspicions if neighbours see the same car outside the Boyd's house for the second time in a week.

As she pushes the front door open, a stony silence rolls out of the flat, the silence you only get when a place has been vacant for some time. She stands in the hallway and thinks about the best way to do the search. She goes into the bedroom, looks in the safe and methodically goes through each document. There is nothing of consequence; house deeds, cash, some contracts and insurance policies. Olivia starts on the shelves immediately around the safe. Most is ephemera. She switches on the computer and searches that too, Claire had been very open about her passwords, fortunately.

By the time the light of the day starts to nudge into dusk, Olivia has been through nearly all of the shelves, papers, drawers and possible hiding places she can find in the flat, but has not found anything useful. She starts on a final set of shelves in a tiny bedroom by the front door. They contain mostly paperback books stuffed in with no gaps to spare. She pulls one out and the row all come out together and crash down onto the floor at her feet. She starts to pick them up and shove them back in. As she stands up to replace the first handful, she notices there is an old shoe box on the shelf that had been behind the books. She takes the box down and opens the lid. Inside, it is full of papers with handwriting all over them. She pulls one out and can see it is the childish scrawl of a young Claire Harwell as her name, with floral decoration, is on most pages. Olivia picks up the box, sits on the bed, and starts to read through the sheets.

The pages are about her mother, Jennifer, how she loved her, how she didn't know what she would do now she was dead. The words mention Patty and how young Claire was sure that Patty was only trying the get her father's money. There's a vague reference to Jennifer's death and how Patty, 'probably killed her to get dad'. There's mention of Claire's regret that her father and mother were never married, how Jennifer didn't want to get married and how that 'may have made dad find a woman who did want to be his wife'. Some of the words, Olivia has no doubt, are a child coming to terms with her mother's death. But could any of these accusations be true? Did young Claire see and hear more than she lets on? Is she a witness to the fraud, or worse, the death of her mother? None of this is clear, but Olivia knows that she must talk to Claire about all of this to find the truth.

As she reaches the end of the papers, Olivia picks up the last sheet and sees a mobile phone in the box. She leans in and picks it up. She tries to turns it on but there's no charge. She searches for a cable and finds one beside Claire's bed, then switches on the device.

Olivia starts by exploring the messages on the phone, she swipes through each one and can see that this was Stephen's phone, not Claire's. There are many day-to-day messages between them - dinner dates, telling each other to buy something on the way home, or reminders that they're going away at the weekend. She checks each one, there is nothing that could be misconstrued or some sort of code.

Then she checks the photos. More daily normality – pictures of friends at dinner, birthdays, and a couple of Claire at Surridge Place. Olivia finally goes into the file manager app to see what has been filed elsewhere. The words rotate in her head as she flicks through the stores and she ends up saying it out loud, "Normal, normal, norm…"

Then, she stops. A hidden folder is at the end of the listing. She clicks on it. A picture of Greer Alpin appears, smiling at the camera. The next one is Greer in bed, the covers pulled up over her body but it's obvious she's naked underneath. There are a dozen taken in the same room, all of Greer, all laughing or smiling. Olivia swipes some more across the screen. More pictures of Greer, then one that answers the question in her head. A picture of Stephen and Greer together, arm-in-arm, both lying in bed with Stephen holding the camera above their heads and their steady gaze smiling up to the lens. Olivia checks the dates on the images – all within the last two months.

She navigates to the end of the folder but there are no more pictures of interest. She takes photos with her own phone of a few of the images as a piece of advice she was given in her twenties rolls across her mind, 'you never know when evidence might come in useful'. She drops the phone back into the box and puts everything back on the shelf, just as it was, then opens the front door and walks back outside.

Olivia dawdles back to her car, her brain a forest of questions and possibilities. Stephen and Greer were having an affair, it appears, right up to the day he died. Claire was right about his propensity to be unfaithful. But is this significant when it comes to finding out if he was killed or died by accident? Olivia knows that she has to talk to Greer. The woman is already defensive and now Olivia knows why. Even if Greer had nothing to do with his death, she wouldn't want to be linked to Stephen in any way given her political ambitions. In Olivia's mind though, there's only one way to do this, and that is to go direct.

As she reaches the main doors to her block of flats, she can see a blond man waiting inside the reception area. The door slide open noiselessly and she can see that it's Jack as he turns to her and smiles.

"Can we talk," is all he says. They go up to her flat. She opens a bottle of wine and pours them both a glass, and they sit on the tall stools in the kitchen.

He looks as though he wants to say something big and she tries to pre-empt him. "You regretting us sleeping together?" she says.

"No."

"Why the uncomfortable feeling, then?"

"It's fine. What's been happening?"

"Claire Boyd is on the mend, she asked me to look after her for a few days when she's out of hospital."

"Very friendly."

"What about you?" she says. "How's the investigation?"

"I have to ask you something," he says and takes a large gulp of Merlot.

"OK."

"Do you know anything about a break-in the night before last?"

"Any particular one?" She smiles but he doesn't and her face falls. "No Inspector, I don't."

"The offices of GreenLink were broken into."

"I think you'll find I was shagging you at the time."

"Let's not get angry."

"Then let's not accuse each other of a crime that occurred when we were in bed together, shall we?" Her heat rises.

"Olivia, I'm just doing my job."

"OK." Her voice is cold. She sits up. "No, Inspector Savage, I can confirm that I was not aware and had nothing to do with a break-in at GreenLink's offices the night before last. Will that do?"

"I had to ask."

"What evidence do you have that links me to that break-in?"

"None."

"So, have you collected any evidence from the break in?" Her tone is all professional now, the private woman has gone. "Do you have photographs, finger-prints or video evidence that connects to me?"

"Not yet."

She pauses for less than half a second in response to his vaguely accusatory words. "Do you have witness statements, maybe? A blonde in her thirties was seen with a striped jersey and a bag with swag written on it departing the premises?"

"Look, I'm trying to help."

"Help?" she says. "What are you talking about?"

"I was told to come."

"You were *told* to come?" Her eyes have more power than he has ever seen.

"Ralph was saying..."

"Ralph?" She pauses, letting air and time seep in between them. "That would be Superintendent Ralph Peters, would it?"

"I had no choice."

"No choice?" she repeats. "He ordered you to come here, just like before when you accused me of murder, I think it was, that time?"

"He thinks there's a connection and wanted me to follow up," says Jack.

"You've lost me," she says. "Ralph Peters thinks that I am connected to a break-in, without any evidence?"

"I can't discuss internal matters."

She feels the disappointment wave across her skin and rolls her lips inwards to give herself thinking time, then clears her throat.

"If that's all, Inspector." Her voice is depleted now. "Thank you for calling. If you need any more information then, of course, I will gladly come into the station and give further assistance."

They sit for a second, their eyes locked on each other's, both wanting to say something more but neither does.

Olivia stands and holds up her arm in the direction of the door. Jack stands, puts down the wine and walks over to the hooks where he had left his coat. He hauls on his jacket and circles a scarf around his neck. She hasn't moved from her place in the kitchen. He stops for a second and looks at her but her face has no emotion. He opens the door lock and walks out.

CHAPTER TWENTY-FOUR

After getting a call from someone who refused to give their name but who did say that they had information that she may find interesting, Greer is not suspicious. She immediately thinks that Evan must have given her details to someone who had more dirt on the local members in Sussex North to further help sway the upcoming vote to make her official party candidate.

The W/A Bar on Queen's Gate is a ten minute walk from her house in South Kensington. The mid-morning sky has the merest hint of blue towards the west and the day is unusually sunny considering it's only a week before Christmas. She enters the bar and looks around for someone looking expectant but sees no one who fits the bill. She sits on one of the tall blue chairs that face a large almond-coloured marble bar and orders peppermint tea. She doesn't look around the place again - if the person wants to find her, they will.

Someone sits down next to her and Greer turns her head.

"Olivia, this is a surprise."

"It was me who left you the message."

"Of all the people I might have guessed who it was going to be, you would not have been on the list."

"Thank you for coming," begins Olivia. She places an A4 envelop on the bar. "I said on the phone that I had information I would like to talk to you about."

"And that could be useful for my bid to become an MP?"

"I didn't say that."

Greer's eyes are already narrowed with suspicion, and they narrow further. Olivia turns the envelope, flicks open the flap, pushes her hand inside and pulls out four photo enlargements. She peels each one off from the stacks and places them on the counter in front of Greer. The woman surveys the images, her eyes jumping from one to the other, exploring them in detail.

To Olivia's surprise, she smiles as she talks. "I hadn't seen these. This is our last afternoon together. We look happy, don't you think?"

The response knocks Olivia's pre-prepared question structure off-kilter as she had not planned on this reaction from Greer, a woman who had only shown her anger and power up to now.

"You don't deny the affair, then?"

When Greer turns her eyes to Olivia she can see they're slightly watery.

"I loved him," is all she says.

A barman asks Olivia if she wants a drink and she orders coffee. The interlude creates a useful break in the conversation with Greer to allow Olivia to think what she needs to ask now.

"Why didn't you say anything before about this?"

Greer frowns. "Say anything? To whom? You? Why would I?"

"It could bear on the circumstances of his death."

"Could it?" How?"

"Did something happen between the two of you?" says Olivia.

"I told you at Surridge Place that discretion is an admirable quality in people," says Greer. She is dead calm. "The man I loved has died. It was a tragic accident, I was planning to leave my husband in the next few weeks and sue for divorce. Stephen and I were planning to get married."

"He was already married to Claire."

"And planning on leaving her, in fact, he was planning on telling her that it was over on the day he died. I think he was having a drink with you that night, and Ms Hill?"

"That's right."

"If he had reached home, he would have told Claire that it was all over."

"Wait a minute," says Olivia. "He was travelling straight home from Browns Hotel?"

"Yes."

"But he was found at Clapham Junction. That's the opposite direction. There's no route to Hampstead from Mayfair that takes you through Clapham."

"What are you saying?"

"That he wasn't going home."

"Where was he going, then?"

"I don't know, but your brother talked to him that night."

"Evan?"

"Yes, earlier in the evening. Evan told me."

"You know Evan?" says Greer.

"He told me that he believes Stephen was killed."

"He's in hospital, you know?" says Greer.

"What do you mean?"

"The fire."

"What fire?" says Olivia.

"There was a fire in Evan's flat the other night and he's badly burned. Is that something to do with you?"

"I didn't know anything about it until you just mentioned it."

"How do you know Evan?" says Greer.

"I met him."

Greer's face has grown in concern over the last minute. "Why?"

"No one would tell me the truth."

"The truth about what?"

"Stephen's death, by person or persons unknown. It wasn't an accident," says Olivia. "The man you loved was mixed up in something, I don't know what, but it was enough to get him killed."

Greer stops and sips her tea. Olivia can tell she is debating whether to reveal something significant or not.

"He needed money," says Greer eventually. "He was in debt. He'd borrowed from GreenLink accounts and couldn't pay it back."

"How did he borrow from GreenLink?"

"Jeremy agreed to lend it to him."

"Why would he do that?"

Greer breathes in and out, controlling the breath so it lasts for a few seconds. She raises her hand to the barman who walks over.

"Two brandies, please," she says, and waits while he pours them into two glasses. Greer picks up the drink immediately, takes a swig and closes her eyes as the liquid tangs against the sides of her throat.

"There are some non-executive directors who are not declared."

"What's that mean?" says Olivia.

"The official records don't show them."

"And why is that?"

"Stephen was one of them, as well as two other friends of ours. They had put in personal funding but it was lost."

"Why have undeclared non-execs?"

"They managed a private fund that invests in companies that are owned by various politicians. Investments that those politicians wouldn't want to be associated with."

"Investments in crime?"

"The details are always sketchy, intentionally so. The whole idea is to keep it all under wraps."

"Was Stephen killed as a consequence of this secret fund?"

Pools of moisture cling to the lower waterline of Greer's brown eyes.

When the words, "I don't know," come they are barely audible.

"Are you involved, Greer?"

"I'm not."

"How do you know about all this? And why have you not gone to the police if you're not involved?"

"They're part of it. There's a guy called Ralph Peters, he covers for them if anything ever turns nasty."

"Why have you suddenly told me all this when you've only ever tried to put me off the scent up to now?"

"Honestly?"

"Of course."

"Life in politics is only ever about the degree of risk," says Greer. "One puts forward one's views, some people agree, some people disagree. The art is to get as much of what you want and carry enough people along with you. The question is, what do you do with those who don't agree with you? The people who can weaken you in the future? There are only two options: attack or undermine. GreenLink, and my association with it, albeit on the margins, has been an advantage. Jeremy's father has helped me put forward my candidacy, the Harwell's have given me credibility locally with folks. Now, I don't need them anymore. So, attack or undermine? I can't attack them, they're too established in the world of politics, so my only option is to undermine them. I'd already decided to do something about all of this corruption before today. You just happened to come along with your photos and remind me about the man I loved. I'm not a robot, underneath all of this bravado I'm human. Stephen meant something to me, he was part of my plan for the future. I'll find another bloke of course, but I did love him. So, making them pay for his death, whether they were indirectly or directly involved, makes me happy."

"Is it only about looking after number one?"

"That's all it ever is," says Greer.

The women pause their conversation, both take gulps of brandy and let their minds roll through the ideas they've talked about. They think about how this changes the landscape of what is going to happen.

"I'm going to see your brother," says Olivia. "I need to hear his point of view."

"He's not involved, as far as I know."

"He found out what was going on though," says Olivia. "What will you do about GreenLink?"

"Use it to my advantage." The woman smiles at Olivia. "Think I'm mercenary?"

"Yes."

"It's about survival, Olivia."

*

Before visiting the hospital, Olivia is booked in to attend a legal seminar. Even though it is the last place she wants to be, she committed to attend as there are relevant sessions on change to the procurement processes for large public contracts that she needs to be up to speed on as it will affect the work she is being paid for. Her taxi pulls up outside Central Hall, Westminster. She walks into the vast entrance hall and up the curved staircase to the first floor. She shows her ticket and takes a seat on the front row of the upper balcony. The woman on the door had handed her a programme of the speakers and Olivia scans through the list, noting the key people she came to hear. As it turns out, the important talks are after lunch and there is nothing worth hearing before then. Her eyes track across the immediate next sessions. There is coffee is five minutes, then a session about, 'Judicial Reviews – there place in legal practice'. Then she sees a name she recognises, the speaker is Patricia Harwell.

Olivia immediately gets up and goes out to find the coffee area. Patricia is sitting alone at one end of the room, reading through her slide deck in preparation for the session.

"Hello, Patricia," says Olivia once she reaches within a few feet of the woman.

"Olivia, have you come to see my talk?"

"Yes, thought it might be interesting. Are you busy or can you chat?"

"Yes, fine, I was only going through the slides to fill the time."

Olivia sits next to her on the sofa. "How's Claire?"

"Out tomorrow actually," says Patricia. "Thank God."

"I went down a few days ago and she was making a great recovery."

"It's worrying when your children are unwell," says Patricia.

"Claire was saying how much she loves the relationship she has with you," says Olivia, starting to tiptoe across the minefield. "I had a long chat with her about fifteen years ago and you were the one person she said helped her pull through."

Patricia is suddenly listening more than talking. It's now or never thinks Olivia.

"Did you know her mother?"

"I didn't." The woman's voice has taken on mild frostiness.

"A lovely woman, apparently."

"Mmm."

"Claire still has photos of her."

"Yes."

"What a tragedy to die so young," says Olivia. "What was she, in her thirties?" The conference has broken for the coffee break and ones and twos, then dozens of people start to flood into the refreshment room.

"I believe so. I really need to talk to a couple of people before my session."

"Do you know how Jennifer died?"

"I can't help you, I'm sorry."

"Was she Miss J, Patricia?"

Patricia stands. "Good to see you again, Olivia."

Olivia stands too. "Was Jennifer Peters, Miss J, Patricia? The woman who died fifteen years ago?"

"I must dash."

"Should the case be re-opened, My Lady?" says Olivia, using the in-court mode of address for a High Court Judge. Patricia stops and looks at the floor. "There may be new evidence in Claire's belongings, and you may know more about the case?"

Patricia says nothing more, her eyes flick momentarily to Olivia's then she walks away across the room and towards the auditorium.

*

Jeremy climbs off Violet and lays next to her in the bed. She pulls the covers over them.

"I don't know what I'd do without you," he says after his breath and heart rate have subsided. She smiles at him.

"Good. I like you being dependent on me." She drapes a long arm across his chest. He turns to her and kisses her on the forehead and they smirk quietly to each other.

"I have the evidence about your father on the way," she says.

"What evidence?"

"Documents from the private files in GreenLink."

"How did you get those?" says Jeremy.

"I have my ways," she says. "And I have lined up a journo to publish them."

"You have been busy."

"Just protecting you, darling."

He turns to her. "Yes, you are. Thank you."

"It may be published as soon as tomorrow."

"OK," he says. "Have you got a plan B in case your source doesn't cough up?"

"I always have a plan B," says Violet.

*

The lift inside the Chelsea and Westminster Hospital takes Olivia to the third floor. She follows the signs for the Burns Unit and asks a nurse at a reception desk which bed Evan Rice is in. The woman directs her to the last bed in the ward, next to the window. Olivia walks up and dumps her coat on a plastic chair by the bed. Evan is lying on his back with bandages covering the top half of his face, both shoulders, and all down the left hand side of his chest. His eyes are closed but the nurse had said that he sleeps a lot and Olivia was welcome to try to get him to talk, but don't expect him to be able to have the energy for much conversation yet. Olivia leans over him and inspects the damage that is not bandaged. There are red marks that disappear under the white fabric almost everywhere across the skin that remains exposed.

Olivia waits for a few minutes to see if he wakes but Evan doesn't stir. She leans back over him and whispers his name. No reaction. Not even an eyelid flutter. She says it again, this time mildly louder. He does react this time. She can see his eyes moving under the lids. Then he opens them.

"Ms Delaney?" he barely annunciates the words.

"Mr Rice. I came to see you."

He keeps his eyes open and looks at her face, tracing the outline then the details of her features.

"Can you talk?" she says. He makes a quiet affirmative sound. "Was this an accident, Mr Rice?"

Evan's eyes are still, looking up at her face. He says something but she can't hear the words. Olivia leans closer to his mouth. "No," he says quietly.

"Someone did it on purpose?"

Affirmative grunt, but his consciousness is ebbing and his eyelids flutter.

"Who?" Olivia leans right in again.

"Boyd."

"Mr Boyd?" she says. "Stephen Boyd?"

His eyes are closed now. Evan doesn't make an affirmative grunt this time. Olivia looks up at the monitors next to the bed, the heart rate trace is still flicking up and down as the light works across the glass.

"Mr Rice?"

No response.

What could he have meant? Stephen Boyd had set the fire in the flat? It doesn't make sense and Olivia concludes that the delirium is still spinning around inside Evan's head. She is frustrated that he couldn't say more and what he did say was nonsense. She waits for a few minutes to see if he regains consciousness, and says his name a few times but there is no reaction. She goes back to the nursing station and reports what has happened in case it is important but the staff say it's typical at this stage of recovery.

Olivia makes her way out of the building and onto the Fulham Road then cuts down Beaufort Street to the King's Road. She starts to walk east through Chelsea and back up towards Sloane Square to give herself a chunk of time to think about whether she's any nearer knowing who killed Stephen Boyd.

What does she know now that she didn't a few days ago?

Stephen and Greer were a couple, they had both planned to leave their respective partners if tragedy had not stuck. Stephen was in debt and owed money to GreenLink, and more than that he owed it to the people who operated on the dark side of GreenLink's balance sheet – driving hidden projects with private money to generate big profits on the black market. This explains the blackmail notes to Claire. Someone who knew about the dark side operations and wanted to cash in.

Was Stephen killed because of his debt? Possibly. Was the fire in Evan's flat a result of Evan knowing too much? Also possible - Evan had told Stephen about GreenLink, not knowing that Stephen was part of it already. Both men had been attacked due to their knowledge by someone covering their tracks.

What of Greer Alpin now? The woman had turned on a dime as her American friends would say. Greer seems happy to talk about the corruption but isn't motivated to go to the police as the knowledge is more use to her as a blackmail tool against Sir Bruce and Gerald Harwell to get more of her own way.

Lastly, the crimes of fifteen years ago. Is Patricia Harwell guilty of anything? She was part of the investigation team and ended up marrying one of the suspects. That's not a crime, but Claire's teenage notes lay out the events in a different light. If Claire saw anything back then, anything that is incriminating, then Patricia's defensiveness earlier today at the conference makes sense. She had been keen to keep anything that had been hidden away back then, firmly under the carpet. If Stephen had found out something from his wife about those events, then he could have been killed because of that knowledge, or maybe it was the other way around and he was blackmailing his parents-in-law. Without a testimony from Claire, there's no new evidence and the case will not be re-opened by a judge if there's nothing new to consider. Talking to Claire as soon as she's out of hospital is critical now.

The death of Stephen Boyd is becoming clearer in Olivia's mind. Was he killed for what he knew? That is looking possible. But what exactly he did know, and who took it upon themselves to stop him reporting it, is the biggest missing piece in this jigsaw.

CHAPTER TWENTY-FIVE

"You want lunch?" says Ellen. Tom looks up from his desk in the big office they share on the first floor. He smiles at her.

"Where are you taking me?"

"The canteen," she says. They both laugh.

Once they have chosen mac and cheese with bacon and poured plastic cups of water out from a tap that is positioned to spill as much as it fills, they sit down at a table between two pillars, that is the only place that offers anything that could be described as privacy in the staff canteen of the Department of Business, Energy and Industrial Strategy.

As they sit Tom notices a burn on her hand. "That looks nasty."

"Yeah, I burnt myself cooking the other night." She gives a vague chuckle. "Doesn't hurt though. My mum always said she had asbestos hands when I was a kid." They smile at the idea.

There's a pause, then she says. "What do you think about us?"

"I like it."

"Why?"

He looks at her quizzically, trying to fathom if this is idle chat or a structured interview. "Being with you makes me happy."

"How?"

His eyes take on a bemused air but he is happy to play along. "You're funny." She raises her eyebrows. "In a cute way." Her face takes on a comedy be-very-careful look. "What do you think of me?" he says.

"You think a lot…"

"Good."

"…about yourself," she says. "Too much." She pauses then adds. "I think you are trying to find something that you lost five years ago, but you'll never find the same thing. I'm not sure you'll ever think you have found the same thing again."

"That's deep for ten to one on a Thursday," he says.

"And I think you avoid talking about the pain you feel and use comedy to deflect."

Tom eats a mouthful of mac and cheese.

"Am I close?" she says. He barely nods but makes eye contact as he does so and blinks too often. "I want to talk to you more about it." He makes another tiny nod to acknowledge her point. "Not now, but soon."

They finish their lunches without any more deep psychological discussion but fall back into the safety of daily banality.

As they put their plates on the trolley for the kitchen staff to wash later, they talk about Stephen and how terrible it all seems. Ellen is careful about what she says as she's acutely aware that she's never told Tom of her closeness to the dead man.

 "…then Claire's accident happened," says Tom. "Do you think it was connected?"

"To Stephen's death? Of course not," snaps Ellen with enough passion for Tom to turn to look at her as they walk along the corridor back to their office. Tom pushes down on the handle of their office door and they walk in.

"Everyone connected with that family ends up getting hurt," she says. "It's like a merry-go-round. Claire comes out of hospital today and Evan Rice, Jeremy's brother-in law, gcts badly burnt in a fire the other day. They're just bloody criminals, the lot of them."

Tom stops and turns to her. "What?" he says.

"Oh ignore me, just ranting."

Tom says nothing more for a minute and they go back to their respective desks. Then she notices he has started to pack away his things. "Look, I'm off this afternoon," he says. "Christmas shopping, you know?"

He smiles at her with no emotion behind his eyes.

*

"Where have you been?" says Poppy as Ethan arrives at the café half an hour late. "You can get me another chai latte."

The place is packed and Poppy is on a table in the middle of the large room. Around her are couples, families and business people picking over their Danish pastries and sipping their chosen drinks.

"Sorry, stuff's kicking off."

"What stuff?"

"That fraud thing."

"What's happened?" she says as he sits down opposite her.

"I got some evidence," says Ethan.

"Cool, you can write the article now, then?"

"Yup, all good," he says.

"How d'you get it?"

"Let's just say that their security isn't all it should be."

"What d'you mean?" says Poppy.

"I went to their offices."

"And stole it?"

"Borrowed it, I prefer to say," he says.

"What the fuck, Ethan?" she says. "You stole stuff from them? You're no better than them then, are you?"

"I'm the good guy here, Poppy."

"Says you."

"They've killed people," says Ethan. "Your mum said."

"They *could be involved*, is what she said."

"They did it, I know them."

"It doesn't fucking excuse you breaking the law, Ethan."

"Relax, I thought you were cool, stuff happens, you know. You gotta make opportunities."

"You're no better than them, can't you see that?" Her voice rises on the air.

"Keep your voice down," he says.

She ignores his request and talks even louder. "And you now a common thief, Ethan Poole."

"Shut up, Poppy."

"Ethan Poole of the International Courier newspaper."

He stands up, leans over and grabs her wrist. "Fucks sake."

"What? Shut up or you'll make me?" Her voice remains loud and she stands too.

"You're just a spoilt little schoolgirl," he says equally loud as she had done, talking to the café customers more than Poppy.

"And you fucked me!" She stands up. "I think we all know which one of us is the low-life, Ethan Poole." Her eyes blaze with victory. She gives him one last look, then turns and walks away to the street.

*

The taxi turns the last corner into Well Walk and stops outside the Boyd's flat. The driver gets out and opens the boot, then puts a case on the pavement. Claire pulls out the handle on the case and drags it after her as she makes her way down the side path to the front door. As the door slams behind her, she lets go of the suitcase and leaves it in the hallway before walking around the quiet rooms of the flat. Her memories come and go, remembering scenes that took place within these walls.

Her phone's ring tone cracks through the silence. She walks back to the hall and picks up the device from the side table where she had left it.

"Hello?" She listens. "Yes, I just got home."

"Not yet, no."

"I couldn't in the hospital."

"I know."

"Yes, I know." The insistence climbs in her tone.

"I'm going to bed. I'll do it tomorrow."

"No, you look, I'll fucking do it tomorrow." She pushes the end call button and takes a large breath out.

The phone is silent for two minutes then it rings again.

She swears under her breath. "Stop calling me!" she says.

"Hey, it's me," says Olivia in her ear.

"Sorry."

"Getting annoying calls?"

"No, it's nothing," says Claire. "A friend, he's needy."

"A close friend?"

"Long story."

"Anyway, I was thinking of coming over to make sure you're OK," says Olivia.

"Sure, yeah."

"Five o'clock?"

"See you then."

*

Greer is waved through security after her car has dropped her off outside of the Houses of Parliament. All of the previous times she has been in this building have always been as an outsider, not an elected member. Soon that will all change. The plan to get her there is coming together. The locals are being corralled to agree that she is the right woman to represent the interests of the good people of Sussex North. Soon, the voters will soon be harangued with press coverage telling the story of her struggle as a young woman in an unforgiving world.

Sir Bruce is sitting by one of the windows in the Terrace Cafeteria reading a newspaper.

"Bruce." He looks up, over his half-moon spectacles.

"Greer, my dear." She sits and orders coffee for them both.

"How are you, Bruce? I worry about you, you know."

"No need to worry about me, Greer."

"You cope with so much," she says. "All those plates spinning."

"I bring my experience to bear on it all," he says. "A younger man couldn't cope. You need to know how things work, how people will respond." She takes a sip of coffee. "I did want to talk to you, my dear."

"Oh?"

"The constituency party."

"What about them?"

"A bit of wavering."

"I'm sure you can bring your expertise and gravitas to sway the waverers," says Greer.

"A bit more serious than that. They want a local chap as their candidate. Alan Selman?"

"I met him," she says. "Nasty little man."

"A local nasty little man, though."

"I'm sure you can persuade them, Bruce. A man like Selman isn't going to give them the cut-through that I can bring. He has back-bencher written all over him, he'll never be anywhere near a cabinet."

"I think that's their point. They want someone to focus on local issues, like Mike has done."

"You risk sounding like a defeatist," says Greer.

"I think they may have the advantage of us," says Sir Bruce.

She puts her hand, palm down, on the table between them. "Am I hearing this correctly, Bruce? You're changing your position on my candidacy?"

"I think Alan will be a good candidate, he'll provide continuity with Mike's good work."

Greer stops and her mind rattles through her options.

"Bruce," she begins. "I hear GreenLink has been involved with extra-curricular activities, outside of its formal balance sheet. Did I understand that correctly?"

He smiles. "Your dear husband has been putting his fingers into pies that he shouldn't, I believe."

"No, Bruce. You have. You've been getting your dirty little hands on all sorts of things. Things that, I'm guessing, you don't want to be out in the open."

He smirks. "Be very careful, my dear."

"This is what's going to happen, father-in-law," she says. "You're going to endorse me as candidate and your activities are not going to be spread all over the papers. How does that sound?"

"You're not the candidate, Greer. I am putting my weight behind Alan," says Sir Bruce. "If you want to destroy your family, have your husband's name dragged through the mud then go ahead. It's Jeremy's name on all of the papers. He's been screwing his tart for two years, he wants a divorce from you. I'll tell the journalists that I have been pleading with the two of you to make amends and not ruin your lives, but you insisted on revealing his crimes as revenge for him wanting a better life with another woman. Your bitterness and deceit knows no bounds, my dear. It has only been my insistence to do the right thing that means I can hold my head high."

"You won't win this battle, Bruce."

"As I said, my dear, experience is a valuable asset."

"You should think carefully about what you decide to do," she says.

"I already have."

"You'll be ruined."

"You're hardly clean yourself, are you, Greer?"

"What are you talking about?" she says.

"Your relationship with a certain man who is now sadly no longer with us."

"I don't know what…"

"Stephen Boyd was your lover, my dear," he says. "It would a tragedy for that to come out as well. There's some doubt about whether it was an accident, apparently. Did he get too big for his boots? Did he need to be silenced, Greer?"

She picks up her Prada Galleria bag and stands up. Greer looks at him. For a second, they just watch the other, both wondering what will happen after today.

"Goodbye, Bruce." She turns on her heel and heads for the door.

*

Tom's flat is cold tonight. He turns on the electric bar heater under the window and pulls the blinds down over the sloping roof windows above his head. He wasn't feeling very well this afternoon and went to bed when he got back early from the office. He won't go in tomorrow, he decides, he hasn't had a day off sick all year, they owe it to him. He looks in the cupboard above the hob and surveys the two tins of beans, one tin of soup and a bundle of brown pasta. He chooses the soup and heats it up on the hob, then cuts slices from the end of a loaf and dunks the crusts into the tomatoey redness as it steams before him.

His mind is full of Kate, her smile, her smell, the softness of her skin on his fingertips. He thinks about Ellen and wonders if he trusts her. Is she genuinely interested in his life? There's been no one since Kate and it feels risky to trust anyone again, but Ellen is cute and seems to like him.

Kate sits across the table from him. Her eyes on his. She looks beautiful in this light. He rests his hand on the table and his fingers touch the handle of the knife.

*

Well Walk is icy and dark as Olivia walks from Hampstead tube station. The Heath lays brooding at the end of the road. She turns down the side passage and pushes the doorbell to the Claire Boyd's flat.

They take seats overlooking the garden. Claire isn't back on alcohol but offers Olivia a glass of Merlot.

"How are you?"

"It gave me a lot of time to think while I was in hospital," says Claire.

"About the blackmail?"

"No, he hasn't contacted me again."

"Good."

"I was thinking about my life, about Stephen, about what I'm going to do."

"What are you going to do?"

"I might sell this place and move on," says Claire. "He had a big life insurance policy so I don't need money, and this place is worth a million."

"Where will you go?"

"France? Italy maybe. I could buy a place and bring up my child, invest the money and never work again."

"Would that make you happy?" says Olivia.

"You don't know until you try it. It was so perfect here with Stephen. It's not the first time I've been through crap times and I came out OK before."

"Yes, I know, I was talking to Patricia," says Olivia.

Claire turns and looks at her. "What about?"

"Fifteen years ago."

"Why were you talking to her about that?"

"It could connect to Stephen's death."

"How?"

Olivia takes a punt.

"I didn't know she was your step-mother."

"Yes, mum died," says Claire.

"What happened?"

Claire stops and thinks about how to describe something that has meant so much in only a few words. "They were in bar somewhere. Her and Dad. He's never told me what happened in detail. I asked him a thousand times but he wouldn't talk about it. Patricia did though. She helped me through it, got me to talk, got me to say everything I was thinking."

"Are you still curious about your mother's death?"

"Not now," says Claire. "I moved on, just like I want to do again."

"You know Patricia was in the police?"

"Yes, police lawyer wasn't she?"

"She was part of the team investigating your mother's death."

Claire looks bemused at Olivia. "I know, that's how they met, Dad and her."

"You know your father was being investigated?"

"If this is you trying to help me after I have come home from hospital then it's weird," says Claire. "Can we talk about something else?"

"I just wanted to understand what went on."

"Well, it's ancient history."

"Stephen may have found out something about the events of that time and talked to your father."

"You've lost me," says Claire.

"I believe he may have been killed for what he knew."

"I'm too tired for all this now."

"Was your mother, Miss J, Claire?"

Claire's face drops and her mood shifts instantly. "What do you know about that?"

"I know Miss J was the code name for the woman killed when your father and Bruce Alpin were meeting someone about bribes. Whatever happened, Miss J was killed in suspicious circumstances. The investigation never found out how she died or who her killer was. The team was wound up very quickly and. In my view, there's sufficient evidence that the senior investigating officer covered up what really happened to protect someone."

Claire's face is static, listening to the words.

"I believe Miss J was your mother. I believe that she died on that day and that Bruce Alpin and possibly your father were involved in her death."

"You don't know what you're talking about." Claire is calmer than Olivia would have predicted.

"Then, tell me what you know," says Olivia. "I believe that you saw something or heard a conversation back then. You're the only witness to what really happened. What was it, Claire? Did you hear your father and Patricia talking? Or see something?"

"I want you to leave."

"A crime was committed, and the guilty parties got away with it."

"Get out!" Claire stands up with help from her arms as her strength is not yet fully back.

"You can bring them to justice," says Olivia.

Claire grabs Olivia's wrist and pulls her arm until Olivia stands. "Keep out of my business!"

"Why are you protecting them? One of them, at least, is a criminal."

"You don't know what you're talking about. You haven't seen what the police knew."

"What did the police know?"

"You need to go!" Claire drags Olivia towards the door.

Olivia pulls the rip cord. "Did you know that Stephen was having an affair with Greer Alpin?"

Claire stops, her gaze on the floor.

"He was going to leave you."

"No, he wasn't."

"He was, and he was on his way home to tell you that on the night he died."

"No."

"Yes," says Olivia. "I've spoken to Greer, there are photos of the two of them."

Claire's energy slips away and she grabs for the door frame beside her. "No."

"I'm sorry."

As the words leave Olivia's lips, Claire's body collapses against the frame then sideways on to the floor with a heavy thud. Olivia checks her breathing, the woman has fainted. She grabs her phone and calls for an ambulance.

CHAPTER TWENTY-SIX

A breeze plays at Claire's window and catches the edge of the curtain, momentarily letting blue winter light pour into the bedroom and across the woman's face as she lays asleep in her bed. Olivia walks in from the kitchen with a mug of tea and sits back down on the chair that she dragged in from the dining area sometime in the middle of the night as her place to sleep. After the ambulance crew had checked Claire over, they had wanted to take her to the Royal London Hospital so the doctors could see her, but Claire was awake by then and insisted that she would be alright at home. Olivia had promised to stay with her and call if Claire's condition worsened. It had meant a sleepless night for Olivia as she sat by the bedside and read various books from the shelves throughout the flat.

Claire opens her eyes and takes a few seconds to wake fully and focus.

"You OK?" says Olivia.

"Have you been here all the time?"

"I told the ambulance crew I'd stay."

They sit in silence for several minutes. Olivia wonders if Claire remembers the conversation they had last night that caused her to faint, and doesn't want to pressure the woman again yet.

"Let me see the photos," says Claire.

"Are you sure?" Claire nods.

Olivia gets up and goes to the tiny bedroom across the hallway. She returns to Claire's room with the phone in her hand, already powered-up. Olivia flicks through to the hidden folder and hands over the device. Claire holds the phone above her and looks at the pictures in turn. Her eyes are dry at first but fill with water the more images she sees. Eventually, she stops and puts the phone down on to the duvet. Claire closes her eyes and Olivia waits to let Claire get used to the ideas that are now in her head.

"My life's a mess," Claire says after a while. "Nothing I thought was true, was, in fact, true. How long do you think this had been going on?"

"A year, maybe?"

"And I didn't notice." Claire pauses. "Who else knows about this?"

"No one."

"You said you'd spoken to Greer?"

"Yes."

"Why?"

"To find the truth."

"How did you find out?"

"I found the phone," says Olivia.

"You were snooping around my flat?"

"I thought you might have something to help identify the blackmailer," she says. "It's what I do, Claire, bring people to justice. Bring hidden things into the daylight. Sometimes it means pain for the people around the guilty. I'm sorry you had to hear it from me."

Olivia goes and makes tea then brings it back into the bedroom.

"Do you know why Stephen's phone was in that box?" says Olivia.

"No idea, it's not his normal phone." She turns away from Olivia in the bed and another block of silence drops between them. Outside, rain starts to patter on the glass. "You said that you think he was killed?" says Claire.

"I do."

"Do you think he was killed because he had an affair with Greer Alpin?"

"No. There's nothing to be gained by anyone from that. Crimes are only committed by people for gain, usually money. Stephen's death is more likely connected to the criminal activities of GreenLink."

"Or Bruce Alpin trying to cover up what happened fifteen years ago?"

Olivia looks at the woman in the bed, Claire's eyes pleading for her to say no, but Olivia can't lie. "Yes, that's possible. Stephen might have found out about it and told your father or Sir Bruce that he was going to the police."

Claire's eyes are wet and light catches on her tears.

"You said yesterday that the police knew what really happened back then," says Olivia. "What did you mean?"

"There was one guy who did all of the interviews, blond bloke. He spoke to me but I didn't tell him anything, he didn't seem that trustworthy. I was only eleven at the time, so grown-up men were a bit scary anyway."

"But was there something that you heard? Even if you didn't tell the police?"

Claire's eyes are dark with sorrow and memory. She takes a breath. "There's a tape."

"What tape?"

"From the answerphone in Dad's study. I stole it."

"Do you still have it?" says Olivia.

"Yes."

"What does it contain?"

"Recordings of messages and there's a call that Dad must have recorded."

"And what are they saying?"

Claire looks straight ahead. "I've never told anyone about this."

"What's on the tape?"

"They're talking about a bribe to destroy evidence, and he says they need to meet up somewhere out of the way."

"Where's the tape?" says Olivia. Claire gets out of bed and walks to the wardrobe along the back wall. She moves a chair and stands on it to get to the top storage. She fishes around in the cupboards then pulls out an old suitcase, a child's suitcase.

"My school bag," she says and pings the two locks open as she dumps it on the bed. There are only a few items inside: a teddy bear, school certificates for swimming, and a school tie with signatures of school friends all over it. Claire pushes open a top pocket in the lid and her fingers disappear inside then pull out a mini-tape cartridge, the type used in answer phones in the past. She holds up the tape to Olivia.

"I'll can get it copied," says Olivia. "Can I give it to the police?"

"What are we doing here?" says Claire, ignoring the question.

"Bringing them to justice. They may have killed your mother, if what's on the tape is incriminating then someone will go to prison."

"It won't bring mum back."

"No, it won't," says Olivia. "But you can move on, have your new life."

"With no family."

"It depends who did what," says Olivia. "But if your father and Patricia are implicated then they have to pay the price."

Claire turns the tape over in her fingers, her mind trawling the pros and cons of what she is about to do.

"Go on, take it," she says and holds the tape out in her hand.

*

The journey from Hereford Square to White's Club is taking longer than usual in the London traffic. Jeremy taps his fingers on the wheel of the Range Rover and wills the lights to change ahead of him. Eventually he turns off the roundabout at Hyde Park Corner and along Piccadilly. The phone call from the man at White's had been odd. He had insisted that Jeremy visit the club to see his father but he wouldn't tell him anymore. Jeremy stops the car in the loading only spaces next to the club and walks up the steps. In the reception area, the same man who had been on the phone is waiting for him, looking nervous.

"Mr Jeremy," he says. "Thank you for coming. Will you follow me?"

The man turns and walks up the stairs from the reception area, up one more flight then left along a corridor of bedrooms. There's a Do Not Disturb label hanging from the handle on Room 205. The man takes his master key from a chain on his belt and unlocks the door.

As Jeremy enters the room, he can see his father asleep on the bed. He looks at the man who has led the way to the room.

"Your father is dead, Mr Jeremy," says the man. "The club doctor was called immediately. The breakfast girl found him this morning. There was no pulse. I'm sorry."

Jeremy walks over to the body. "What happened, Mr Kendall?" he says.

"Sleeping pills, the doctor said, sir."

"Who else knows?"

"No one, Mr Jeremy."

Jeremy rubs his hand across his face and looks at his father.

"Mr Kendall."

"Sir?"

"Would you call the police?"

*

An hour later, Detective Inspector Fiona Hale and Jeremy sit in the room next to where Sir Bruce's body lies. The two rooms have an interconnecting door and Jeremy watches two white-suited forensic scientists take samples and finger prints from the bed and surrounding area as they collect evidence. Sir Bruce is covered with a sheet.

Inspector Hale is tall, her red hair is tied back in a ponytail and her hazel eyes flit between Jeremy and the scene in the distance.

"When was the last time you saw him?" she says.

"A few days ago."

"What happened?"

"We argued."

"About what?"

"The company. I wanted him to step down as Chairman."

"What was his state of mind on that day?" says Fiona.

"Angry."

"Generally, I mean," she says. "Happy? Confident?"

"His usual bullish self. He was a man of strong opinions, Inspector."

"What do you think happened here?" She nods at the body.

"Suicide, the doctor said."

"You agree with that?"

"I'm not the expert," says Jeremy, he looks quizzical.

"Did he have enemies?"

"Plenty."

"Are you one of them?" she says. There is no smile on her face.

Jeremy turns to her. "I didn't kill my father, Inspector, if that's what you're implying."

"Why would you think that?"

"From your words."

"You think he was killed, don't you, Mr Alpin?"

"I don't know." Jeremy opens his palms upwards as he speaks.

"Where were you last night, sir?" she says, watching for non-verbal signals of stress or lying.

"At home."

"Alone?"

"My wife was out."

"Do you have staff, sir?"

"Not live-in."

"No alibi then?" she says, watching.

"Do I need one?"

"We all need an alibi at some stage. I'd like to continue this at the station, sir, make sure we've got all of the details."

"I have meetings, I'm afraid."

"They'll have to wait, sir."

"I can come down later."

"I'm sorry, I must insist."

"Why the hurry?"

"I had a word with the club doctor, Mr Alpin. He confirms that his previous statement about sleeping pills was intentionally incomplete as he didn't want to upset the club management, but there are signs that he was forced to take the tablets and the alcohol. This is a murder investigation, sir. Shall we go?"

*

Poppy comes up from the tube lines at Westminster and out into the coldness of the day. She walks towards the river but turns left just before the bridge and along the Victoria Embankment, then turns into New Scotland Yard.

"Can I help, miss?" says the policewoman on the desk.

"I'd like to report a crime," says Poppy.

An hour later, Poppy has given a statement to a policeman with bright blue eyes, who asks her to wait in the interview room while he gets a print out so that she can sign her statement. Another policeman comes in and offers to get her a cup of coffee, but she declines. The room is a pale green colour which seems to have been painted sometime when that colour was fashionable, but Poppy can't think when than would ever have been the case.

The door opens with a rush of air from the corridor outside.

"Poppy?" says the woman.

"Yes."

The woman offers her hand to shake. "I'm Fiona," she says. "I'm looking into your statement."

"OK."

Inspector Hale sits down opposite her and reads from a print out of the statement that Poppy made earlier. "You have said here that your boyfriend stole some papers from the offices of GreenLink Industries."

"Yes."

"And he is a journalist, and he is writing a piece on Sir Bruce and Jeremy Alpin who are directors of the company?"

"Yes."

"Do you know any of the people I just mentioned?"

"No."

"Did your boyfriend tell you what was in the stolen papers?"

"No."

"Why do you think he did it?"

"His dad was killed when he was investigating the same company and Ethan thought they'd killed him. He was intent on exposing them."

"Passionate, was he?" says Fiona.

"Obsessed, really."

"Due to your age, Poppy, I'd like to contact your parents, is that OK?"

"If you like."

"Can you give me a number?"

Poppy flicks through her phone. "This is my mum's," she says and puts the phone on the table facing Fiona, who writes down the number.

"I'll go and call her. You OK here?"

"Sure. How long is all this gonna take?"

Fiona thinks. "An hour or two. Do you want some food?"

Poppy nods. "Sushi would be good."

"I'll see what's in the canteen," says Fiona, but Poppy doesn't hear and is already flicking through her mobile.

*

Olivia sits in the reception area of New Scotland Yard until a policewoman collects her and takes her to an interview room on the second floor. Within a minute, Inspector Hale comes in, shakes hands and sits across from Olivia and places a paper file on the table between them.

"As I said on the phone, Ms Streete, your daughter came in this morning and reported a crime."

"What was the crime?"

"Can I ask you some questions first?" says Fiona.

"Go on."

"Poppy says she has a boyfriend who is a journalist, Ethan Poole, is that right?"

"I don't know his surname, but yes Ethan."

"How long have they been together?"

"Only a couple weeks."

"What do you know about him?"

"Nothing, except what she's told me, which is what you said just now. He's American, he's a journalist. I think he's in his twenties."

"She's eighteen, is that right?"

"I note your inference, Inspector. I raised with her having an older boyfriend at her age."

"Are you concerned that she has a boyfriend who you've never met?"

"No," says Olivia. "She's a sensible girl."

"Is it a romantic relationship?"

"Sexual, you mean? Highly likely."

"Does she live with you?"

"Her father. We're divorced."

"I did a quick search before I came in," says Fiona, opening the paper folder and reading from it. "You're a lawyer working in Whitehall and you made a statement to Inspector Savage in the British Transport Police a couple of weeks ago about the accidental death of a Stephen Boyd?"

"That's right."

"And, I believe, you're now friends with his widow?"

"We've become friends and I have helped her through the grieving process."

"Help me understand," says Fiona. "You're a witness on a case of accidental death and you befriend the man's widow – and now, your daughter has reported the theft of documents from a company that the family is connected with."

"I didn't know Poppy had reported that."

"A company who lists Sir Bruce Alpin as a director."

"OK."

"What do you know about Sir Bruce Alpin?"

"I've never met him."

"Where were you last night, Ms Streete?"

"With Claire Boyd, all night."

"Oh, you're a couple?"

"No." Olivia smiles. "She's just back from hospital and I'm looking after her."

"Can Mrs Boyd confirm that you were there?"

"She was asleep, I was in the chair next to her."

"Am I missing something?" says Fiona. "You have multiple connections to the Boyds and GreenLink, and you have no alibi for last night?"

"What happened last night?

"What am I missing, Ms Streete?"

"It's a long story, Inspector."

"I've got plenty of time," says Fiona. "Start at the beginning."

"Fifteen years ago, a young woman died. She was called Miss J in the police file on the case."

"How do you know that?"

"I've seen the file."

"A confidential police document?" says Fiona.

"It was lent to me by Inspector Savage. It's a closed case," says Olivia. "Two men were questioned at the time because they had been in the same bar as the dead woman. Those men were Sir Bruce Alpin and Gerald Harwell. There was a cover-up by the police and the killer of Miss J was never found."

Olivia fishes the old folder from her bag and places it on the table.

"Here is the case file, take it. It's been laundered of any criticisms of Sir Bruce or Harwell, and most of the details of the police investigation."

"None of this is provable, Ms Streete."

Olivia puts her hand into her bag again and puts the answerphone tape on the table.

"This is an answerphone tape from Gerald Harwell's phone line from fifteen years ago."

"How did you get that?"

"Claire Boyd, she's Harwell's daughter."

"What's on it?"

"A recording of a conversation between her father and a policeman where Harwell offers to pay a sum in cash to the officer in return for him making evidence go away."

"I'd like to listen to it," says Fiona.

Olivia pushes the tape two inches towards the Inspector. "This is a copy for you."

"You don't trust me with the original, Ms Streete?"

"The original was returned to Claire Boyd as it's her property."

"Tell me about Sir Bruce," says Fiona, reaching out and putting the tape in her hand.

"I don't know him at all. He was an MP for years, he's the father of a man called Jeremy Alpin who is CEO of GreenLink, and Sir Bruce is the Chairman."

Fiona looks at the folder on the desk and there's a pause in their conversation.

"You asked me to come in to discuss my daughter," says Olivia.

Fiona's phone buzzes in her pocket. She pulls it out and reads from the screen. "We've arrested your daughter's boyfriend. Confidential GreenLink documents have been recovered from his hotel room."

"What's in the documents?"

"That's police business, Ms Streete."

"If those documents prove that Sir Bruce and Gerald Harwell are corrupt then it could show that the death of Stephen Boyd wasn't an accident, and that he was killed because he found out what was going on and was going to report it."

"Another accusation without evidence, Ms Streete."

"They killed him to cover up the death of Miss J," says Olivia. "If the tape confirms that they bribed the police, and the documents show they have been breaking the law within GreenLink, then it all fits."

"It's circumstantial," says Fiona. "As I'm sure you are aware with your legal background."

"And you are in a position to now find the proof," says Olivia.

Fiona doesn't react and it leaves a space between them.

"Can we talk about Poppy?" says Fiona. "What's she like?"

"She's a teenager, so slightly self-obsessed, but no more than any other."

"Good at school?"

"What's this got to do with anything?" says Olivia.

"Is she?"

"Yes, As and Bs in her exams. Why?"

"Trustworthy?"

"Moral, as you can see. She's reported her own boyfriend to you. She was brought up to respect the law, Inspector, like her mother."

Fiona smiles. "You know I have to ask these questions."

"She's not implicated," says Olivia. "An eighteen year old wouldn't report a crime that they are part of. I can help you, Inspector. I have many years' experience of evidence collection from my time in the US in court and here as a lawyer."

"Maybe you can," says Fiona.

CHAPTER TWENTY-SEVEN

The clock in the newsroom shows just before Noon. Adrian is clicking through a draft article about how a boy band singer has been caught in a hotel in California with the girlfriend of one of his bandmates.

"Where's that piece on the rising cost of Christmas, Layla? I need it."

"Doing it," calls a woman from one of the computers scattered across the room.

Adrian's desk phone rings, he picks up the receiver and puts it under his chin but carries on editing the words on screen with his keyboard.

"Yup?"

Gradually, his attention to the call moves from uninterested to attentive to enveloped. He stops typing and puts the receiver into his hand.

"When did this all happen?"

"And no press have been briefed on it yet?"

"Who's the officer in charge?"

"I know her, she's tricky."

"Has the son been arrested?"

"OK, yeah OK. I owe you one, Mich. Yeah, bye." He stands up and walks to the centre of the newsroom.

"Everyone!" he calls out. Gradually the dozen people in front of him stop typing, or end the calls they're on, until all the people are looking at Adrian in silence.

"We have the biggest story of the year, breaking now. We have an exclusive early lead on it. Sir Bruce Alpin has been found dead this morning, a suspected overdose. However, and this is the bit that makes it big - potentially, it could be murder."

The journalists break out in to chatter across the room.

"Dan is lead on this." He looks across to a man by the window who gives thumbs up. Layla and her team will be on it full time from now. Get rid of your other stories to someone. Kev, you and yours will need to pick up those. Sorry, mate, next time you can lead a big one."

"Any suspects, Adrian?" calls Dan from his desk.

"Apparently they have the son under arrest. So it could be a juicy family battle. Pull on all of your contacts. I want hourly report backs please!"

The room bursts back into life and Adrian returns to his desk. He picks up his mobile and walks to a balcony the other side of a glass wall at the back of the building. He selects a number and dials.

"Hi Violet, it's Adrian Gilbraith."

"Mr Galbraith."

"Sir Bruce Alpin, you were going to send me some documents on him."

"A slight problem."

"Oh?"

"My source was arrested this morning."

"Was he now," says Adrian. "Can I ask who it was?"

"I'm sorry, I can't tell you."

"I'm sure you've heard the news," he says.

"What?"

"Sir Bruce is dead."

Adrian can't detect any reaction over the phone and it annoys him that he didn't reveal this fact face-to-face where he would've been able to tell much more from the woman's reactions.

"I didn't know," is all she says. No emotion, no shock and no disappointment are displayed in her voice tone.

"Apart from the evidence that you were going to share with me, do you personally have anything you want to say about Sir Bruce? I could interview you."

"I'm not sure."

"We're going big on this story, it's going to run all over Christmas. A well-known politician found dead in a hotel room, maybe with a back-story about his corruption and under-hand deals over many years."

"Let me think."

"There's no time to delay, Violet. Meet me this afternoon. If you have information about him, now is the time to get the record straight about what he has done, before there's briefing to the media to protect his legacy."

"Who'd do that?" she says.

"Anyone who has benefitted from his crimes, anyone who is also implicated. If he's corrupt, they'll all go into self-preservation mode."

"OK."

"Do you know if there are others who are involved? Other well-known figures?"

"There are."

"Who?"

"I'll tell you when we meet," she says. They arrange to meet later in Soho and end the call.

*

The Thames looks like black silk between the river banks from The London Eye on one side to New Scotland Yard on the other. Fiona Hale sits with headphones on that are plugged into an old telephone answering machine that the technical department had found lodged at the top of a dusty set of shelving in the basement storeroom.

She presses the play button and picks up a pen from the desk, holding it ready to make notes about what she's about to hear.

The tape has a few seconds of white noise, then silence, then the first message starts with echoes from fifteen years ago.

"Gerry, Dan Palmer, just checking about the timing for tonight. I have seven in my diary. Can you call me back and confirm. Cheers."

"It's Patty. Can you call me? There's some wording in your statement that I need go over. Thanks."

"Mr Harwell, it's Angela from the Garrick, I wanted to talk to you about the bar bill from last week. I'd appreciate it if you call me back."

"It's Bruce, Gerald. We need to talk. There's an Inspector who's willing to help us. Savage he's called, Jack Savage."

"Mr Harwell? St Stephen's Entrance Security, sir. You have a visitor but I know you're not in the House today, sir. I've taken a name and told them there's no point coming here without something in the diary. Thank you."

"Dad? I'm calling from the school office. Can you call me here? They can get me out of class when you call back if it's during the day. I want to talk about mum and what happened. Are you coming to see me this weekend? Bye, love you."

Then the messages stop and the tape goes silent for ten seconds until Fiona hears a click and a recording of a phone call starts that Gerald Harwell must have made as the device allowed for call recording as well as messages.

"Mr Harwell?"

"Hello, Jack is it?"

"Mr Alpin and I were talking, and he said that the two of you might be interested in a discussion, off the record."

"Can you help us?"

"Let's talk about that."

"OK, what do you want to know? Bruce and I think we could find ten thousand, would that be enough?"

"Hang on, hang on. I'm not going to talk about anything over the phone."

"OK, do you want to meet?"

"Yeah, there's a place I know, discrete."

"Where?"

"The Bluebird Bar, off the Buckingham Palace Road. You know it?"

"No."

"Walk down from Victoria, you'll see a sign on the wall. Meet there at nine."

"We'll be there. Do I need to bring the cash?"

"A down-payment would be handy."

The tape goes silent as the recording stops. Fiona plays it back and listens to the call again to make sure she noted down all of the points of evidence.

The office door opens and Detective Sergeant Terry Moore walks in. He is shorter than average for a man, with slight build and black curly hair over small wire glasses that make his eyes appear to be larger than they are.

"Guv, I spoke to the journo. He's raving on about corruption and how he almost had them," he says. "They've been at it for years apparently, he reckons, all the usual posh bloke crimes, false accounting, bribery, fiddling the books, he says. But, he doesn't seem to know that Sir Bruce is dead. I didn't mention it and he talked about the bloke in the present tense all the time. He also talked about a man called Gerald Harwell being part of the whole thing."

"I've got to talk to the son in a minute, Terry. Let's see what he says."

"OK, guv."

"Can you do something for me?" she says. "This is a copy of a police file. Can you go through this and compare what's in it versus what is in the online copy of the same file?" She holds out the folder to him.

"What am I looking for?"

"Anything that doesn't match up, missing pages, different words; things added in where they shouldn't be."

"On it, guv."

Fiona takes a pad and pen and walks along the corridor to the interview rooms. Just before walking in to Room 4, she looks at Jeremy Alpin sitting on the other side of the glass and wonders about his ability to lie.

"Mr Alpin," she says walking into the room. "Did the officer tell you about your right to a lawyer?"

"I don't need one."

"I'm going to record this discussion." She turns on the recorder. "22nd December, Detective Inspector Hale and Mr Jeremy Alpin are present. Mr Alpin has declined to have a solicitor with him. Could you confirm that for the tape, sir?"

"That's right."

"Mr Alpin, you reported your father's death this morning to us. Let me take you back to the last time you saw your father before today. Where was that?"

"At White's Club."

"And what did you discuss?"

"I proposed to him that he step down as Chairman of our company, GreenLink Industries."

"And why was that, sir?"

"A number of directors had complained to me, as CEO, and the majority of the board felt that my father's best years were behind him."

"Did he agree to your proposal?"

"No."

"What did he say?"

"He refused to step down."

"Were you angry?" she says.

"Yes, I was."

"Were you violent at all, sir?"

"Of course not," he says furrowing his brow. "I walked out."

"And where did you go."

"To a hotel."

"Why not home, sir?"

"I needed to get away."

"Were you on your own in the hotel, sir?"

"No, I was there with a friend of mine."

"Who was that, sir?"

"Is this needed?"

"Just so we can verify what you say, sir," she says. "Standard procedure."

"Her name is Violet Dudley."

"Can I ask, sir, is that an intimate friendship?"

Jeremy's eyes show signs of anger. He pauses, in his mind, he hadn't thought about involving Violet in all of this.

"Yes."

"What do you know about the circumstances surrounding your father's death, sir?"

"I was called to the club this morning, they had found him first thing when a maid took in his breakfast."

"There were signs around his mouth that someone may have forced him to take the pills and brandy," she says, watching every muscle movement on Jeremy's face. "What do you know about that, sir?

"Nothing," says Jeremy. "You told me that earlier, that's all I know."

"And where were you last night, Mr Alpin?"

"At home, there was no one else there."

Fiona writes down a note on the pad. "Let's turn to your relationship over the years with your father, sir."

Jeremy shifts in his chair and wonders how much to talk about.

*

Terry Moore checks his watch, it shows just after two. He looks at the words on the screen that list the differences between the paper version and the electronic version of the case file from fifteen years ago.

The door to the open plan office swings open and Inspector Hale walks in. He follows her to her office at the end of the room.

"Guv, that file you gave me has had twenty-four pages removed compared to online. There are big gaps in the statement dates from Bruce Alpin and Gerald Harwell."

"Right. Let's update ourselves, Terry. The file has been doctored, removing the deceased and Harwell. I have interviewed the son, he has no alibi, and he has motive. He could get into the club easily because they know him there, but I spoke to the staff on shift last night and this morning, and no one saw him," she says.

"What about his family members, Guv?"

"We've got an officer going to talk to the daughter-in-law, but the deceased's wife died years ago. I've listened to this tape and that implicates both men, plus..." She stops. "Terry, push the door to, would you?" He follows her instruction. "Everything I say from now on is strictly confidential, Sergeant."

"Ma'am."

"The tape implicates a service officer in British Transport Police who worked for the Met back then, Jack Savage."

"Shall we bring him in, Guv?"

Fiona considers the question while her sergeant looks on, waiting for her command. "Yes, Terry, go and pick him up. Take Manish."

Sergeant Moore walks out of her office and calls out. "Mani, with me." A man at one of the desks stands up and hurries out after the Sergeant.

*

Winter sunlight breaks through the clouds over Surridge Place and slides across the lawn outside the window. Patricia sits on the sofa with her shoes off and her legs up. She turns another page in the thick ring binder on her knees and reads more words on the case she is hearing tomorrow at the High Court. From behind her, somewhere in the house, she hears a door slam and footsteps hurry down the main staircase before Gerald appears in the door to the lounge. He walks to her, pulls up a chair, places it beside her and sits.

"Patricia."

"You look like you've seen a ghost, my darling," she says.

"Some terrible news." She waits. "Bruce."

"What?"

"Passed away, my love."

She raises a hand to her mouth. "No!"

"This morning at the Club."

"What was it?"

"Sadly, he seems to have taken his own life."

"Poor man!" Gerald reaches out and takes her hand, his face pushed into a crumpled sadness. They sit for a moment as they share their shock. Eventually she says. "Should we do anything?"

"What can we do?"

"I could call Jeremy, see how he is?"

"I believe that he's in police custody."

"What? Whatever for?"

"I don't know."

"How did Bruce kill himself?" she says.

"Pills."

"Are you sure Jeremy's in custody? If it's a straight suicide, there'll just wrap it up into a case file with a doctor's affidavit. There's no investigation, unless there are other circumstances. How are you getting your information?"

"A friend."

"Who? A working police officer?"

"Yes."

"Did they call you?"

"I'm worried, my darling," he says.

"Why?"

"There may be implications from the case fifteen years ago."

"The fraud case? That was closed off. How does Bruce's death bear on that?"

"He may have lied at the time," says Gerald.

"Lied to the police?"

"Yes."

"About what?"

"He seems to have paid a bribe to have evidence destroyed."

"How do you know this?"

Gerald looks away to the window.

"Gerald?"

"Were you involved?"

"I knew he was doing it."

"You need to go to the police, immediately," she says. "This is highly damaging. Are you saying that for fifteen years you have known that Bruce bribed a policeman and you didn't report it? Gerald, you and I met during that case. We've lived together all these years and you didn't say anything?"

"I'm sorry, my darling."

Patricia's features are screwed up into pain. "What have you done, Gerald?"

"I'm going away, my love."

"No, you'll face this like a bloody man."

"I've packed a case."

"Gerald, don't. You'll make it look far worse than it is."

His eyes come up to meet hers. No words are needed to convey what is in his mind.

"How bad is it, Gerald? Did you just turn a blind eye back then or were you part of it?"

"I think it's best if I say no more."

"And what about the girl? The girl who died. Please don't tell me you knew something about that too?"

He stands up. "My train leaves in half an hour," he says. "Michael is bringing the car around to the front."

"Gerald!" He walks away. She calls after him. "Gerald!" She hears the front door open and slam shut then the Bentley move off across the gravel on the driveway. Patricia walks to a telephone handset that is in the hallway, dials then waits for the call to be answered.

"Deputy Chief Constable, please," she says into the mouthpiece, and taps her fingernail on the base of the phone, thinking through what on earth she is going to say, and the consequences for everyone involved.

*

The coffee shop in Golden Square is half-full, mostly with media types wearing all black who have come out from their offices in this part of Soho to have meetings in the early afternoon. Adrian had got here early, he prefers to give himself thinking time to help his brain order his thoughts. Unlike Violet's entrance in the cocktail bar where they met previously, she slips into the café almost unnoticed. She is wearing a red polo neck jumper and pale leggings with a fitted black jacket and a black fur hat.

"Mr Gilbraith," she says as she sits opposite him.

"Won't you call me Adrian?"

"As you wish."

"Coffee?"

"Americano, black." He signals to a waitress who comes over the takes their order.

"Sir Bruce, then?" he begins. "I assume your source was Jeremy Alpin."

"No."

"He's been arrested."

"I know."

"What do you know about the crimes Sir Bruce has committed?"

"He has been involved in crime for twenty years," she says. "Property fiddles, money laundering, black market supplies for clubs and bars. My sister was part of his business empire. She ran one of the clubs that he had pushed through planning, but she didn't know anything about his corruption at first. He bribed people to get clubs approved, then set up companies to supply the drink and food to the club. Parts of the supply were legitimate, but Sir Bruce wasn't happy with just food and drink, he wanted the big money in clubs – drugs and girls."

"Your sister became an escort?"

"No, she didn't. She was older than me, I looked up to her, she had always done everything first, boyfriends, drinking, leaving home. Then one day I got a call from the police to say that Julia had been found dead - killed, unlawfully. The police investigated but they never found the killer. I came to London to try and find people who had known her. Her friends became my friends; slowly, her life became my life. I joined the same club behind the bar, then became a dancer. It didn't take long for the truth to come out, that as well as the dancing, the club was a front for prostitution."

"Aren't all clubs the same?"

"No, that's not right. Some are just sleazy but they're only dancing clubs. The press always put two and two together and make five."

Adrian ignores the dig at his profession. "Did you find out if Bruce Alpin was responsible for your sister's death?"

"I spent years trying to do that," she says. "No one would talk, they all knew what had happened but were scared they'd end up dead too."

"Excuse me for asking," says Adrian. "But, your occupation. Did you start that as part of Bruce's business empire?"

"Not directly."

"What do you mean?"

"As a dancer, I did get propositioned, but I know how men work and just avoided it. Then the club had to close for six months after a fire, and I was out of work. I kept in touch with the girls I had worked with and one of them introduced me to escorting. It was just that at first, having dinner with rich, lonely men; nothing more."

"And then one night you were offered more money to go further?" he says.

"I was young, the money was good. I even enjoyed it," she says. "Now, I have no other saleable skills." She smiles.

"We both know that's not true, Violet."

"Don't humour me, Adrian."

"What happened after that?"

"Years passed by without me really noticing. I had money, I didn't forget about Julia, but I had never found out anything of substance to help me find her killer, and it became harder and harder to discover anything new. Then, a year ago, I met Jeremy Alpin through a friend."

"Is he corrupt too?"

"No, he's not. He's resolutely innocent. We fell in love. He hated his father, Bruce wouldn't let him decide anything even though he became CEO - so Jeremy worked out a plan to get him out of the company. Bruce would have none of it and threatened Jeremy. He said he would publish documents to show that Jeremy is the criminal."

"He threatened him to keep quiet?" says Adrian.

She nods. "It made me start researching Bruce's business dealings again, and I used my network of rich men to find out more about my sister's death. It became obvious that Sir Bruce had been involved back then and there'd been a cover-up. Someone even got a court order to remove her name entirely from police records, she was just a faceless corpse to them – a body who was expendable. It's disgusting what they did, all the records only now show her as Miss J."

CHAPTER TWENTY-EIGHT

Detective Sergeant Moore shows his warrant card to the constable on reception at the Head Quarters of the British Transport Police and is waived through. He and DC Manish Shah run up the stairs at the back of the reception area and crash through the doors on the fourth floor into the open office. He walks to the first desk he can see, where Lois is sitting.

"We're here to see Inspector Savage." He shows his warrant card again.

"He's out," she says. "Came in earlier then got a call and had to go somewhere."

"Do you know where?"

"Sorry. He didn't say."

"Damn it!" Moore says mostly to himself.

"Can I help?" says Lois.

"Which one's his office?"

"Why?"

"We need to see if he's got some papers for one of our cases."

"Over there in the corner, T41." She nods her head towards the canal end of the building and Terry and Manish follow her directions. In the room, they scour the paperwork that is on Jack's desk and go through the drawers and cupboards in the office, but find nothing. After half an hour they return to Lois.

"What time did he leave here, constable?" says Terry to her.

"Twelve?" She says screwing up her face as she thinks.

"Was he walking or go by tube or what?"

"Driving definitely," she says. "He took one of the pool cars - I hold the keys."

"Which one?"

"Hang on." Lois leans over and pulls out a large A4 book then leafs through several pages of handwritten grids where keys have been issued to officers when they take a car out. "Here it is, G15."

"Reg number?"

"SZ 47 ETN, it's the one he usually uses, he hasn't got a car so he takes it out quite a lot."

"Thanks, constable," says Terry. "Mani, ring that in can you? Put out a stop and detain on the occupant."

"Is he in trouble?" says Lois.

"Can't say, sorry love," Terry calls back to her as they hurry out.

*

Tom hasn't been in this alleyway next to the Bluebird Club during the day before. All the times he has visited have been the night time, the same time that Kate would have been laying here with her face bloodied from someone's fist. He trusted her. He still can't understand why she left him; he had put his whole life, his whole soul into their relationship. She was ungrateful in the end, after all he'd done, she just chucked him away on the scrapheap. At lcast he had known was love was like before he knew the truth about her.

The back door to the bar clatters as the bolts are pulled back on the other side, then it opens and Marie pushes the door with a crate of empty beer bottles in front of her. She dumps them noisily onto the ground next to the row of commercial waste bins on wheels.

"What you doing here?" she says to him. "Haven't you got a job to go to?"

"Yeah, day off."

She picks up an empty crate, puts it on its end next to him and sits down. "What you thinking about?"

"You know."

"Fucking hell, Tom, bloody move on, man."

"I will."

"Do something," she says. "Go and find a hooker, get pissed, move to the Caribbean. You're just wasting your life here."

"I am gonna to do something about it."

"What?"

"Sort it, once and for all."

"Like what?"

"I've met someone."

"Thank fucking Christ!" she says. "What's she like?"

"Kind, intelligent."

"Then fuck off and build a new life with her. Once I've saved up I'm going to go and open a bar in Greece, we've all got dreams, mate."

"I'm seeing her later."

"Then tell you what you think of her, if you haven't, tell her you have plans – and tell her she's part of them."

"I *have* got plans, and she *is* part of them."

"Cool." Marie stands up and moves towards the open back door. "Sort it, mate. See yer."

"I will," he says softly but only he can hear the words.

*

The sky over London has darkened since lunchtime and coldness now hangs around the corridors of the Chelsea and Westminster Hospital grasping at the passers-by as they flit between wards. Evan pulls a blanket up around his throat. He has been feeling a lot better since they increased his pain killers yesterday. His face is still bandaged but his voice has returned after drinking numerous glasses of water under the glare of a stern Matron who had insisted that burn victims need excess liquid. The doctors have said good things about his recovery and psychologically he thinks this is what happy must feel like. The flashes of memory from the fire are getting less frequent. At night he still sees the hairs on his arm burning but for less time, and he still thinks he can smell his skin burning occasionally, even now, laying here under clean linen.

He isn't expecting anyone he knows to visit him. He intentionally asked the nurses not to contact anyone because he isn't sure that the whole thing was an accident and he doesn't want to broadcast his whereabouts. Apart from that Ms Delaney who he vaguely remembers coming to visit him before he could talk again, there has only been a message from an ex of his, Cat Beecham. She had said that she's in London and will come and see him. His brain clicks through the happy times they had had together. He'd always liked her.

The last face Evan is expecting to see is his own sister's. But nonetheless, Greer is standing at the end of his bed as he comes out of the day-dream.

"Hello, Evan "

"Sis, my goodness, this is a surprise."

She holds up a brown bag. "Grapes. Isn't that what you're supposed to bring?" She deposits the bag on the side table and drags a chair from the next bed to sit near him. "How's my little soldier?"

He smirks. "You used to call me that." She returns a smile with more warmth that he was expecting. "Getting there," he says.

"Thought I'd come and update you on the family."

"Oh yes?"

"My dear husband is being held by the police."

"Did he refuse to get you a new handbag?" says Evan.

She makes a mock smile and tips her head to one side. "Very fucking funny. Also, something more serious, Sir Bruce is dead."

"Blimey. Did Jeremy kill him?"

"No one knows," she says. "I haven't been able to get to see him. They took him straight from White's Club to Scotland Yard."

"I'm not surprised."

"That he died?"

"That someone killed him," says Evan. "He wasn't a nice man, Sis. You know that."

"Yes, he was an arsehole."

"You know I found some dirt on him?" says Evan. "I was going to send it to the police."

"What dirt?"

"GreenLink fiddles, fraud type stuff. One of my contacts found it."

"Did you ask them for it?" she says.

"Another client wanted dirt on him."

"Did you report it?" she says.

"No, I never got the chance, but I told an old school friend about it. One of the few people I have ever trusted and thought he'd know what to do. That's where it all gets crazy - he died, then my fire."

"Who was it you told?"

"Stephen Boyd. You know him, don't you?"

Greer closes her eyes.

"Sis? You OK?" She says nothing. Evan can't get out of bed so has to wait for her to recover her composure. After a minute, she opens her now red eyes. "What is it, Sis?"

"I did know him, Ev." Her voice is oddly quiet. "He was a good friend."

"Sorry, I didn't realise."

"When did you tell him?"

"The day he died," says Evan. Her eyelids hang heavy over her dark blue eyes. She walks to the window and looks out. The rain from earlier is slowly changing to white, high up in the clouds. She watches the scene for a minute as, slowly, snowflakes start to flurry in the air outside. Greer turns back to her brother. "Sorry, I probably never told you how much he meant to me."

"No worries, Sis."

She gets a tissue from her bag and blows her nose.

"Who was this client who wanted dirt on GreenLink, anyway?" she says.

"A woman called Rebecca Delancy, lawyer, she had clients who wanted leverage in the sector," says Evan.

"Had you dealt with her before?" says Greer.

"No, came out of the blue."

"What do you know about her?"

"Nothing really. There's a bit on her website."

"What's the address?" says Greer getting her phone out of her coat pocket.

Evan recites the website address and she types it in then hits enter. Greer navigates from the home page to the About Us tab, and there, centrally placed is a picture of Rebecca Delaney.

"Very interesting," says Greer.

"You know her?" says Evan.

"Oh yes, I know her."

*

"This story goes live at four," says Adrian to the newsroom. "I need those last two pieces, people!" Around him, his staff are busily typing words and dragging and dropping design elements on new pages that are almost ready to go. The headline at the top of the first page shouts, 'MP commits suicide over fraud and murder allegations.'

Adrian reads through the words on a screen in front of one of the journalists, leaning over their shoulder. "On that second line, take out the second bit. Yes that. Add in the section we moved earlier, about him being well-connected across Westminster," he says, then calls across the room. "Where are those images of Alpin, Sash? We need three after the headline."

"Adrian?" another staffer says to him over his shoulder. "A bloke to see you."

"Not just now, Sally."

"You'll be interested in what I have to say," says Jack from right behind Adrian. "I know about Bruce Alpin."

Adrian turns. "Who are you?" he says.

"A friend."

"Don't fucking start all that," says Adrian. "I don't deal with sources who won't give me their name, one of my ground rules."

"I was on the police team who investigated him fifteen years ago."

Adrian keeps looking at Jack, now his attention has been captured. "Come into the meeting room," he says and the two men walk in, shut the door and stand facing each other. "What do you know?"

"There was no cover up."

"Of the girl's death?"

"Yes, that and any fraud," says Jack. "We found no evidence of false accounting, money laundering, bribery or anything."

"What about Miss J? We know her name and we're going to publish it."

"You can't, there's a court order banning publication of her name for seventy-five years."

"Why so long?"

"You'll have to ask the judge that."

"He died ten year ago," says Adrian. "Look, what are you hoping to achieve coming in here?"

"You can't publish," says Jack. "People will get hurt if you do."

"Which people?"

"I can't say."

"You're giving me nothing, mate, apart from a load of random statements about what I can't do."

"You'll be arrested if you contravene a court order, and fined, maybe imprisoned."

"I know the law around publication, you're talking bollocks." As the last word leaves Adrian's lips, Jack lunges at him and swings a fist up and across at his face. Adrian dodges the incoming punch and pushes back against chairs and a table in the middle of the room. Jack comes for him again, grabbing at his shirt. Adrian's fingers curl around one of Jack's wrists and the editor pushes the arm away and tries to twist it behind Jack's back but Jack twists out of it. Adrian rolls his arm into an arc and surrounds Jack's neck with it, then pulls the man down towards the floor. Jack's feet slip and he collapses onto one knee, but spins and pulls Adrian off-balance and the two of them crash to the floor amid the scattered furniture. Adrian swings a punch and lands it on Jack's cheek. Jack echoes the move and brings his arm back for an assault, but the door opens and Layla runs into the room to help. Jack hits her and it lands on her shoulder, he tries to kick out at Adrian but his leg goes wide. Layla is up again and runs at Jack he is pushed back momentarily against the glass wall, but her hands can't latch on to his body and Jack slides away, out of the door, runs the length of the office and crashes out through the door to the reception area. They all hear the outside door crash back against its hinges, then he's gone.

Adrian lays on the floor and Layla stands next to the door, both panting. She puts a hand to her shoulder. One of Adrian's eyes is bloodshot and his shirt is ripped on the shoulder.

"What on earth?" Layla says eventually. "Who was he?"

"Sent to stop us publishing this Alpin story."

"What?" She opens her eyes wide at her boss. "Someone comes in here trying to beat you up to stop a story going up? Fuck, this must be some story."

"You know what we can tell from this, Lay?"

"What?"

"It's all fucking true. No one tries to stop publication if your story is bollocks."

"You still want to go ahead?" she says.

"Two hundred percent." He stands up and pulls his torn shirt across his body. They smile at each other. "Proper journalism!" he says.

CHAPTER TWENTY-NINE

A grey ceiling hangs over London. The last of the scattered sunlight at the end of a short, December day, fades away and a dark curtain descends across the city. The snow is falling steadily now, the flakes larger than they were an hour ago and large enough to remain cold after they hit the ground. On Hampstead Heath the grass turns white and walkers scatter to their homes, away from the desolation of the grassland in winter. Only a few people are left outside to achieve what they set out to do a long time ago. On the road in front of the Boyd's flat, a car pulls up and stops. The driver switches off the engine and waits, watching the snow.

At the end of the road, the Wells Tavern enjoys a position only a minute away from the start of the Heath. Ellen is exactly on time and gives Tom a big smile as she walks into the pub and unwraps the scarf from around her neck.

They talk about Christmases they've known, holidays they've loved and what they were like as children. Ellen buys another round of drinks and thinks that maybe this will work out after all, maybe Tom is getting over his ex and can move on.

"It's crazy all the things that have happened over the last couple of weeks," she says. "Stephen's death, his wife having that gun accident, now Jeremy Alpin's dad dies, weird."

"Not that weird."

She turns to him. "Why do you say that?"

"None of them were that nice," says Tom.

She looks confused. "They weren't nice so they deserve to die?"

"Karma, you know?"

"That's a horrible thing to say!" she says. "Stephen was alright."

"They're all connected."

"Those accidents?"

"None of those were accidents," says Tom. "Stephen was killed by someone, Claire's gun was booby-trapped, and one of the people Sir Bruce Alpin had screwed down the years finally caught up with him."

"God, you're in a cynical mood tonight."

"I'm just a realist," he says.

"I bet they were all in it together."

"All in what?"

Tom takes a swig of his beer. "You'll think I'm crazy."

"I do anyway," she says smiling and putting her hand on his.

"No one wants to take responsibility," he says.

"For what?"

"Stephen wasn't clean, he had his fingers in dirty pies."

"I know that already."

"You do?"

"I saw some messages," she says.

"When?"

"In the flat."

She instantly regrets the words and feels a tide of emotion cross her body.

"What? In what flat?"

"Let's talk about something else, Tom."

"When you did you see those messages?"

She breathes out. "I wasn't going to tell you." She stops and looks at his wide eyes, knowing that her next words are a mistake before she says them. "We were together for a while."

"You and Stephen Boyd?"

"Years ago, before he knew Claire." Tom is silent and drinks a mouthful of beer. "Years ago," she repeats. They sit in silence. After a minute she says. "*You* talked about *your* ex."

"She was special," says Tom, then after a pause. "Anyway, they killed her."

"Who?"

"Alpin, Boyd, the rest. They just throw people away and don't care. Someone had to do something to stop them."

She watches the waves of anger and fear ride across his face.

"Its people like you, not wanting to see it, that's the problem," he says.

"Stop it, Tom."

"What do they say? You're as guilty as they are if good people stand by and say nothing."

"Tom, look…"

"Frightened, Ellen?"

"Bored of listening to you," she says and picks up her coat and bag. "Thanks for the drinks." She stands up and walks towards the door. Tom grabs his coat and follows her outside. "I'm going to walk to the tube."

"I'll walk you," he says.

"No, it's fine." She goes off into the darkness.

"That's the wrong way anyway," he calls out after her. "That's the way to the Heath." But she is out of earshot and has disappeared around the corner of the street. He shakes his head in disbelief and thinks whether he should walk after her.

Olivia sits on one of the two squashy sofas in Claire's lounge, a coal fire burns in a grate to one side. Her phone pings a notification inside her pocket and she reads from a news app about Bruce Alpin's death. Claire emerges from the bedroom and sits opposite her.

"Have you seen the news?" says Olivia.

"No?"

"Sir Bruce."

"What about him?"

"Dead."

"Killed?" she says without her eyes leaving the fire.

"Suicide it says here."

"Do you think it's connected to the death of my mother?" says Claire turning to watch Olivia.

"Maybe," says Olivia. "Do you think he was murdered?"

"I think that he was a corrupt man."

"It'll all come out now," says Olivia. "Now this is in the public domain, there'll be journalists digging up his past." Olivia reads more from the news story. "It says here about Miss J." Claire's eyes are a world of emotion. "It doesn't say she was your mother, Claire. It was a woman called Julia Dudley, apparently.

"That's not right," says Claire. "Alpin killed her."

"The tape only talked about cover ups for bribery, not murder."

"Who's side on you on?"

"I'm being objective."

Claire turns back to the fire and remains silent as she lets her passion recede.

"I'm going to the loo," says Olivia. She gets up and goes to the bathroom. She's washing her hands when she hears the sound of breaking glass from the lounge. She hurries back to where Claire had been sitting. The lights are off and only the light of the fire in the grate illuminates the room. In the shadows, she can see Claire on the ground and a figure over her wearing a balaclava and all black clothing with their hands on her throat.

Olivia's body has moved before her conscious mind has created the thought to intervene. She launches herself at the figure. They hears her approach and turn towards her. Olivia tries runs straight for them but is met with a sharp blow to her forearm and feels herself falling backwards after the intruder grabs her shoulders and pushes her away. The figure starts to move towards the French windows over the broken glass scattered across the floor. Olivia regains her balance and pursues them. As the intruder grapples with the door to the garden, Olivia catches up and pulls at their coat. The figure turns again and this time launches a wild swing of a punch which lands in Olivia's face and a ring on their finger cuts her cheek with enough force to send her onto the floor. She lets out a cry of pain and scrambles up, but the intruder has gone and only a broken, swinging garden door remains to show they had been there at all. Olivia lets out a large sigh and puts her hand on her face and wipes away the blood from the cut. She goes to Claire. The woman is unconscious but breathing. Olivia calls an ambulance and sends Inspector Hale a message to update her. She makes sure Claire's stable then grabs her coat, leaves the door on the latch and walks out into the night.

Olivia stands on Well Walk and looks back towards Hampstead village but there is no one to be seen. The snow is getting heavier now and the silence that comes with settled snow sits like a blanket across the street. Olivia turns her head towards the Heath. At first, the same scene, no one there, no one moving. Then a shadow darts out from one side of the road to the other in the distance, a running figure wearing all black. She takes off in pursuit.

The first section of path that Olivia runs down is a broad bridleway that goes downhill into a dark valley. Trees sway either side of her as the sky turns more stormy and the wind catches the bare branches. She runs for a few minutes then slows to a walk. She's in the bottom of the valley now, the path sloping up in front of her to a summit in the distance. She stops and looks back the way she came. There is no sign of the figure in black, she exhales and considers going back to see if Claire is alright. She looks up to the hill. In the distance, moonlight bounces off the ground from where the trees end and the open heathland starts. She watches for a second, then walks on. As she is half way up the hill, someone comes out of the tree-cover ahead and out onto the bridle way, probably a hundred yards away. Olivia takes up a steady jog. Her quarry reaches the edge of the woodland and pushes on further out across the Heath. When Olivia reaches the top of the hill, she stops and looks out across the open grassland. She can see the twinkling lights in the houses of Highgate to the east, but a further rise in the land obscures the rest of the city to the south.

She sets off along the main path, constantly searching the surrounding land for signs of activity. The snow is laying thick and covering the grass now - whiteness for as far as she can see, giving the darkness an eerie reflected light off the ground. She pushes on across the open land and reaches smaller trees and bushes that form a wind break near the next high ground. As she approaches, someone bursts out from the shrubbery, straight towards her. They hit her with their full body weight to her stomach. Olivia is winded and they fall back together into the snow. She tries to reach out but fails to get traction and gets the back of a hand in her face before a fist then comes at her to her stomach. She coughs and her body curls up before she feels a boot in her back and hears the sound of footsteps running off.

As she lies there, a trickle of blood from her lip skates down her skin and drops onto the snow. Her eyes are closed. Olivia doesn't know how long it is before she opens them again. She didn't sleep but she is colder now. She stands. Her body telling her that is unwise but she ignores the pain and walks off towards the peak of Parliament Hill.

When she reaches the highest peak on the Heath, she stands and looks across the vastness of London below her. Thousands of lights in the night, marking out the famous buildings, iconic against the skyline. The flakes are falling densely now and her view is obscured from snow hitting her eyelashes, but she can see enough to spot a torchlight coming up from the road below, slowly moving nearer to her eyrie.

The torch bearer reaches twenty feet away before they speak. "Olivia! I thought it was you."

"Jack, what are you doing out here?"

"I spoke to Claire, she told me what happened and said you'd chased after a guy who broke in."

"Is she OK?"

"Yeah, tough as old bricks, that one."

"Did you see someone on your way up here?" she says. "Wearing all black?"

"Nope, seen no one. Have you been down to the ponds? They could be there."

"I've only come up from the village to here."

"Let's both go and see if they're down by the water," says Jack.

"I'm fine. You go."

"Come on, it'll be quicker with two."

"Honestly, I'm going back," she says. "I'll see how Claire is doing. I've lost the trail now anyway."

The two of them stand stock still, each watching the other, each wanting to know what the other is thinking. The moment seems to last for longer than the few seconds it does. Then she sees more torches at the bottom of the hill.

"Look, reinforcements," she says. "I called Inspector Hale, told her what happened."

Her turns to look where she points, on his face is a look in his eyes that she can't fathom. "Jack, I wanted to ask you?" she says.

"What?"

"The fraud case, the one with Sir Bruce Alpin. Were you involved with anything dodgy?"

"What do you mean?"

She thinks before releasing her hand grenade but reckons on the police being a minute away and this being a golden opportunity. "Did you take a bribe to destroy evidence?"

The torches, like fire flies, flicker towards them. He shakes his head. "Of course not," he says. "What makes you say that?"

"Claire has a recording of you, from her father's answer phone."

"I wouldn't worry about Claire now," he says.

"Why?"

He says nothing.

"Jack, now's your chance to come clean."

She turns her eyes to the police coming up the hill. The outline of the figures carrying the torches are visible through the snow storm. She turns back to him but Jack has gone. "I'll search the ponds," he calls back as he runs downhill.

Less than a minute later, Fiona arrives with her officers. "Jack was here," says Olivia.

"Savage?" says Fiona.

Olivia nods. "He's going to the ponds."

"Did he do the assault on Mrs Boyd?" says Fiona.

"Maybe."

Fiona turns to the police. "We follow, spread out across the grassland." Olivia watches the police descend the slope away from her, the lights from their torches scanning out across the snow. She waits for a minute then follows them.

When they reach the water's edge the police start to move around each side of the first pond. Olivia waits at the point they split and watches their progress through the torchlight as the snow storm stops her seeing any more.

Suddenly, Jack's voice is right behind her head. Olivia starts to turn but he grabs one of her hands and flicks a handcuff across it and the metal locks itself. She brings her arm back and manages to wrench her arm free. She swings the handcuff round in the air and brings it down on his face. Jack cries out but she pulls back and repeats the blow. He is momentarily stunned and falls down on the ground. Olivia retreats back towards safety and runs towards where she can see torches bobbing in the air until she reaches Fiona and the officers. Olivia leads the group back the way she came. Jack has gone and Fiona tells the police to continue searching around the water. The snow is thick now, falling incessantly.

"Guv!" shouts one of the officers ten minutes later from up ahead as they all walk along the water's edge. "Body in the water."

"Get it on the bank," says Fiona. The two policemen wade into the pond and drag the floating corpse towards land. They struggle to pull it out but finally get it on the grass. One of the officers feels for a pulse.

"Dead, guv."

A black balaclava is hiding the man's identity. Fiona goes down on her haunches and pulls off the mask. Olivia can't help a breath of shock.

"Know him, Ms Streete?"

"I do," she says. "That's Stephen Boyd."

"The dead man from three weeks ago?" says Fiona. Olivia stares at her and nods. "I can't see a fucking thing in this storm." She turns to her officers. "Lads, get forensics out here, get a tent set up. Ms Streete, let's talk in the car."

Fiona and Olivia force themselves against the wind to walk back around the hill to the road that runs along the edge of the Heath. Olivia can see two police cars parked up near where the grass stops and the tarmac starts. They clamber into one of the vehicles and wipe snow and water from their clothes, hair and faces.

"Now, what the fuck has been going on?" says Fiona. "We find the body of a man who died three weeks ago?"

Olivia looks at her. "The real question is," says Olivia. "Who actually died on the tracks at Clapham Junction then? Can you get into police records online?"

"Of course."

"Can you find out how they identified the body?"

"Two secs," says Fiona. She picks up a keyboard attached to a screen on the passenger side of the police car and types in passwords. She scrolls through screens of records made about the first death of Stephen Boyd. "Normally there'll be a post-mortem. Let's see…" She scrolls some more. "Fuck it!"

"What?"

"No post mortem, no formal ID," says Fiona. "What the fuck? Identified from the wallet on the body." Her words reveal her incredulity and she shakes her head.

"Is that a cover up?" says Olivia.

"Maybe, or just shit policing."

The sound of the window smashing a few inches from Olivia's head explodes into the confines of the car. Glass scatters across the interior, Fiona reaches for a mace canister in the glove box. The passenger side door is torn open and a hand grabs Olivia's upper arm. She is dragged out onto the ground.

"You just wouldn't keep your bloody nose out of it, would you?" Jack's face is pushing up against hers and the cold muzzle of a handgun gouges her cheek.

"Savage," calls Fiona. "Let her go." She trains the mace towards him.

"You just had to go on asking your fucking questions, didn't you?"

"Jack, don't be stupid," says Olivia. "Where's this going to get you?"

"It's going to stop you talking anymore."

"Did you kill Stephen and Bruce Alpin?" says Olivia. "What were they going to do? Did they find out about your corruption, Jack? Did they threaten to go to the authorities? Did Ralph say he couldn't protect you any more, Jack?"

"Be quiet!"

"Fiona here will stop you, Jack, if you kill me, this won't be the end of it. You'll go to prison for the rest of your life if you kill me, but maybe she can get a reduced sentence for you. Let me go and we'll help you." Jack is lost in thought. "Maybe you didn't mean to kill them, Jack? Maybe they got angry and it was manslaughter. Is that what happened, Jack?" Is that what you did?"

"Drop the gun, Savage," Fiona calls from her position six feet from him.

"It'll be OK, Jack," says Olivia. "Give me the gun." She moves her hand towards his, places her fingers on his skin. Slowly, gently, she moves towards the handgrip of weapon. Jack doesn't move but watches her face. Tears well in the corner of his eyes. Olivia slides her hand onto the gun and pulls it away from him.

"It's over, Jack."

CHAPTER THIRTY

Over the River Thames, the snow swirls as it is caught by gusts of wind and the lights across London outline the streets and houses of the vast city.

"Happy Christmas, Grandma," says Poppy as she hands Olivia's mother a box with bright paper around it. The old lady smiles at her and begins the ritual of unwrapping, watched by the family.

"Thank you for inviting me here today," says Ellen quietly to Olivia as they stand behind the sofa with glasses of Prosecco, watching Olivia's parents and daughter open presents.

"My pleasure," says Olivia. "After you said you'd be on your own, it's the least I could do. How are you feeling about it all?"

"Tom was just obsessed with his ex, I thought it could have worked out but he seemed to get more and more crazy about the whole thing as time went on."

"Do you know what really happened to her?"

"It was a tragedy," says Ellen. "He finally told me yesterday. She died in a back alley next to a club in Victoria where she worked. On his deathbed, Tom's dad told him that Stephen had killed her. His dad worked for GreenLink but they sacked him for being drunk at work, and his dad knew Stephen was part of the GreenLink operations. I reckon it was just his dad's way of getting his own back and playing on his son's obsession with his ex-girlfriend. It was Tom's dad who came into the Christmas party last year and was shouting at Stephen, you know?"

"I thought you knew more about that bloke than you were telling me," says Olivia. "Why the secrecy?"

Ellen shrugs. "I dunno. I was cut up about Stephen's death, I guess. But I still don't understand how he died twice."

"I have my theories," says Olivia.

The sound of the door entry buzzer ripples through the flat. Olivia walks to panel and sees Inspector Hale's face in the tiny screen. She presses the button that opens the street door, then opens her own flat front door and leans on the frame with her wine waiting for Fiona.

The lift arrives and Fiona steps out. "Working on Christmas Day, Inspector?"

"I know, shit isn't it? I was on duty anyway, I often opt for this shift because no one else does and it's preferable to my family." Fiona smiles and Olivia raises her glass to her.

"Come in," says Olivia. "What brings you here?"

"I thought you'd be interested in an update."

They walk through into the kitchen. "Prosecco?"

"I'd better not. Got any coffee?"

Olivia pours out a mug of coffee from the machine on the kitchen counter and they both sit at the breakfast bar that looks out over the river.

"Jack has confessed to the fraud of fifteen years ago," begins Fiona. "He says Peters pressured him in doing it though."

"Did you arrest Peters?"

"He's disappeared," says Fiona. "Must have had a plan B in case he was ever found out. But we have other evidence that I won't share with you, that he's been a bent copper for a couple of decades. We should've got him before now, that investigation will run and run."

"Did Jack confess to anything else?"

"Yes, he killed Boyd on the Heath the other night."

"Boyd faked his own death to avoid being blackmailed by Jack, didn't he?" says Olivia.

Fiona takes a sip of coffee. "Exactly. How did you know?"

"It's the only logical explanation," says Olivia. "Jack somehow found out that Stephen Boyd and Evan Rice had discovered his bribes, and maybe that Jack was involved with the cover-up of Miss J's murder. That's when Jack started to hassle them and threaten them to keep quiet. Jack must have thought Stephen was the bigger threat and put him particularly under pressure."

"That lines up with what Jack has said so far, except the Miss J bit," says Fiona. "He fervently denies anything to do with that. As far as he can recall, they never really found out what happened to her. When we catch up with Superintendent Peters, he may know more."

"What about Claire's parents, Gerald and Patricia Harwell?"

"We sent officers to their place in Sussex but Gerald had gone," says Fiona. "His wife had called the Police Commissioner and told him, so we had an early warning that he had run and he was picked up at St Pancras boarding the Eurostar for Paris."

"Did he admit to anything?" says Olivia.

"We'll get him on accessory to fraud and bribery. He wasn't the ring-leader, that what Bruce Alpin. But Gerald Harwell knew about the Jack Savage bribes – as we know from your answer phone tape, so we'll play that to him and see what he says."

"Nothing on the son, Jeremy? Or Bruce's daughter in law, Greer?

"No, they haven't been mentioned," says Fiona. "What do you suspect was their involvement?"

"I don't suspect them. I'm certain Jeremy is clean, he just got mixed up with the consequences of his father's corruption, but he somehow managed to not know about any of it."

"The documents that were stolen from GreenLink tell a different story," says Fiona. "They have Jeremy's name on them all."

"I'm surprised," says Olivia. "Jeremy didn't behave as though he was trying to cover up any crimes when I met him, and I'm used to seeing through people who lie. He seemed genuine."

"We'll see," says Fiona. "I've let him have today at home then he's agreed to come in to the station tomorrow morning to be interviewed."

"His wife seems more suspicious, but I've no evidence," says Olivia. "She lied to me, I could tell. Did you know she was having an affair with Stephen Boyd?"

"I didn't," says Fiona, raising an eyebrow. "She's out of the country, flew from Heathrow to Barbados two days ago. We'll see her when she gets back. The Barbadian police have her under surveillance to make sure she returns."

"How did Boyd fool Jack with the man on the tracks at Clapham?" says Olivia.

"We've got a proper ID on the body now, a homeless guy who lived near the station. Post-mortem says he died of alcohol poisoning. His face was then obliterated after death, presumably to allow for the swap and make it look like Boyd had died on the tracks. Jack knew it wasn't Stephen straight away when he saw the guy, but didn't want to bring any attention to the case, so didn't do a post mortem as it risked implicated him. That was Jack panicking as he thought it would come out that he had been threatening Boyd in the days and weeks before his apparent first death. There's only one angle I can't work out," says Fiona.

"What?"

"Why did Stephen Boyd attack his own wife the second night he died?"

"He didn't."

"Your witness statement says he did, Miss Streete."

"No, my witness statement says a man in a balaclava attacked her."

"And you were present when I pulled off the mask and we discovered it was Boyd."

"Jack swapped his balaclava and put it on Stephen's body after he'd killed him to cover his tracks."

"How did you know?"

"The attacker in the flat had a ring on his finger that cut my face. The body in the water had no rings."

"Very Sherlock Holmes," says Fiona. "Why did Jack attack Claire, then?"

"He knew she knew all about what he'd done. He got it into his head that he could silence everyone who was a witness," says Olivia.

"We'll ask him about that too," says Fiona.

"There's one thing you haven't mentioned."

"What?"

"Who killed Sir Bruce Alpin?"

"Yeah, that's taken a slight back seat to the Boyd murder," says Fiona. "Any ideas?"

"Jack maybe? Covering his tracks? That's another reason that Gerald Harwell ran, to avoid the authorities and a murderer who may have come after him too."

"Let's see," says Fiona. "No peace for the wicked. I need to get back."

They both stand up and Olivia leads her back to the front door.

"I may have some more questions after the holidays," says Fiona.

"Sure. Thank you for confiding in me," says Olivia.

"You've been a massive help." Fiona puts out her hand and they shake.

"Happy Christmas!"

As she shuts the front door, Olivia's phone buzzes in her pocket. She checks the screen and sees it's a call from an unknown number.

"Hello, is that Olivia Streete?"

"Speaking."

"I understand you're a friend of Claire Boyd's?"

"Who is this?"

"Could you give her a message?"

"Only if you tell me who you are," says Olivia.

There's a pause on the line, then the woman speaks. "My sister was Miss J."

"I read about it in the news," says Olivia.

"Can you pass on a message?"

"Sure."

"Tell her, I did it for us."

"What do you mean?"

"Miss J was my sister and Miss J was also Claire's mother," says the woman. "She met Gerald Harwell when she was a dancer in a club. She got pregnant by him and had Claire. He insisted she changed her name to cover up the scandal of him sleeping with a dancer. Gerald was embarrassed by it and kept it all secret from the press when he was an MP. Eventually, when Claire was only eleven and away at school, her mother, my sister, was killed." Another pause. "Now, at last, the man who killed her is dead."

"Did you kill him?"

"He killed himself, Olivia," says the woman. "Can you tell Claire?"

"I will," says Olivia. "Why can't *you* tell her?"

"I'll be gone overseas. I'll throw this phone away as soon as we've finished this call. My flight's been announced, I need to go."

"I'll have to tell the police you called."

"They won't find me." The line goes dead. She taps the silent phone against her teeth, thinking about what the woman had said. She calls Fiona and tells her what has just happened and the Inspector says she will deal with it.

Olivia walks back to the lounge and the scene of the family's present giving. She discovers it's her turn. As she rips open the wrapping, the others cheer and smile. The first one is from Poppy and it's underwear.

"I thought you might need it!" her daughter calls across the room. Olivia makes a glum face then they all laugh.

THE END

OLIVIA STREETE WILL RETURN IN

THE ROME CONSPIRACY

Death and double-dealing in The Vatican

Printed in Great Britain
by Amazon

87052467R00192